FORGED BY THE PAST

A TIME TRAVEL ROMANCE

SPIRITS THROUGH TIME

AIMEE ROBINSON

AMR PUBLISHING LLC

To the dreamers

SPIRITS THROUGH TIME SERIES

Charmed by the Past

Sirens of the Past

Forged by the Past

CHAPTER 1

The plop of her soon-to-be ex-husband's designer dress shirt
hitting the mud was the most satisfying sound Beth Carmichael
had ever heard. Hands down. The sound was more delicious than
freshly popping popcorn and more enticing than the doorbell when
she was expecting her latest shipment of addictive artisan chocolates.

All of that muck and worm food drenching those silk fibers? She
could lick her fingers clean just thinking about it.

"Don't forget the Italian leather loafers and cuff links!" Beth's best
friend, Amanda, who had been her monumental pillar of support
through the worst week of her life, waltzed through the back glass
door of Beth's house holding another cardboard box. The door
shoomped closed as Amanda slid the thing home with her hip before
trotting over to where Beth was sitting in a collapsible camp chair.

"Honestly, who the hell wears cuff links to work anyway?" Amanda
parked it in the camp chair next to Beth and started rummaging
through the goods. A white jewelry box emblazoned with a preten-
tious logo appeared in Beth's hand a moment later.

Looked like the cuff links were going in.

"I'll tell you who wears cuff links to work." Beth unboxed the two
pieces of bright and shiny and chucked them, one at a time, aiming for
a bigger mud splash with each throw. When they both lightly tapped

the surface of the puddle, her heart sank like she'd hoped the cuff links would.

She needed to get the garden hose out and water that puppy down for the proper satisfaction.

"Allergists. That's who wears cuff links to work." Unsettled by the lack of dirt-to-water ratio in the barely mud pit, Beth leaned over the arm of the camp chair and picked up a stick. Squinting with determination, she poked the blunt tip of the wood against the floating fabric. The soft silk protested before it was dragged down and entombed in the sparse mud. Once that was adequately submerged, Amanda threw two pairs of dress slacks on the surface. More of Kyle's finery ready for its spa treatment.

"Oh, please." Amanda scoffed. "I could write scripts for ninety percent of the stuff they recommend for their patients. Do you even know what those monthly allergy shots are good for?" Amanda was gearing Beth up for their favorite line.

"Sending allergists' kids to college," they said in unison before laughing. The joke had been an oldie but goodie between them. She and Amanda had gone through nursing school together before Beth changed her concentration and decided to focus on becoming a certified nurse-midwife. Amanda stuck with the nurse practitioner route, but they had kept in touch and were both still fortunate enough to see each other frequently at Commonwealth General Hospital in Boston, where the midwifery group Beth worked for had hospital privileges.

The warm June air was pleasant but not stifling. Beth appreciated the courtesy of good weather as she and her best friend fawned over a muddy hole the same way parents would set up shop to watch their kids play sports and enjoyed the view from the sideline. As Beth's laughter died down, her attention returned to the mud puddle overflowing with thousands of dollars' worth of designer duds that her soon-to-be ex-husband, Dr. Kyle Donovan, valued more than her.

Perhaps it had been her red hair that was the draw all along. For some unknown reason, men always found redheads exotic and enticing. Too bad Kyle didn't hold the rest of her in the same high regard, from her passion for pursuing midwifery down to the curves that

2

placed her just shy of off-the-rack mall sizing and landed her firmly in the lower rungs of plus size. What had Kyle's aunt called her again?

Ah. Rubenesque.

The signs had been there, sure. But when a gorgeous doctor who worked at the hospital where she yearned to be accepted began to show an interest in her, all sense had ricocheted from her brain.

Like a wedding band off a cheating husband's finger, apparently.

Served her right for laughing at those early asinine icebreaker jokes when no one else would.

Beth's stomach soured as she used her weapon of mass destruction to further submerge Kyle's precious ensemble below the puddle's murky surface. Each poke reminded her of every shortcoming, every flaw that highlighted her as less than in the eyes of Kyle and his peers.

Beth was beyond proud to be a certified nurse-midwife. According to the Massachusetts licensing board, she was a full-fledged nurse. Oh, who had then gone on to earn an *additional* master's degree in midwifery. Delivering well-women care and obstetrical services was her passion. She was an empowered practitioner who, in turn, loved empowering her patients to make whatever choices were right for them.

Too bad her OB/GYN colleagues at the hospital didn't see her and other midwives in the same light. Regardless of her medical background, extensive track record in delivering healthy babies, and improved recovery times for the new mamas, to many of the hospital obstetricians, she was just a nurse. Heck, when she was involved in joint consultations with OBs at the hospital, more often than not she turned into the gauze gofer.

"I was never going to be enough," Beth whispered more to herself than Amanda. Her eyes started to glaze over the pile of brown garments in front of her as her hand controlled the stick of its own accord. *Poke. Poke. Poke.*

"Aw, sweetie. I know it hurts, but don't let that douchebag make you ask questions about yourself you know damn well don't need answers. Kyle's an asshole who never deserved you. Period. End of story. But just wait," Amanda said with a gleam in her eye as she set down the box at her feet. "I'm coming up with the perfect anonymous review to post online. The benefit of being 'just a nurse'? Patients won't bother complaining about you to the world. But a doctor, and a fancy one at that? Hell, people eat up bad reviews about them like whipped cream on a sundae. I'm thinking I should title my review 'The Allergist Asshole Who Can't Shoot Straight' or maybe 'Run Away! This Allergist's Treatment Is Worse Than a Venereal Disease.' I'm still fine-tuning the details."

Amanda's smugness was gratifying, and the comfort via retaliation offered by her best friend was a soothing balm to her hurt pride, but Beth's professional doldrums still weighed her down. Kyle had always had difficulty understanding her frustrations. Other midwives in her practice mostly stuck to themselves and had no preference over delivering babies outside the hospital versus in. But Beth yearned for peer-received acceptance in a more clinical setting. Validation that her higher calling was high enough for others. Kyle tried to be supportive, but he was also firmly planted in the white-coat-doctor-who-enjoyed-his-two-hour-lunches department. A stark contrast to her daily blood-soaked disposable hospital gown attire and two-in-the-morning baby arrivals.

But still, he listened. And made her laugh, even if his jokes were on the corny side of cornball. He was a connection, someone to snuggle with when the nights grew cold, and a steady arm to hang on when they went to dinner. So, boy, did this whole thing just *hurt*.

After Beth and Kyle's year-long engagement, not to mention the down payment on the newly built single-family craftsman that *she* had sprung for because he was too busy to sign the papers at the time, the hospital Kyle worked at had taken on a slew of new nurses. One of the new nurses to join Kyle's floor was Stephanie, who had just moved to Boston from California. A month later, unbeknownst to Beth, Stephanie and Kyle had both joined the mile high club, thanks to Kyle's frequent-flier miles he told Beth he had used up long ago so she had to pay full freight for their honeymoon airline tickets.

Turned out allergists actually made very good money. And if you were a nurse named Stephanie, you got to reap the benefits of that. Not that the money mattered to Beth so much, but honesty definitely did.

Stephanie was tall to Beth's average height. The woman's figure reminded Beth of the curving highways hugging the Pacific cliffs and pushed the limits of the standard-issued hospital scrubs. They also pushed the limits of Beth and Kyle's relationship. After she and Kyle said their I-dos during their gorgeous Memorial Day weekend wedding, Beth had walked in on the two of them, with Kyle mid-thrust in the reception hall's bridal lounge where Beth had stashed her purse and other belongings.

Silly her for wanting to touch up her makeup on her wedding day. And for *not* wanting to see her sparkling new husband's bare ass as he pumped their guest full of all sorts of thank-you-for-coming.

And that had only been a week ago.

"At least the resort in Jamaica had a reasonable cancellation policy. And the flights you could reuse. There's just one more detail I'm unsure about." Amanda handed Beth another glass of chardonnay. The cold smoothness of the glass brought Beth back to the conversation.

"What's that?" Beth asked, chuckling at the mounded-over mud puddle in front of her. Amanda must have thrown some more designer logs on the fire when Beth wasn't paying attention.

"We're a week out from the wedding, lover boy hasn't come back to the house yet, and we still have not done a precious thing to his brand-new Tesla."

A sharp laugh erupted from Beth. Her chardonnay sloshed over her fingers, but she hardly cared.

Because when your life was falling apart, your philandering husband of one week hadn't shown his face yet, and you had a brand-new wedding dress you'd starved yourself to squeeze into taking up all your closet space, you had to laugh to keep from crying.

CHAPTER 2

Beth peeled off her second skin of nitrile gloves and disposable gown as she looked back over at mama and baby. The newborn was resting sweetly skin to skin on his mother's dark chest. The delivery had been hard. They were always hard. But, boy, had this one been *fast*. It made sense since this was a second baby for the happy couple and first deliveries tended to take longer, but man, that one had thrown Beth and the birthing center staff for a loop. No way she'd tell the smiling mama this, but going from zero to fully dilated in forty minutes would test even the most skilled of midwives.

That mama was what Beth and her staff referred to as a drive-by.

"How's everyone doing?"

"Better now that you're finished with those stitches down there. Those hurt more than that ring of fire you warned me about."

Beth chuckled softly. "Tearing is never fun and especially not when you don't have time for the epidural I know you wanted. But everything looks good now. The nurses will come over in a few minutes to check on you. And how's Daddy doing?"

The mom's eyes briefly left the snoring bundle of mush on her chest to glance over at her husband, who lay curled up on the couch, sucking wind through an oxygen mask while beads of sweat dotted his bald head.

"I guess we know blood isn't his thing. For my C-section the first time around, it was much more clinical, less . . . juicy. And the screen helped . . . Darren didn't have to see anything the doctors didn't want him to see. But I'm just so grateful for you encouraging me to try a vaginal birth after having a cesarean. All the obstetricians I spoke to about my preference weren't very supportive."

"Of course, Monica. That's what I'm here for. I love empowering mamas to make their own delivery choices, and I saw no medical reason you couldn't pull it off. I'm proud of you."

"I'm pretty darn proud of me, too," Monica said, gazing down at her newborn son.

"All right, my work here is finished. Kelly will be in shortly to check on you . . . and Dad," Beth said with a grim smile before leaving the exam room.

The sun on Beth's face added to her high as she scooted down the steps of the birthing center to go grab some lunch. She always relished in the afterglow of a healthy birth along with the family. At twenty-seven, she was right where she wanted to be career wise. Her daily grind settled her, grounded her, and through some of her tougher deliveries, even bolstered her confidence. Confidence that, yes, her skills made her worthy of professional peers to sit up and take notice.

Especially despite philandering husbands who embarrassed their wives among all their shared industry connections. With the new nurse. Who had not once been asked to be a gauze gofer.

The heavy soles of Beth's clogs thudded against the sidewalk as she finished braiding her long hair down her back. It wasn't her best work. With the way the hair tie pulled at some strands, she could tell the plait wasn't even. A quick reach around her neck revealed one section of hair noticeably thicker than the others. And two mini clumps failed to even stay bound. Her fingers trailed over the bumpy braid and came away unsettled and frustrated. They were itching for a redo.

Beth harrumphed as she tugged her hand away from the hot mess behind her back. Even her hair had trouble falling in line with expectations.

The scents of cardamom and cilantro rose up to greet her as she rounded the corner. Her stomach did a Simone Biles somersault at the prospect of fresh falafel slathered in tahini and crammed into pillowy pita pockets. Avi's Shuk was her favorite lunch spot when she was working at the birthing center. With her stomach leading the way, Beth picked up the pace. The rough starchiness of her hospital scrubs rubbed together, the sound reminding her of dry sticks anxious to start a fire.

Not entirely inaccurate given that, if she didn't get some fried chickpeas in her belly soon, she couldn't rule out arson as a reasonable response.

The bell above the shop sign jangled as the door opened, allowing two customers to exit right as Beth approached the short steps leading up to the door.

"Beth?"

Her white clog nearly tripped on the middle stone stair when her name rang out unexpectedly. From the voice of her ex-husband. Who she hadn't spoken to since he cheated on her at their wedding a week ago.

Beth silently cursed as she lowered her foot and backed her way down the stairs. Her eyes hadn't yet left the ground. Because why add a painful picture to the already depressing audio file she was clearly about to be subjected to?

"I'll just run in and use the ladies' room real quick."

The woman's voice in close proximity to Kyle caught her attention. Beth whipped her head up and saw the side of Stephanie's face as the woman retreated back into the restaurant. A brown paper takeout bag hung loosely from her wrist while her other hand held a cardboard drink holder with . . . oh gee, looky there . . . two drinks.

Perfectly acceptable items to take into the bathroom. Especially when the soon-to-be ex-wife was staring daggers in the woman's wake.

"You couldn't even leave me Avi's, huh? Had to add our favorite restaurant to the list of things you needed to shit all over? Hadn't you marked your territory enough?" Disgust dripped from her words like motor oil, black and thick and leaving imprints wherever they fell. Beth crossed her arms over her chest, but she still couldn't meet Kyle in the eye for longer than a second. He was like a disease to her, a virus that could infect her calm and confidence and cut her down at the knees. So she backed away until she occupied a patch of the concrete sidewalk that was a solid three concrete squares away from the steps.

"C'mon, Beth. You never let me explain, never answered my phone calls." Kyle had the nerve to sound desperate and slightly remorseful in his plea. She made the mistake of looking up at him.

And immediately took in his brand-new wardrobe. With the upgraded button-down shirt and finely pressed dress slacks with a seam so crisp down the legs she imagined it could tear through paper. Polished shoes, neatly trimmed hair, and not a bit of facial fuzz in sight. If she got in close enough, she'd no doubt scent his cologne and, if she went in even closer, would detect the faintest hints of the baby powder he used to wipe off the little hairs that loved to cling to his chin after he shaved. He looked good. Damn good.

And wasn't that just the biggest kick in the pants.

Beth stared down at her wrinkled navy-blue scrubs, with her chunky white clogs peeking out beneath her baggy pant legs. Disheveled wisps of hair tickled her upper arm, reminding her how unruly her appearance must have looked.

All in front of the soon-to-be ex and his new next. Wonderful.

"Look," Kyle hedged as he impatiently ran his hand through his hair and quickly looked back toward the restaurant entrance before returning his attention to her. "It just . . . happened. I know that sounds shitty, and, yeah, call me all the names in the book. I deserve them. But with Stephanie—"

Beth's hand shot up in front of his face.

"Don't. Don't you even say her name to me. Don't even *breathe* her name. Your bronchioles don't need the added effort sifting through your bullshit explanation." Tears started to prick the corners of her eyes, so she stared down at his shoes instead of his face. She pinched her lips together, breathing out through her nose, until the tips of his loafers entered her vision. Begrudgingly, she looked up.

"We just didn't click as well, you and I." There was sadness in his voice, heavy and thick, but no remorse. The melancholy was out of obligation. "You were like a best friend, Beth," he said, hands extended out at his sides. "I could open up to you about anything. Crack beers with you, watch movies, joke about work. But I needed—"

"To fuck someone else on our wedding day."

Kyle winced, but thankfully, he didn't deny it. She had literally caught him with his pants around his ankles. Beth stared at him as the silence dragged on between them.

Go on. I dare you. Say it.

"No. I mean . . . yes, I did that. But not because I don't love you. Stephanie and I, we just . . . fit better."

Beth's anger momentarily tagged out as confusion tapped gloves and stepped up. "Fit better? As in your dick in her vagina? Because I wasn't aware that our parts didn't match up."

Kyle bounced on the balls of his feet as he looked nervously around at the patrons leaving the restaurant. "Don't make me say it, Beth. C'mon."

"Say. What." What the hell was he getting at?

"She and I just fit . . . better. You get my meaning?"

Kyle stared at Beth. The man was desperate for her to catch his meaning from his all-over-the-place hand gestures and bouncing eyes. But she was clueless as to what he was getting at. She'd have had better luck deciphering sign language. While he continued to flail his arms in her direction, she raised an eyebrow at him.

"Stephanie and I fit better, all right? As a couple, as colleagues. And . . . yeah, in body type."

Holy. Shit.

"What? Body type?"

"She's not as big as you. I mean, she's curvy, but not . . . um . . . as heavyset? Is that the right phrase? Look, you're beautiful, Beth. You know I've always thought you were beautiful. But attraction, even at a primal level . . ."

The fucker didn't have the balls to finish that sentence. Good. Because Beth was done hearing it.

"I don't need the explanations. I don't need any excuses. I just need you to leave. No, as a matter of fact, let me take that last one off your hands. I'm out."

A quick turn on her heel and Beth all but sprinted in the direction she came from. Hot tears fell from her eyes and threatened to blur her vision into obscurity, but like hell she'd allow that in that moment. The skin on her palm pinched as her grip tightened against her handbag's shoulder strap. She couldn't safely run in her clogs, but she could damn well speedwalk. Anything to get her away from the steaming pile of shit that had somehow piled up in front of her favorite lunch spot.

Beth's head spun from the confrontation. If the body's automatic response to protecting itself was fight, flight, or freeze, she had miraculously managed to do all three simultaneously. She was nothing if not the overachiever, apparently.

Hooray.

Desperate for a change of scenery where she wouldn't run the risk of Kyle following her, Beth slowed down and glanced at the wooden antique shop sign hanging to her right. No way would he follow her there. Kyle was practically allergic to anything with a manufacture date older than his latest smartphone. A brief squint at the store hours confirmed they were open. Without a second thought, Beth gripped the worn bronze door handle and slipped inside.

A bell announced her arrival as she softly closed the door behind her. The wood on the door was worn and hardly fit tightly inside the doorjamb, but the knob released cleanly, nonetheless. The shop windows had a slight tint to them, blocking out the afternoon's harsh sun. Various trinkets adorned the bay window's display. A gramophone no bigger than Beth's hand. A rag doll. An assortment of candlesticks, teapots, jewelry boxes. All well-worn, though in usable condition.

"Hello there. Are you looking for anything in particular this afternoon?"

The clacking of wooden beads drew Beth's attention away from the window display. An elderly man was behind a sheet of bead strands, which hung over the top of a back door. Gnarled fingertips peeked through the strings and parted the beaded curtain. The whole ensemble was apropos of what one might find in a tarot card reader's lounge. The man, though, hardly looked like a turban and crystal ball would do him justice. Nor did his expression. From head to toe, he was all about tweed and sweater vests. As if the profession came with a standard uniform of drab wool attire. But he definitely looked like he was in the right place, that was for sure.

"Um, nothing in particular, no. Just . . . looking around." Beth's unease was so obvious that she was surprised the shopkeeper hadn't booted her out yet while crying, "Hooligan!" With her red hair and blue scrubs, she stood out like a sore thumb among all the delicates and untouchables.

"Ah, I see," the man said, adjusting his glasses. "Well, let me know if there's anything that catches your eye. You know, you'd be surprised what people come looking for in this part of the city. Tourists, especially."

"Let me guess. 'Sir, do you know where Paul Revere did his midnight ride?'"

The shopkeeper chuckled hard before pointing to a stack of cards at the table next to her. She squinted down at the cards, picked one up, and smiled as she read it.

A Map of Paul Revere's Boston circa 1770s

"Ah." Beth's lips thinned out before she placed the card back on the table.

"Well, if you need anything, just ring the bell on the counter. I'll come right out."

Beth nodded and peered back out the window, trying to squint through the slight tint to see whether Kyle had followed her. Rough, cold metal rasped against her fingertips, which were still resting on the table with the tourist cards.

The odd sensation against her fingers had her glancing back down. To her surprise, the whole table was a little mini shrine to American Revolutionary War artifacts, all labeled with roundabout dates and descriptions.

"Wow. He wasn't kidding about keeping the tourists happy."

Her fingers skimmed over long iron nails, rusted and misshapen by modern standards. There were horseshoes, musket balls, and even a pewter toy soldier. All standard-issue bits of colonial America.

Except for the small ax at the end of the table.

It was the tiniest ax she'd ever seen. No, scratch that. It was the only ax she'd ever seen, actually. But in movies, they always seemed bigger, more deadly. This one was small, almost dainty. The head of the ax was no more than four inches high and didn't look powerful enough to chop a carrot, let alone something more menacing . . . like a redcoat. Was this a hatchet, then? Like hell she knew the difference between the two, though she seemed to recall hatchets being more like tools as opposed to weapons.

But she wasn't sure this was either.

She gently raised the ax off the table and stared down at it more closely. A muted thrill shivered through her at the thought of holding anything remotely close to a weapon while Kyle was within a two-block radius.

Note to self: take up ax throwing.

The iron of the blade had slight hammer marks, which were there but very faint to detect amid the encroaching rust. None of that stood out as abnormal. What *did* surprise her, however, was the handle. It was metal as well, not wood. All along the spine snaked intricate etchings and engravings. Beth squinted more closely at the imagery. Patterns of what looked to be branches and ivy twirled around the length of the handle.

The detail was astonishing, especially when she peeked at the card next to it to try and glean more information.

Bag ax - mid-to-late 1700s

Beth turned the card over and was surprised there wasn't more detail written down. She couldn't place why that disappointed her. Was this a tool? A weapon? A piece of art made for a loved one?

"Sir, I have a question about this . . . ah . . . ah . . . *choo!*"

The muskiness in the shop had finally wormed its way into her sinuses, and her nose wasn't having any of it. Beth put the ax down quickly but still kept her fingers clutched around the handle as another sneeze overtook her. Two more sneezes erupted out of her, nearly causing her handbag to knock over a nearby handmade nutcracker. Beth held her hand over her nose and mouth and, with her eyes still closed, exhaled slowly as the sneezy tingles finally began to retreat. She dropped her hand and glanced down at the ax handle still gripped in her other palm. Pale green dust peeked out between her fingers.

"Ugh, what is tha . . . tha . . . ah *choo!*"

Both her hands flew to her nose and mouth, knocking the ax to the floor. Mortification warred with self-preservation as Beth tried to prevent snot and spittle from spraying all over the place. But the antiques had the upper hand, apparently. A few more forceful sneezes in her hands and Beth's lungs kicked it into high gear.

She inhaled a deep breath into her lungs.

Tingling tickles assaulted her nose and throat. Dry, hacking coughs rumbled through her body, bending her at the waist like a lawn chair. The heaving came harder as Beth tried to steady herself on all fours. In between the racking coughs, she'd throw a glance at the beaded curtain.

C'mon, come back upstairs. Please . . .

Soft chatter of a baseball announcer floated up toward Beth's ears. Faint crowd noise erupted into louder cheering as the radio the shop-keeper must have been listening to gave the play-by-play of the Red Sox game.

If Beth could hear it so well from out in the front of the store, the man must have had it cranked in the back. No way would he hear her.

Hurried, heavy exhales puffed out of Beth's lungs in short bursts as she laid her head on her bicep. Her vision blurred before her heavy eyelids closed the curtains. As her body melted into the floor, her shaking fingers wrapped around the handle of the ax just as her mind slipped into unconsciousness.

CHAPTER 3

Despite her profession, Beth had never been a fan of needles. Oh, she could appreciate the benefits of what those needles brought, sure. They were handy for delivering a nice dose of local anesthetic or for stitching up split eyebrows. Those tiny acupuncture needles even went a long way toward stress relief . . . or so she'd heard.

Because like hell she'd ever try.

Needles were the harbingers of a great compromise: endure tiny (or not so tiny) pricks in exchange for improved healing or saying bye-bye to a boatload of pain and stress.

As Beth battled the most massive headache of her life, she'd jab every epidural-gauge needle in the world directly between her eyes if they'd make the pounding stop. The tinny crackle of the shopkeeper's radio had long since faded away. That was encouraging. He'd surely heard her fall. At the very least, he had to be concerned she'd taken out a sizable chunk of his Paul Revere-obilia when she went down.

But she'd been lying on the ground for several minutes already and he hadn't yet come over . . .

Her mind, for all it was doing to tone down the rave inside her skull, backtracked on the mental slip.

Lying on the ground . . . not the floor.

Beth's other senses decided to get with the program and help her poor addled brain out. A cold, rough surface supported her right cheek. Well, "supported" was a loose concept. A more accurate description would have been "squashed her cheekbone like a disgruntled plastic surgeon after their patient tried to pay with grocery store coupons."

A whining groan squeaked through Beth's parted lips as she forced her eyelids to rise and shine. The pounding in her head grew less frequent but more insistent. The rapid pitter-patter had branched out, apparently, and went the gong route every thirty seconds. Another knock on her cranium and Beth was fairly confident her molars would say, "Enough of this crap!" and jump ship. The bright light assaulting her vision wasn't helping the situation either. Fat lot of good those tinted store windows did.

With her eyes all the way open, she took in the length of her arm outstretched before her. But the image was off. Because her pale arm lay limp as a dead fish across a sea of gray cobblestones. Not the cheap laminate flooring of the antique shop. Beth inhaled slowly and ticked her jaw back and forth. Each time her chin touched the cold ground—for it was definitely the ground—unease blossomed in her stomach.

A sharp neigh, followed by loud snorts, broke through the cozy reunion of her jumbled senses. Beth scrambled at the noise, crawling away from it until her back hit the curved side of a large oak barrel. Startled, she turned around. Five more just like it were neatly stacked in a row next to it.

Along a street she'd never seen before. And didn't remember walking to.

"What the hell?"

Beth's bottom lip had all but dried out with the rapid ins and outs her lungs were doing as she took in her surroundings.

In front of her was a massive covered wagon. From her position on the ground, she got an eyeful of wheels bigger than any car tire she'd ever seen. There were four wheels total, with the back two measuring as wide as she was tall. The front wheels were only slightly smaller, as if that was some comfort. Beth squinted at the contraption as her eyes followed the curve of the wagon's body. It reminded her of those sea dragon rides at amusement parks, with the swooping ends flaring out like bat wings.

Really long, pale bat wings.

Horse hooves clomping against stone drew her attention around to what she thought was the front of the thing. And, yup, judging by the eight gigantic horses attached to that specific end of the wagon, she got the orientation right.

And that was about all she got right.

Beth shot up from the ground. Her quivering legs fought to hold up her ramrod straight spine. She leaned back against the curve of the barrel, the height of which still came up to her shoulders, and tried to mold herself around the wood, as if that would magically make her an invisible spectator of the confusion before her.

Hollow heels clacked along the cobblestone street to her left, though she could hardly tell whose shoes were doing the clacking. Men and women bustled up and down the thoroughfare, both of whom sported heel heights Beth hadn't dared to wear since she was in college. But the shoes were the least of her confusion. Stockings, bonnets, tricornered hats, skirts on top of more skirts, *muskets*. The whole block looked like a movie set for Steven Spielberg's next Revolutionary War movie.

Horses drawing carts trotted by while a man on horseback in your standard-issue dead presidential wig cantered casually in front of the covered wagon near Beth.

Was that a *sword* on his hip?

Beth whipped her head around in desperation, praying to see the same antique shop door behind her. Where she could simply slip back in, close the door, send a few more curses into the world about Kyle, and renege on the whole let's-talk-about-Paul-Revere conversation she'd had with the shopkeeper.

Beth stared up at the looming brick wall in front of her. The lack of a door, with its handy hours of operation hanging in the glass, added to her rising hysteria.

Until the tip of her white clog nudged something metallic.

By her feet lay the decorative ax she had been holding before things had gone all topsy-turvy. The scrolling details caught a glint of light as the sun's rays passed through the shadows of the alley. Hesitantly, Beth crouched down and picked up the ax, pinching the handle with two fingers.

It was the same, thank goodness. Just like her white clogs and navy-blue scrubs. But that was where the similarities ended. Everything else around her, literally *everything,* was different.

What on earth is going on?

"Gerald, what do you suppose that woman over there is wearing? I've never seen anything like it before in my life. Are those trousers?"

Hushed tones around Beth began to bubble up in her ear. Curious whispers magnified into speculative conversations.

On instinct, Beth's hand made a death grip around the ax before her gaze addressed the murmurs. Small clusters of women and men formed along the street, each person slowing their steps as they took in the sight of her. One man, who had been hauling large canvas sacks into the back of a wooden cart, stopped mid-heave to stare and hadn't even noticed the tear in the bag—or the grain slowly pouring out of it. Another woman paused her rug cleaning mid-beat to gander Beth's way.

The fact that the woman was beating the dirt out of a rug at all was a giant red flag of nope-not-right, but less so than the white bonnet the woman wore or the layers of colonial-era skirts kissing the tops of her boots.

"I couldn't say, Regina. But I never could keep on top of your fashions. Though it all is quite peculiar. Perhaps . . . miss? Are you all right?" The man, who sported a tricornered hat, a forest-green velvet waistcoat, and white hose, edged from the woman's side and began to walk in Beth's direction.

Dust kicked up under her clogs as she turned around and ran. Whatever hair still managed to stay in her braid was a blessing because the remaining metric ton of it slapped her every which way as she zigzagged through the streets. She hadn't a clue where she was heading, but panic was an excellent motivator to get her butt in gear.

Beth spared a quick look over her shoulder. There were no footsteps behind her, no calls out to her, and the relief was immense. As she rounded a street corner, she turned her head forward before committing to the slow down.

And slammed face-first into a solid wall of warm, breathing man.

Beth was knocked off balance by both the living rock wall and her missteps, having stomped on top of the man's boots in her haste to slam on the brakes. She lost her footing and teetered backward, fully prepared to wind up on her ass.

A hot, firm hand encircled her right wrist, while another rested steadily against the curve of her hip. The contact was scorching. Both grips squeezed ever so slightly as her rocking slowly ebbed to a stop. Only once her feet were both solidly on the ground did the pressure at both poles ease. But only slightly.

Beth's eyes tracked the length of the arms extending out from her body. Tanned forearms with a smattering of black smudges fed into shirt sleeves loosely rolled at the elbows. The white fabric of the shirt lay baggy along the arms but was cinched tight beneath a buttoned-up leather vest, at the top of which revealed the deep V of the shirt's opening.

A quiver born of panic and anticipation, if that was possible, had Beth tracing up the column of the man's neck, which was neatly wrapped in a white handkerchief.

But it was the strong angle of his chin that stopped her dead. His jaw was cut sharply, all harsh lines and unforgiving slopes. Wisps of black hair dangled about his face, while the rest was tied back in a leather tie at the nape of his neck. His eyes, hazel pools of uncertainty, stared back at her. A sharp crease between his brows fed the magnified unease in her gut and threatened harsh judgment against the otherness she couldn't hide.

Words tried to form. An explanation, an excuse, hell, even a decent lie through the teeth would have been handy. Anything to get her out of the scorching cage she was in.

"I . . . um. I don't . . ."

More stuttering tumbled out of Beth's mouth as the man in front of her just stood there and had yet to let her go . . . or say anything. A sharp tug of her wrist and twist of her hip did all of diddly squat as she tried to break free. The man cast a glance at her body, no doubt

19

sizing up the clearly nonperiod blue scrubs and noncolonial white clogs. Wherever she was, whatever living colonial farm she must have stumbled onto, she stuck out like a sore thumb. As she racked her brain for an explanation this man would buy, the hold at her hip retreated and rose up to inspect the small bag ax still clutched in her right hand.

The man's fingertips, dusted in what reminded Beth of charcoal ash, slid up and down the handle of the ax. The touch was less of an inspection and more of a caress, and for the first time since she came to, thoughts other than fear and confusion danced through her mind. His trimmed fingernails traced the intricate curves and carvings as his jaw fell open more. That damn jaw again, with its dark stubble and dimpled chin, captured all her attention. His left hand, still firmly gripping her own, started to ease, almost as if he meant to cradle the ax in his hands. And every time the pads of his palms or side of his hands made contact with hers, a scorching tingle shuttered through her.

"How?"

The single word was all the man said, and he hadn't even looked at her when the word stumbled out of his lips. His amber gaze still settled on the ax like it was his lover or some other cherished thing.

For a brief moment, Beth wondered what it would feel like to be looked at by this man the way he ogled that ax.

And then she did what any modern, sensible woman would have done.

With all the strength she could muster, Beth jammed her knee into the man's very soft and totally unprotected nads and sprinted like hell.

CHAPTER 4

The blazing sun had begun to sink lower in the sky as the afternoon drew to a close. Beth huddled behind an empty cart that was lying on the side of a less-than-busy street. The shadow cast by the cart's large wooden wheel was the only reliable concealment she'd been able to manage. There were no horses attached to the cart, and the only inkling of its earlier use was the scattered tufts of hay in its bed. All signs pointed to the fact that no one was coming back to this cart anytime soon.

Good. Because she desperately needed the time to sit, regroup, and contemplate all the absolutely scary thoughts banging around her head. Ever the pragmatist, she thought out all she knew to be true.

Fact: she was in a Boston antique shop before she blacked out, and the year was solidly 2022.

Fact: to the best of her knowledge, all the people she'd seen since she'd woken up were wearing what she would best describe as colonial dress.

Fact: she was most definitely *not* wearing any style of colonial dress and had never in her life.

Fact: wherever she found herself, her purse—and all the wonderful modern marvels held within—had not made the trip with her.

She briefly entertained the idea that she was on a living historical farm. When she was in elementary school, her fifth grade class had taken a field trip to one. For the low, low price of a public school education, she and her classmates got to spend the day churning butter and cracking jokes about chamber pots. But she hadn't known any to be in downtown Boston near the birthing center.

The second option—again, briefly entertained, as it was a giant football stadium of a stretch—was her somehow being involved in a Revolutionary War reenactment. But she didn't travel in those circles and knew next to nothing about where they took place. She chalked that one up as the proverbial snowball hanging out fire-side.

The third option, and the scariest one of all, she wouldn't admit to herself just yet. Because before she started spouting off thoughts that were inexplicably crazy, she needed to switch gears. She needed a plan.

She needed to find some clothes that were less blue.

People couldn't help but notice her clothing. Like the man she'd run into. Literally ran into. Like a frickin' Mack truck.

Beth scooched her butt back closer to the cart's wheel and drew her knees up to her chest, wrapping her arms around them. Her navy-clad knees poking out the top were a blazing homing beacon against all the tawny tans and rusty reds of the landscape around her. Yet as frazzled as her mind was, her senses couldn't help but zero in on what they'd gotten a noseful of earlier. Beth inhaled deeply as she recalled the heady scent of the man in the street.

Dark, smokey notes had wafted up from his clothes . . . No, that wasn't right. Was it his skin? Cologne?

Cologne. Ha! That's a good one. And where would he have purchased it, Beth? Ye olde department store?

Beth shook her head in a mix of annoyance and frustration. She didn't know where the scent had come from, but it reminded her of fire, though not in a Smokey Bear kind of way. Hardly. No, the scent was more tantalizing and complex, like when the final wisps of a scented candle were extinguished. The remaining smoke still wafting up from the wick would be a subtle mix of charred carbon and what-ever fragrance the wax had been dipped with. The harshness of scorched cotton fibers mellowed by, say, lilac or vanilla. A yin and

22

yang of complexity, similar to throwing pine needles on a budding campfire, with its earthy essence and harsh phosphorus enticing people to sit closer just to watch its sparks.

The irony of the analogy wasn't lost on her. That man in the street lit Beth up like a Christmas tree. And the sensation scared the crap out of her. Almost as much as when his eyes had jerked toward her ax and refused to budge. Since the little thing had a head no longer than the length of her palm, she hardly thought he'd needed it if he really intended on doing her harm. Since his arms were so damn big, he could probably fell a tree just by pushing it. But like hell she wanted to volunteer that information.

She had every intention of hanging onto her rusty old baby ax with its little baby blade, thank you very much.

Raspy footsteps shuffling along the cobblestones drew her attention. Beth crouched low and peeked through the slats of the wheel. A woman's black buckle shoes and white stockings came into vision first. As Beth angled her head upward, she got an eyeful of the rest of the ensemble, more skirts, aprons, and caps she'd seen on other women in the street, but this woman was carrying a rather large wicker basket in front of her.

And it was overflowing with clothes.

Beth scrambled around the wheel as the woman walked past the cart. Cold stone dug into her knees as Beth got a better look at the basket. Hanging over its side were swaths of fabric Beth hoped were skirts, along with loose apron strings and ruffled edges of what she'd seen on some women's jackets. But the woman herself wasn't dressed as fancy as others she'd seen.

Was the woman . . . Gosh, was she a . . . servant?

Beth swallowed down the thought as quickly as it rose up. She promised herself she wouldn't entertain the idea of option number three. Not yet. Because how in the holy hell was it even an option?

First, clothes. She needed to get on board the whole when-in-Rome train *fast*.

As sneakily as she could, Beth rose from her hiding place and followed the woman. She allowed her target to get pretty far ahead before she risked sprinting to the next hiding spot. Since she'd left her phone in her purse, she had no idea what time it actually was, but she figured it was a few hours after lunch, creeping into late afternoon, judging by the sun and fewer people on the streets.

The woman with the basket slowed her pace, and Beth panicked for a moment when she thought the woman was about to enter the beige townhouse on the corner. But instead, the woman passed the three small steps leading up to the door and turned right, walking around to the back of the property. As Beth caught up, though more slowly than she would have liked, she rounded the corner of a wrought iron garden fence and ducked down low behind a nearby shrub. Inside the fence, the basket of laundry had been placed on the ground by the rear door of the property, near a washbasin, and the back of the woman's skirts kicked up as she walked inside the house.

Beth scanned the perimeter. No one. A slight moment of silence didn't reveal any clopping of horse hooves or the rumbling of carriage wheels. The woman hadn't yet returned from inside. It was her only chance, so she took it.

The iron latch on the gate was scorching hot, having no doubt baked in the afternoon sun for hours, but that didn't stop her. Once inside the garden, she ran to the basket and grabbed whatever she could. Three-quarters of the fabrics in there looked like curtains or frilly pillow shams, but she didn't care. If her fingers could grab it, she palmed it. Beth's arms were laden with what she hoped were the components of a working outfit. Then she scrambled out of the garden, her white clogs nearly tripping over an apron string, and scurried back to the safety of her bush.

Her stomach soured at the prospect of taking her clothes off in public, but she was out of options. She quickly laid out her loot, assessed what she guessed should go where, and started stripping. Her exposed skin pebbled in the shade, even though it was nearly summer. Adrenaline tended to wreak havoc on a body's innate workings, apparently.

Once her blue scrubs were crumbled under the bush's lower branches, Beth grabbed the skirt and pulled it over her head before shimmying it down to her waist. Fastening the thing was a head-scratcher, as there were no buttons or buckles. But there was a long length of string. Hell, everything she grabbed had a string dangling from it. She felt like a damn marionette. With a shrug, she wrapped the string around her waist once and did her best to tie it off in a knot at her hip, silently cursing how her belly wouldn't allow for more slack on the string. Beth took it as a win when she did a slight shimmy and the thing still stayed in place. A white apron with, yup, more strings seemed self-explanatory, so she wrapped it over the skirt and tied it off the same way.

Beth crouched in the bushes, all colonial on the bottom and half-naked on the top as she took in the two articles of clothing before her. One seemed like a short jacket with elbow-length sleeves, but there were no buttons or fasteners to keep it closed. How the heck did that work? The other piece she was fairly sure she knew how it worked, but she looked at the thing like it was a poisonous animal about to bite her.

Was that a real corset? She ran her fingers up and down the boning of the garment and shivered with every new pass. Honestly, how the hell was she supposed to get in that thing, let alone breathe in it? And didn't women usually need someone else's help to tuck things in nice and tight?

A loud bang brought her head up. The woman was at the back door, which had beat against the wall when she opened it. She bent over to grab the basket and walked back into the house.

Crap. Beth was running out of time. Okay, it was go time. The words of one of her midwifery school instructors floated through her mind when students would complain to her about questioning their decisions.

Make your decision the right decision.

Beth grabbed the white-and-pale-blue striped jacket and threw it over her bra. The thing was an inch shy of closing over her large chest, but since she couldn't see a way to secure it shut anyway, it hardly mattered. Next, she grabbed the corset and threw it over her head. As she tried to shimmy the damn thing over her wide shoulders, with her arms straight out above her, she'd never had more sympathy in that moment for all the babies she helped deliver. All those wriggly worms having their chubby bodies squeezed through a tight birth canal.

This . . . frickin' . . . suuucks.

When one shoulder popped out, then the other, Beth exhaled a sigh of relief. The torture tube was still bunched up under her chin, and her boobs were going through all sorts of *not having it*, but with a few more tugs and loosening of the strings, she managed to get the thing to lie somewhat flat over the jacket. Then she grabbed the bonnet-hat-thingy and popped it on the crown of her head, fully aware how her disheveled hair had mostly come undone from its braid and hung wildly around her shoulders.

Beth stood up and looked down at herself. The toes of her clogs poked out beneath the brown ankle-length skirt, but it couldn't be helped. She hoped they'd be obscured enough by the fabric and no one would really notice.

As Beth hesitantly walked out from behind the bush, she couldn't help but wipe her sweating palms down the front of her apron. A low grumble made itself known in the base of her stomach, and she was reminded of how she'd missed out on eating lunch.

Which then reminded her of *why* she'd missed out on eating lunch.

Hunger and worry knotted her insides together as she laid her hands against her stomach. The rough fibers of the corset's laces abraded her palms. And as she stood there, clogs on cobblestones and her boobs in a vice, it was yet another reminder of how lost she was.

What do I do now?

"Miss McCrary? I say, are you Miss Elizabeth McCrary?"

Curiosity got the better of Beth as she looked up and followed the direction of the voice. From out of the back door of the house she was still standing in front of, an older woman walked down the short steps. The trill in her voice was harsh as she hobbled down the path, all bosom and billowing skirts. She looked like a squat, moody version of Mrs. Potts from *Beauty and the Beast*, except for the whole being-a-tea-kettle thing.

And she was heading right for Beth.

"Good God, what on earth have you done with your stays? My goodness, this will never do. Have you forgotten how to dress yourself?" The woman, who was several inches shorter than Beth but several octaves louder, put her hands on Beth's shoulders and quickly spun her around in inspection, tsking nonstop. Beth was so stunned, she had no choice but to let the woman turn her like a top.

"When I had spoken to your uncle inquiring after help for Mr. Richmond's house, he said I would recognize you by your red hair, but he failed to expand on your inability to dress your own self. Where is your uncle, anyway?" The woman looked down the road and then back, obviously expecting to see the remnants of a carriage that wasn't there.

"Well, no matter. Help is hard to find and we are in great need. Come, let us get you inside. No doubt the ride from up north was long." The woman laid her hand on the small of Beth's back as she escorted her down the walkway leading into the back of the house. Beth's feet moved forward without her commanding them. Mrs. Potts was certainly a pushy one.

"Is your trunk arriving separately? In the meantime, you can borrow from Annabelle if you need anything, though . . ." The woman paused and ran her eyes up and down Beth's form. "Annabelle is not quite as . . . buxom. You'll have to make do. Come along now, Elizabeth."

"Beth."

"Sorry?" The old woman quirked her head, nearly missing what Beth had said.

"I'm . . . Beth."

As Mrs. Potts climbed the top stair, with Beth slowly rising on her heels, the woman turned around and placed her hands on her wide hips. The brief smile she flashed was a welcome ray of sunshine in a world of cloudy confusion.

"And as I'm sure your uncle informed you, I'm Mrs. Potter, the housekeeper. Now, let me take you to Annabelle and see if we can't set you to rights."

Mrs. Potter. Well, Beth hadn't been far off.

What she wouldn't give for an enchanted rose and magic mirror.

CHAPTER 5

"Have you really never had to fasten your stays on your own? My, I had no idea things were so different up north. You must have had quite a lot of sisters to help, I imagine. Where did you say you were from again?"

Annabelle stood in front of Beth, roughly tugging each lace of the corset taut—correction, *stays*. With each tighter pull of the strings, Beth took the opportunity to inhale deeply, allowing her chest its final moments to fully expand. Kind of a last hurrah bachelorette party before the ball and chain, or boning and ties in this case, were clamped down. The only saving grace of the whole procedure was Beth's relief, and mild embarrassment, at how the jacket she'd chosen was supposed to go *over* the stays, not the other way around.

Oops.

"I'm from . . . um . . ."

Tug tug tug. Deep breath in. Tug tug tug.

"Salem," Beth exhaled, throwing out the first up-north town that came to mind.

"Oh, yes. I've heard of it. On the coast, right? Not as busy as Boston, I imagine. There, now let me just get some pins . . ."

Annabelle leaned down to her right and pulled on yet another string attached to her waist. This time, at the end was a red round ball with pinheads sticking out of it. Once she tugged it up, she removed a few straight pins, planted them between her lips, and let the pincushion drop.

"The jacket will fit much better now that the stays have flattened out your figure," she mumbled around a mouthful of pins.

How the hell has my figure been flattened out? My tits are so high under my chin a sudden yawn could knock out a tooth.

More tugging, more tying, and Beth glanced down at her torso. Annabelle had woven the pins into the two flaps of the jacket, securing them together. To Beth's great astonishment, the woman was right. It fit much better, though she still was showing an awful lot of—

"Here's a kerchief. You can tuck it in the front, underneath your jacket, if you'd like." Annabelle draped a white square of fabric over the back of Beth's neck before walking around to her front. With a knowing twinkle in her eye and a quirk at the corner of her lips, Annabelle demonstrated tucking one corner into Beth's stays, underneath the jacket. "Though there's only so much bounty we can hide." A sharp wink jostled Beth back online, and she quickly mimicked the tuck on the other side.

"Thank you," Beth whispered as Annabelle crouched and laid at Beth's feet a pair of black leather shoes sporting a big ol' pilgrim buckle front and center.

"No need. I'm happy to help where I can. I just hope the shoes fit. Your feet seem to be about my size, at the very least. Though you'll have to tell me of the materials of your shoes. I had never felt anything so sturdy, nor seen anything so interestingly shaped."

Beth slid her stockinged feet into the worn leather and did her best to shrug off Annabelle's mention of the clogs, which Beth had managed to kick behind the bed the moment she was brought into Annabelle's room.

"Yeah, well . . ." Beth let the statement die on her lips. The unease in her circumstances was finally threatening to shine through. She had questions, *so* many questions, but she hardly knew where to start or how to ask.

Beth took in the woman before her, as well as their surroundings. When Mrs. Potter escorted Beth into the house through the back door, Annabelle had appeared by her side as if magically summoned. A handful of staff hustled about, but after a few whispered words exchanged between the two women, Beth's elbow had been gripped by a delicate, yet firm palm and escorted down the hall. Some turns and curves in the hallway later and the two of them were tucked away into what Beth would learn was Annabelle's bedroom. A moment after that, the young woman came forward with proper clothing to right Beth's obvious wrongs: petticoats (okay, not just skirts, apparently), stockings, garters, and a shapeless white shift that would put Casper the Friendly Ghost to shame.

Annabelle couldn't have been much older than her early twenties, yet she carried herself like a Mrs. Potter in training. Her maneuvers had an air of authority, yet with a gentle kindness and understanding a matron wouldn't have the patience for.

For lack of a better plan, Beth exhaled a slow breath and cautiously dipped her toe in the uncharted waters. "May I ask . . . where we are?"

Annabelle cocked her head to the side and furrowed her brow slightly. "Do you not know?"

"I mean, my . . . um . . . uncle just told me he'd be sending me on a long journey. He didn't share many details."

Liar, liar, petticoats on fire.

"How curious. Well, this is Mr. Richmond's home, though I can't imagine how you wouldn't know that."

"And Mr. Richmond is . . . ?"

"My goodness, your uncle really hadn't told you much," she said, with her hands on her hips. "Very well. Mr. Paul Richmond is one of the wealthiest whalers in Boston, with a fleet of nearly fifteen ships. He employs all who serve in this house, including Mrs. Potter, the housekeeper, John, his valet, and the rest of the staff. I had thought you would have known who you were sent to work for, surely. Mrs. Potter spoke very highly of your uncle, Mr. McCrary, who informed her his niece was in want of employment in service at a reputable home."

"Whaling? As in hunting whales? From the ocean?" Beth's stomach had started to flip over on itself, like a gymnast with a bad case of the twisties. Soft pants puffed through her parted lips in an effort to tamp down the hysteria.

"Yes, from the ocean," Annabelle said, exasperated, as if she were explaining to a three-year-old why water was wet. "After all, where do you think the boning in your stays comes from?"

Beth dropped her chin and immediately ran her fingers along her ribs. Or the rigid casing entombing her ribs. *I'm wearing whale bones.*

"Miss McCrary, are you all right? Here, have a sit down."

Annabelle ushered Beth over to a small wooden chair in front of a desk. Firm palms pushed down on her shoulders as she was urged to sit. In the sea of information that had just been dumped on her, one more thing pricked at her ears. Beth raised her eyes to the woman across from her.

"McCrary?" Beth whispered.

"Is your name not Elizabeth McCrary, niece of Jonathan McCrary?"

Oh, no. They must think I'm someone else.

"Annabelle, what's today's date?"

The woman's features twisted in surprise, but another sigh escaped her before she acquiesced to Beth's question. "I can't fathom why you wouldn't know, but far be it for me to deprive you."

Beth stared at Annabelle's lips and held her breath steady in her lungs. Then an assortment of words and numbers, definitely more than needed to answer Beth's simple question, tumbled out of the woman's mouth and knocked Beth clear in the gut.

"It is the tenth of June, in the year of our Lord seventeen hundred and seventy."

Soft clacking resounded in the hallway outside Mr. Richmond's study. The house's staff bustled about, while Beth sat in a plumply cushioned wooden chair in front of her new employer's desk, a long-handled broom lying at her feet. After Annabelle had dropped the Hiroshima-sized bombshell on Beth's freshly bonneted head, logical thought had gone by the wayside. Her situation had gone from fuzzy and strange to a thousand-piece mosaic jigsaw puzzle missing half the pieces.

None of it made any sense, but here she sat, with directions to sweep the study of an employer whose house she now lived in and who, oh yeah, killed whales for a living. The whole thing would have been laughable if Beth would have been able to peel back some curtain somewhere to reveal this was all one big joke.

But it wasn't. Option three, which she now thought of as her nuclear option, glowed radioactive green all around her. It was in the ornate oil paintings of old-to-her ships on the wall; the maps of Boston Harbor and the greater Atlantic Ocean, dated 1768, sprawled out on the desk; and the open ledger poking out underneath the maps detailing recent ship-related purchases, all of which were written in extremely slanted cursive from what was clearly a quill. The curlicues were too epic and beyond a ballpoint pen's ability.

After Beth dressed properly, Annabelle had escorted her to the kitchen where the staff was preparing supper. Beth had been informed that Mr. Richmond would not be home for the evening meal, so no formalities need be taken. Regardless, Beth had only managed to choke down a heel of bread and a few bites of hard cheese, and even those sank like lead in her mostly empty stomach.

Annabelle had perhaps sensed Beth's discomfort and immediately thrown a broom into Beth's hand, with instructions to sweep the master's study. Idle hands were the devil's work, Annabelle had chided and encouraged Beth to keep busy before retiring for the evening lest her tired mind wandered too much and prevented her from being useful before bed. Beth had been given a small room next to Annabelle's but hadn't spent any time in it yet.

Because she was too consumed with the nuclear option.

Clanging and shuffling filled her ears. More noise from the house as rooms were closed down for the evening and pots cleaned and stowed. The faint rumblings of a routine that was not hers in a house she had no business squatting in reminded her of the antique shop back in Boston.

Well, I suppose I am still in Boston, aren't I?

The clacking of the beaded curtain that separated the shopkeeper's back office from the rest of the store seemed a distant memory. Recalling the tinny broadcast of the baseball game that resonated from the back radio magnified the distance further. The cold, abrasive iron of the eighteenth-century nails and the smooth uniformity of the musket balls on the shop's front table had distracted her.

But nothing had distracted her quite as much as her baby ax, which she still had tucked inside the pocket pouch of her skirt.

Beth shifted slightly, and as if bidden from its hiding place, the blunt end of the ax's metal handle poked her in the thigh, making itself known. Beth moved around in her seat and freed the weapon, though she doubted the thing could do more than mildly indent, let alone chop. Her fingernails scraped along the ornate engravings, tracing the patterns in a soothing motion, following the curving vines as they wandered up and down the handle.

The engravings had become a sort of stress relief. Each time she ran the pads of her fingers over the designs, her hand would flow with the current, following every turn up and down the handle until, finally, her hand would land home when it returned to the beginning of the pattern.

Like a yellow brick road for Dorothy Gale.

When Dorothy landed in Oz wearing nothing but a bright blue pinafore dress, she was given a pair of kick-ass shoes and told to follow the yellow brick road. When Beth landed on a cobblestone street in a Boston she didn't recognize, wearing nothing but her navy-blue scrubs, instead, she was given a pair of big-buckle shoes and told to get to sweeping. Since then, one thing had become perfectly clear.

Dorothy's tornado ain't got nothing on Beth's nuclear option.

Because last she checked, time traveling back to the pre-Revolutionary War era couldn't be solved by clicking one's heels.

CHAPTER 6

Beth's shoes scraped across the worn wood floor as she navigated the halls of Mr. Richmond's manor the following morning. Her body was running on fumes, but her mind was going a mile a minute. After she finished sweeping and tidying Mr. Richmond's study, Beth had thankfully retired to her small room for the night. With no clock to check the time (besides, what would she do with the information anyway?) and nothing else to occupy herself, she had lain on the small mattress and stared at the ceiling.

For hours.

From out her small window, darkness had bloomed into blushing grays, pale ambers, and bright oranges as the sun got its rise and shine on. She didn't know how many hours she actually slept, but the dull hum in her head and the knot in her back told her they had been scarce and fitful.

Bright-eyed and bushy-tailed she was not. Did they even have coffee in 1770 Boston? If not, she could at least rely on some tea. Lord knows Boston had been all about the tea back then.

Or now.

Hushed whispers grew louder as Beth turned the corner into the kitchen. Annabelle and Mrs. Potter were standing by the stove, their heads bowed in murmured conversation. Mrs. Potter's lips were compressed into a thin line as she worried her hands down at her waist. Annabelle was staring at the floor with her brows down, nodding slightly, as if she were trying to parse out a solution to a difficult math problem in her head. When Beth entered the kitchen, they both ceased their mumbling and looked up at her.

She froze, not sure what to expect. They both looked at her, but neither said a word. She quickly glanced down at her outfit. Yes, her inner petticoats were hidden, both garters were on her stockings, stays were covered up (live and learn on that one), and she'd managed to get the straight pins in the right position to keep the jacket closed. It all seemed correct by what Annabelle had shown her. She briefly paused in her assessment, then swung her hand up to her head. When her fingers brushed the cotton covering her hair, she exhaled in relief. She'd even managed to remember her cap. Points for her!

So, why the stern looks?

"Um . . . good morning?" Beth threw the greeting out there on a wing and a prayer that it hadn't changed much over the centuries.

More silence.

Unsure what to do, Beth recalled her old ballet and tap days from when she was a child. Dance had been just another extracurricular she'd taken and, like all the others, never panned out beyond the three-week mark. But she did remember two things: shuffle-hop-step and curtseying.

Were they expecting her to curtsey? Hell if she knew, but it couldn't hurt. It was a sign of respect, especially in days gone by, right?

Putting her right foot back, she grabbed the folds of her skirts, bent her knees, and leaned down.

Except she forgot about the stays. Or her inability to bend properly at the waist.

With her downward momentum halted, Beth kind of hovered in a squatting position over her ankles. Her knees screamed in agony and her thighs burned from the surprise yoga pose they were called into action to perform.

Respectful she was not. If anything, Beth looked like a disoriented sorority sister popping a squat over a dirt hole at a backyard fraternity party because she was too drunk to walk up the stairs of the frat house to use the bathroom.

Or not to pee on her shoes.

Thankfully, Beth didn't have to worry about peeing on her shoes. She'd already had the wonderful chamber pot introduction that morning and *nailed it*, for what it was worth. She'd been around enough bedpans, after all.

But Mrs. Potter and Annabelle seemed less than amused, and more than a little confused, by Beth's outward display of whatever-the-heck-that-was, so she quickly backtracked. Offering up a silent prayer, Beth willed her straining thighs into giving just a little bit more. After a few grunts, she was standing tall again, though her legs were gelatin and her back would have flipped her off if it could.

"Elizabeth," Mrs. Potter said with her chin raised, despite Beth's prior correction of her name. "We received word this morning that John, Mr. Richmond's valet, has taken ill."

"Oh, I'm sorry to hear that. Is he all right?"

"His horse threw a shoe and went down, taking John with him. The fall has severely injured John's leg, and he shall not be able to perform his duties until he can walk freely again. Several weeks at least, Dr. Powell said. Of course, it doesn't help matters that the good doctor is in such short supply these days, what with all the boycotts and militia injuries running him ragged, the poor man. We're very fortunate to work in Mr. Richmond's employ, as he has made a very good living taking advantage of our maritime city. He's always looked out for his staff, thank the Lord. John shall be just fine." Mrs. Potter nodded profusely, as if she had to convince herself of her own words, and crossed herself.

"It shall be a bit harder picking up John's duties," Annabelle filled in. Before she continued her thought, an idea flitted across her features. She cocked her head slightly and a smile crooked her lips as her gaze landed back on Beth. "Why, *you* can deliver the ship's plans to Mr. Brannigan and work with him on the orders. Oh, that would help immensely!" Annabelle clapped her hands together under her chin.

"I'm sorry. Ship?"

"An excellent idea, Annabelle!" Mrs. Potter chirped as she walked toward a desk in the corner. After grabbing a few pieces of paper from a drawer, she shut it with her hip and shuffled over to Beth. "These are the items Mr. Richmond is in need of for his newest ship. He's contracted with a shipbuilder, but their supply line is limited due to the British Navy's needs. As part of the arrangement, Mr. Richmond said he'd provide the necessary components for the ship. All the shipbuilder need provide are the men and labor to build it. Here," she said, thrusting a loose stack of papers into Beth's hands. "Now, I shall go through them precisely line by line lest you forget. The amounts must be portrayed exactly as they are to Mr. Brannigan, the blacksmith."

Beth glanced down at the off-white papers in her hands. Her eyes flitted across the black ink on the page. Several numbers stared back at her; quantities and volumes of various bracings, bolts, and anchors, all itemized by types of metals. Most she was familiar with, like iron and copper, but some were foreign. Still, the list seemed straightforward. And if all she had to do was deliver this to a local merchant and he'd take it from there? It was a very manageable errand, with her only having to maybe speak with the blacksmith. The fewer people she needed to talk to, the better.

". . . Copper is strongly preferred, and bronze would be best for the nails. Though iron nails are better than no nails at all . . ." Mrs. Potter kept rambling off the list, covering each line verbatim, as if Beth couldn't read what was right in front of her.

Oh.

Beth was hardly up to speed on colonial literacy rates, but she probably wasn't far off in her assumption that members of the serving class weren't necessarily literate. By virtue of her ability to read and write, she could be more useful in her situation. A greater use would give her a fighting chance of sticking around longer, at least long enough to figure out how this had happened to her.

" . . . the wood should be painted yellow, hence the preference for bronze—"

"I can read this list, Mrs. Potter. I understand the items you wrote out."

The matron paused her recitation and stared, mouth agape, at Beth. "You can read and write, my dear?"

"Yes, ma'am."

Mrs. Potter's hand flew to fidget with the ruffles at her neckline. "Wonderful! I do apologize. Of course, you can. I nearly forgot myself for a minute. Your uncle would have made sure of it, naturally, with his merchant connections and barter arrangements. Well," she said, clapping her hands and scurrying for a quill on the desk. "Here's where you'll be taking this list. The blacksmith is Mr. Thomas Brannigan and his forge is on Cooper Road. Just give him the list and he can take it from there."

Nothing made Beth feel more like an imposter than walking down an eighteenth-century Boston cobblestone road in shoes that were slightly too big, a bonnet that was a hair too small, and very un-colonial boyshort underwear hidden underneath someone else's skirts. Despite Annabelle's directions that the blacksmith's forge wasn't far, Beth had asked the woman to sketch out a map. Thankfully, Annabelle had no trouble drawing and happily obliged.

By Beth's estimation, she had another block or two to go. She was grateful for the outing, even if the world around her was more than a bit terrifying. Men and women, horses and carriages, all mulled about along the streets. The pastel colors and dark blues and browns were a surprising contrast to the vibrant, neon colors she was used to in her own Boston. A salty tang in the air tickled her nose. The harbor was not far, and that was a comfort.

She desperately needed comfort. Of any kind. Fast food and conditioner included. While her thoughts drifted toward what she missed, her baby ax clunked around in her pocket pouch. The weight of it knocking against her thigh had been the only true comfort she'd had since she woke up here. She hadn't shown it to Annabelle or anyone else. It had been hard enough to explain away her bra and clogs, let alone an ornate ax that looked like it should belong here but was speckled in centuries-old rust.

How the heck had she wound up here, and how the double heck was she going to get back home?

Was the ax the key? And if so, how did she jumpstart things to go in the other direction?

Beth let out a huge sigh of frustration as her steps carried her toward the intersection of Cooper and Manor Roads. Across the street, set farther down the road and away from the other connected buildings, was a wooden sign hanging from two black chains in front of a door. On it was an etched depiction of an anvil.

Looks like she found the right place.

Beth walked up to the door and banged her knuckles against the wood. But the door wasn't anything like the doors she was used to back home, where a good rap on a hollow door got someone's attention. Nope. This was a massive entrance made from planks of wood held together with two iron bars horizontally bisecting its middle, one toward the top and one toward the bottom. The top of the door was curved in an oval shape, and the iron handle was as no-frills as they came. She had half a mind to suspect that Bilbo Baggins lay behind the door.

When there was no answer, she knocked again, only realizing that her fist against the wood made no more noise than a kitten scratching at it would. With a deep breath, she grabbed the handle and pushed.

The door groaned its resistance as Beth slowly pushed the thing open and entered the forge. Hot, stifling air immediately assaulted her. The space was dark, except for a few sporadic windows, and anything but dank. Mold couldn't have grown inside that hot environment if it tried. As she adjusted her eyesight to the dark and stepped all the way inside the room, her back rested gently against the door. Resounding clangs of metal on metal drew her attention to the far corner.

Her stomach nearly bottomed out at what she saw.

Powerful thighs stood braced alongside an anvil as a massive arm slammed a hammer down onto a piece of metal. The iron bar took the pounding from the wielder, its bright orange color dimming with each hit. Flecks of metal scattered against the onslaught, dusting the leather apron affixed to the blacksmith's chest.

A chest that was as wide and powerful as the glowing forge was incendiary and nearly made Beth swallow her tongue. The man wore a simple linen shirt, though its sleeves were rolled up to his elbows, revealing taut forearms. He had yet to turn around, so Beth couldn't help but stare at his deliciously curved backside as he brought his arm down again to hammer the iron bar. There was definitely something to be said for the deerskin leather breeches she'd seen some of the men wear in this time. On this man especially, they did a booty good.

Beth walked forward, the list in her hand wilting under the heat, and the skirts at her hip brushed against a horseshoe sticking out over the edge of a nearby worktable. The horseshoe tumbled to the floor and took with it every spare scrap of metal, nail, and whatnot on the table. The noise was immense and echoed throughout the cavern of the forge, alerting the blacksmith to her arrival . . . and her apparent borderline voyeurism.

"I'm sorry! I'm so sorry." Beth dropped to her knees and began collecting the fallen items into her apron. "I knocked, but there was no answer. I didn't mean to intrude."

Once Beth had placed everything back on the worktable, she dusted off her apron and turned to face the blacksmith.

Hard, hazel eyes glowed fiery as they reflected the nearby forge and took her in.

That chest, which Beth had so casually admired from afar, expanded with an enormous breath, increasing the blacksmith's intimidating posture. He exhaled great puffs of air from his exertion, though his jaw remained tense and firm. His grip around the hammer's handle tightened. A flitter of recognition danced across his features as his expression turned to stone before her.

"You." The growl that puffed out of him was deep and abrasive, as if its gruffness could file down metal.

Beth was locked in a staring contest with the man from the street, the very same one she had run into and nearly knocked over while panicked. The one who had most definitely witnessed her up close and personal in her noncolonial blue scrubs and clogs. The one whose smell still lingered in her nose.

And, perhaps most regrettably, the one who she'd kicked in the balls before bolting.

Oh, shit.

CHAPTER 7

Thomas's cods nearly winced at the memory of their abuse from the woman before him. Hence, he was more than surprised to turn around and see her slight fingers scrambling about to gather horseshoes and nails off the floor. Though the lighting was dim, a slight blush crept high on her cheeks as she laid the items on his worktable. It wasn't obvious, but it was there. Was she embarrassed by her clumsiness?

He hoped so.

And what a bastard he was for wishing ill on a woman. Even if his stones would thank him for it.

"You," he breathed out. His heart beat wildly within his chest, and his ears still rang from the hammering. Working molten metal always gave him a rush, and that rush allowed him to be caught unawares, unfortunately. As he had quickly drawn out the cooling iron, likewise had his adrenaline been drawn out through his veins. Over the years, he had learned to tune his mind out to all his surroundings and focus on the metal he was molding. Once his senses registered the abrupt clang of the table items falling, he'd nearly dropped his tongs.

Blast, the knife!

He quickly looked back to his anvil. His long black tongs, which had previously held a lean bar of glowing hot iron, now pinched a black, flaked hunk of metal that would need to be reheated before he could draw it out again. Another delay added to his growing list.

"Come to kick me again?" He couldn't even look at her, his mind was so frazzled. He abhorred interruptions when he was working metal. Emily had always chided him on his foul temper when he got like that. However, she'd always murmured her scolding in his ear with all the disdain of a mother coddling a child's temper tantrum.

God, had it really been five years since she'd passed?

In desperate need of a distraction that wouldn't haunt or attack him, Thomas picked up his tongs, walked over to his forge, and threw the bar into the flame.

"No." The softly spoken word held all the malice of a sprouted, puffy dandelion. "And I'm sorry for that earlier. I was, um, in a hurry. But now, I'm here at Mr. Paul Richmond's behest. I didn't know you were the blacksmith or that you'd remember me."

Her feet dragged through the loose dirt on the floor as she walked over to him. His eyes were still cast on his forge until the corner of a paper appeared in his peripheral vision down by his elbow. Raising an eyebrow, he looked down and grabbed the note.

With his eyes cast down at the paper, he scanned the details while also taking stock of the woman who disturbed him. The woman who saw fit to attack him, only to unknowingly return for what he presumed was business on behalf of an employer. If he didn't lift his head too high, he could see all of her form except her face, as if she were an extension of the note itself.

He held the note away from his body and peered up. To her, he would surely seem as if he were reading the top line on the page. To him, however, he was taking stock of his intruder.

For he would have sworn on the memories of his wife and infant son that he would never see her again. Especially not after she had unmanned him whilst among the public.

Her brown petticoat, though ordinary, lay in a manner that was anything but. The generous shape of her wide hips allowed the fabric to cascade, rather than hang. The sharp curve of her bodice, where her dressing strings were cinched beneath her apron, was pleasing. His hand recalled its brief encounter with her waist and itched to return there. His eyes continued their secretive roaming, traveling northward over her bountiful bosom covered by a blue striped jacket. It contained her well enough, though the sudden hardness between his legs called to mind other features he wished to ignore.

God! It had been too long since he had been with a woman. His darling Emily was his last, and she would be his only. How on earth could he even look at another the same way? No, it would never be in the same way. His Emily was his treasure. He would not allow this woman, with her fiery red hair and abundant charms, or any other woman for that matter, to stir anything within him. Except . . .

Her bag ax. He recalled it swiftly now, as he had never seen anything like it. That was what had given him pause in the street and prevented him from letting her go. The ax she clutched in her hand had a metal handle. Uncommon enough, as most were wood, but not out of the realm of possibility if one had the resources and skills. No, what had captivated him were the embellishments. The vine-like etchings and ornate metalwork had stolen his breath.

For he had longed to pursue that spark of creativity within himself again. Emily had always encouraged him to tamper, explore, expand. Yet the market, being what it was, had no place for decorative oddities and trinkets. No place for a creative blacksmith when such tradesmen were caught between the demands of the colonists for housing materials and the demands of Britain for musket balls. And let's not forget weapons all around. So, in order to support his family, he used his craft to meet the needs of the masses, instead of the needs of his soul.

When Emily died, along with their son, of smallpox those years back, he'd lost his heart as well as his biggest supporter.

How strange and unexpected it was to have those long-dead urges rise up at the sight of this woman and her ax, both of which had literally stumbled right into him.

A loud pop from the forge was all the warning he got before the woman ripped the paper out of his hand. "Since your eyes were roaming elsewhere, I assume you finished reading through Mr. Richmond's list."

Thomas looked up. The woman's red eyebrows slashed angry lines across her pale complexion. Her hand, the one gripping the order, rested in the crook of her waist, with the paper partially crumpled.

Her temper was amusing. And thrilling, for he hadn't had a sparring partner in quite some time.

"Tell Mr. Richmond I'll begin work on his materials within the week." He snatched the paper back from her and walked over to a corner desk.

"That's it? Is there anything more I need to tell him?"

"No."

"Well, what if I'm asked questions? Like, how long will it take for the order to be filled? Or will it all be completed at once or piecemeal? How will it be delivered? What if a certain metal—"

"Stop."

The woman clamped her mouth shut and stared at him.

"Where are you from?"

"Um. Boston."

"Your dialect is . . . unusual."

"Well, I'm from Salem as well."

"Are you?"

"Yes."

Thomas left the list on the desk after making some notes and slowly walked toward the woman. "Name."

"Name?"

"Your name."

"It's Beth Car . . . McCrary. Beth McCrary." Her eyes darted around his forge, as if looking for an escape route.

As amusing as it was to torment her, he let out a sigh of resignation and proceeded to put her out of her misery."Come back tomorrow."

"What? Why? I thought you said you wouldn't begin working on Mr. Richmond's list for another week."

"Tomorrow."

"I'm sorry, but I need more information."

"And you shall have it. Tomorrow."

He turned away from Beth, rolled up a sleeve that had fallen loose, and went back to the forge. After opening and closing his fist a few times, he shook out his hand and gripped the tongs out of the fire before returning the hot iron to the anvil. Mutters and grumbles off to his left were interspersed with grunts as Miss McCrary heaved the door open.

Before she managed to slip out the door, he bellowed out to her one more thing. "And bring your ax."

There was a halt in her footsteps in the dirt and an even longer delay before he heard the wooden door creak shut. Satisfied he was alone again, he let his hammer fall on the iron. The metal hissed and sparks flew.

He had no idea what propelled him to have her return. But as the burn in his muscles reappeared, he held tight to his conviction.

Her ax, and her ax alone, was the only thing that held his interest.

———

Four blocks into her eight-block walk was all it took for Beth to dream up an escape plan, work out how to enact it, and decide on pizza toppings.

Because when she got back to her room, she was determined to will herself, and her baby ax, back home and order a damn pizza.

Maybe she'd splurge on the calories and even order her when-no-one's-looking favorite, the penne vodka pizza. Because if an eighteen-inch-diameter bread circle wasn't carb heavy enough, putting pasta on top would surely fix the problem.

And make her forget about all her other problems. Like showing up for round three to face off with the one man she'd managed to assault on sight. Who didn't look half bad swinging a hammer around and who happened to have the most delicious backside any fabric would be happy to hug.

Thor *had* always been her favorite Avenger, after all.

Thoughts of modern-day heroes encouraged her as Beth rounded the corner of her block and opened up the garden gate at the back of the house. With her steps quicker, almost in time with her speedy heart rate, she bypassed the kitchen and nearly overshot the door to her room when she entered the hallway.

This had to work. Had to had to had to.

She closed herself in and let out a quick breath. In her hurry to get back, she'd neglected to check the pendulum clock in the main entry. Mrs. Potter would probably be calling on her to help with midday chores or meals or some other exhausting thing she wasn't cut out for. She had to work fast.

Fumbling about at her waist, she located the tie for her pocket pouch and yanked that thing loose. The fabric dropped to the floor with a dull thud. She quickly scooped it up and freed her ax from the cotton.

Both hands clenched tightly around the handle, one fist resting on top of the other. Her legs were braced shoulder-width apart, and she slightly jockeyed her weight from leg to leg. If Annabelle had chosen that moment to walk in on her, Beth probably would have looked like she was about to attack a house cat or something.

She squeezed her eyes shut and did three quick exhales through tight lips. Heck, if short breaths helped her patients through a contraction, they sure as hell could help her through a panic attack.

Two soft pumps of her fists around the handle were all she needed before she rounded her shoulders back and waited for the magic to happen.

"I wish to go home."

A few seconds passed before she cracked one eye open. Nothing. She tried again.

"I wish to go home."

Pause.

"I wish to return to my time."

Shorter pause.

"I really want to freaking go the freak home so I can stop freaking the freak out!"

She tried every possible combination she could think of to trigger whatever forces had brought her here to bring her the hell back. Right the hell now.

After what she guessed was probably ten minutes of regripping, repositioning, and rephrasing, she plopped down on the bed and gave up.

Her master plan, the one she *needed* to work because it made about as much sense as everything else had over the last twenty-four hours, deflated as fast as a whoopee cushion. The warm metal against her sweaty palms reminded her that it was probably a good idea to unclench her fingers from the death grip they had on the ax handle. When she looked down, a slight residue was nestled into one of the rust patches along the curve of the dulled blade. She hadn't noticed it before because of the other random pitting along the edge, but this patch was a different color.

Beth brought the ax blade in for a closer inspection. That one spot had a hint of pale green to it, almost as if a colored powder had settled and collected there. But why green powder? Unless the antique shopkeeper moonlighted as Frankenstein's monster during Halloween and had a grand old time terrorizing tourists as the misunderstood creature who wielded a tiny colonial ax.

What an image.

Unconcerned, Beth gave a quick puff and blew the dust away without another thought. But before she could study it any more, hard knocks on her door grabbed her attention.

"Elizabeth, Annabelle needs help with the washing," Mrs. Potter called through the door before her heavy footsteps resumed their trek down the hall.

Beth groaned as she fell back on the bed for an all-too-brief second. "Yes, ma'am."

With the ax tucked back into her pocket pouch, she refastened it to her waist. It was only as she started to close the door behind her that specks of dust danced in the beam of sunlight from her small window. Those tiny flecks tugged at a memory—specifically, how dusty the antique shop had been.

And the pale green dust that had coated the ax handle right before she had a sneezing fit and passed out.

A sneezing fit that was the catalyst, apparently, for dumping her butt in colonial Boston.

CHAPTER 8

The harsh clanging of the hammer against metal didn't bother Emily like it had when she was alive. But back when she and Thomas first met in Baltimore, all the sounds had rattled her. Being fresh from the countryside and new to the region had been an overwhelming experience. In truth, most things about the city had rattled her. She had been twenty-two and a sheltered only child, and the newness to it all had been enough to make her run and hide. Until Thomas had come along. He'd managed to smooth out the city's harsh edges for her and blessed her with a life of joy and wonder.

How she would give anything to soothe his harsh edges now.

Emily's spirit form settled over his worktable, where she sat quietly on top of the desk. It was her favorite observation spot. His forge was in the far left corner, while his grindstone sat directly to the left of the desk. His anvil was the anchor to the small room and sat proudly in its center. Off to her right sat two waist-high quench basins. Emily's nose wrinkled at the memory of the smell. Thomas had always used two barrels, one for water and one for whale oil, to quench his metals. Though she had begged him dozens of times to get rid of the whale oil, he would always fight back, insisting it hardened iron better than water.

It still stunk to the high heavens.

She waved her hand over her nose as a reflex of being in its proximity, though more out of habit than due to any physical offense at the smell. White wisps of vapor floated in front of her as her arm moved. Her spirit form, thankfully, couldn't smell or breathe.

More clanging had her head turning back toward the anvil in the center of the room. Thomas, with his shirt sleeves rolled up and his apron much dirtier than she would have allowed him to keep it, pounded away at what would be another bayonet. She recognized the shape immediately, as Thomas had nearly finished drawing out its length. She could recall the features by heart: seventeen inches long, triangular in shape, circular fastening on the end to adhere to a musket. The requests for them never ceased coming in while she had been alive, and it pained her heart to see that he still made them. A quick glance against the wall behind his anvil confirmed her suspicions. A large stack of quenched bayonets sat, just waiting for the grindstone.

Emily pressed her palms against the table and jumped down. As she walked over to Thomas, the white vapor of her spirit form floating around her, he continued to hammer away at the iron's length. The worked metal had faded in its hues, from a blazing afternoon sun to a dying sunset. Even the metal seemed to sense it was destined to be turned into another mundane weapon and was reluctant to have Thomas work it as he would. When she rounded the anvil, her back was to the glowing forge and she was able to look upon the face of the man she loved, the man she'd left all too soon.

What met her sights crushed her heart, weighing it down like a cannonball in a stormy sea. Harsh, cruel lines stood out along Thomas's brow and around his mouth. His lips were clenched shut and his eyebrows were slanted down. The light from the forge illuminated every severe angle and unforgiving feature. Gone were the coy almost-dimples that would make an appearance whenever he managed to successfully work through a particular design. Gone was the half-smile he would sport when a job neared its completion at the anvil and would find its next life at the grindstone.

Emily's eyes saddened as tears with no wetness welled up before cascading down her cheeks. For the man she loved, the brilliant blacksmith, enamored husband, and doting father of their darling babe, had lost his spark. Depression and routine, instead, had filled the voids left behind after she and their infant son, Elliot, had passed on.

And that only bolstered her decision to do what she'd done. Though never in her wildest imaginings would she have guessed that Miss Beth, the healer from the future, would have been the one to find the ax.

When Emily and their son contracted smallpox on their return travels from visiting her sister in the countryside, it had swept through them swiftly. Mere weeks after the first coughing spells had begun, Emily distinctly remembered lying in her bed, Elliot wheezing in her arms, while the doctor spoke to Thomas in the corner. The words had been too softly spoken, and her senses too dulled by the fever, to make out anything, but she didn't need to.

Death had come for her and their babe.

Elliot had passed first. Through slitted eyes, she recalled Thomas hugging Elliot's still body in his arms. Her giant bear of a husband had wrapped his entire mountainous body around the child, as if his strength and will alone could prevent Elliot's soul from passing on.

But it couldn't, and when her spirit followed suit the following day, her dearest husband had been left to the task of burying his only family.

And when Emily's spirit, restless and confused, found itself inexplicably apart from her body, she had been able to do nothing but watch on in sorrow as Thomas insisted on digging the graves himself. Every patch of grass, clump of dirt, and jagged stone was moved only by his own shovel. Once her and their son's shrouded bodies were laid to rest, only then did he allow the church's help in administering the burial rites.

He had been lost ever since. So she'd followed him these long years. Stayed with him as he'd traveled as a journeyman blacksmith to Boston, which had become a bustling port city with much trade and even more conflict. Both, it seemed, may have been the lure for Thomas, as he had been busier than ever in his business. In the five years since her death, she had kept watch over him and yearned for him to find some solace in his work. Prayed that he would return to the kind of metalworking that fed his soul, instead of that which fed the demands of the city.

But he never did.

Emily glanced around at the shelves lining the walls. Aside from the necessaries of the profession, there was no deviation of product; all she saw were knives, bayonets, musket balls, nails, and more weapons. At his forge in Baltimore, his space had been varied and wondrous. Yes, he'd made weaponry, nails, and other needs of the city, of course. But he'd also made custom molds for marvelous children's toys. Decorative ornaments burnished with engravings that were painstakingly applied. Tin soldiers on horseback crafted from a mold so lifelike, she was sure the horse would leap off the shelf and come alive. Even his weapons had been works of art, with handles crafted so beautifully, or blades curved with such precision, his customers always clamored for more.

Until he left.

Emily recalled the moment the thought came to her, of how she could help her husband. She had been standing outside his Boston forge, holding the spirit of her infant son. There were times when she had been able to hold his spirit in her arms as the babe he had been, mere months old, and times when his spirit seemed called to her own. She hadn't been able to parse it out until a dark-haired woman in a pale blue dress, though different in style, had crossed paths with her. She, too, had been carrying a babe.

She, too, had been a spirit.

Her name was Melanie, and her story had not been much different from Emily's own, as she and her child had died of illness as well, though decades earlier upon a ship traveling from Britain to Boston.

"For wee ones so young, they relied on our life force while they were alive," Melanie had explained, her words softly accented in her native Irish tones. "That is why they can return to us when they pass on, as part of us, if their mother chooses to remain as a spirit. 'Tis a comfort, I suppose, that they still need us, even in death." A sad smile had painted Melanie's face before she shook it off to further enlighten Emily on her new situation. "If you wish to hold your babe in your arms, you just wish it so and it shall be. And if you wish him close to your heart, he shall be returned there. 'Tis as generous an option you'll find in the spirit world. Unless you fancy a bit of time skipping."

That was the moment that had guided Emily's direction and ultimate decision.

To find a kindred soul for her Thomas, one who could ignite the fire within him again.

So, under Melanie's guidance, Emily crafted a plan. Traveling to the past was common for spirits, though frowned upon when they meddled in the lives of the living. Spirits could travel freely, though each time they did, a bit of their essence would be left behind in the form of pale green dust. A mostly undetectable trait. However, if a living person were to touch it, they would be sent to the time of the spirit's choosing whose essence they connected with. It was rather unfortunate for the traveler, as they could never return to their own time.

Unless the spirit's essence was taken into the living's body in some manner. Then the spirit would become a part of them and the living's presence in any time plane would only be temporary. Though the experience was rather harsh, from what Emily had been told.

But that was not what she wanted. Emily had no need for going to the past. Only heartache and sorrow awaited her there. No, she needed what had yet to happen for her plan to work. She needed to see what artifacts would pass through Thomas's forge in the *future.*

"Oh, lass, no good will come from that meddling," Melanie warned. "But who am I to warn you off your own path? As best as I have seen it, all I can say is to stay in one place. It'll be no use following your man around, seeing who he winds up with and whatnot. No, spirits can't travel like that in the future. We'd be bound to wherever our essence would wind up, and there's no way of knowing where that might be. So stick with what you know, lest you want more trouble coming your way."

A sharp hissing broke through Emily's thoughts as steam rose up from the quench basin. Her nose wrinkled reflexively. He'd used the whale oil bin again.

This had to work. When Emily chose to leave her essence in Thomas's forge, she had naively gambled that the building would always be a forge in the future. That a like-minded smith would take over the shop one day, one who might appreciate the intricacies of detailed metalwork. One who could form a connection with Thomas by speaking his own language. A tradesman who could reignite the spark with knowledge of future ironworks and blacksmithing.

She had been so wrong and could never have fathomed something called an antique shop. When she first traveled into the future, she had been nervous about the journey, about what would happen if she somehow got lost. Could that even happen to a spirit? So, she'd stayed close to Thomas's forge and only skipped ahead one year. It was enough to ensure her essence remained, but not so long that she risked a disorienting trip.

It had still been Thomas's forge at that time. She had no reason to expect, foolishly, that it wouldn't remain a forge in the future.

But when the shopkeeper took ownership of the space centuries later, she never would have suspected he'd place metal items from her own time out for sale. Or that such an ornate, decorative ax would have been one of those offerings. It had only been fitting that her essence would find its way onto the ax after her essence had sat dormant in the centuries-old space for so long.

Thomas laid the bayonet blade along the wall with the others and reached for another bar of iron. His shoulders sagged as his head fell forward. He dragged a deep breath into his lungs before turning back to his forge on the exhale. The bar was thrown into the fire as Thomas walked over to his worktable. He primed his tense fingers open and closed before they gripped the cup of whiskey at the edge of the table. In one fast gulp, the liquid slid down his throat. There was no savoring the sip, no stopping for respite. Just a quick swig before he turned and headed back to the iron in the forge.

Emily worried her hands in front of her gown. She had never intended for Miss Beth to find her essence, let alone inhale it into her body during her fit of sneezing in the antique shop. Emily had hoped for a fellow smith or tradesman, not a woman.

But Thomas needed help, and Emily's earthly shell was long gone. Only her restless spirit remained. With no other options available to her, Emily prayed Miss Beth could get through to Thomas, though how she didn't know. The woman was a healer, not a craftsman.

And then she prayed again. Because Miss Beth had unknowingly taken Emily's essence into her body, the woman would not be able to stay in Thomas's time for long. A fortnight at best, maybe an extra sennight if she was lucky, was all Miss Beth had before Emily's essence would be ripped from the woman's body and returned to Emily, landing Miss Beth back in her time.

Melanie had warned Emily not to meddle with time, especially where the living was concerned. What if Miss Beth's intrusion into Thomas's life, only to leave so suddenly, would make things worse? How would he handle another person leaving him so abruptly?

Dear God, what had she done?

CHAPTER 9

The last things Beth needed as she was about to walk into Mr. Brannigan's forge were the sweaty palms she kept wiping on her apron. Or the uncomfortable boob sweat turning her shift into a swamp. It wasn't like she could grab another one from a drawer either. Oh, no. Laundry, she had quickly learned, wasn't called a chore for nothing. But at least one thing was the same.

Colonial Boston was not immune to random June heat waves. Though she had no way of identifying the exact temperature, she would have bet her house on it being somewhere between thighs-sticking-to-leather-seats hot and fry-an-egg-on-the-blacktop sizzling. And it was still morning. Not to mention she was about to enter a stiflingly hot forge. With a stiflingly hot blacksmith—who hated her (with good reason) and only had eyes for her baby ax.

The weight of the weapon lay comfortably against her thigh. The thing was so blunt Beth doubted it could cut a marshmallow, so it was hardly self-defense material. But it was a comfort nonetheless and all she had of her own in this strange new old world.

As Beth stared up at the wooden door, wondering whether to try the whole knock-without-being-heard bit again, the door flew open. She let out a brief squeak as Mr. Brannigan met her eye in his standard blacksmith attire of leather breeches, charcoal-stained linen shirt, and apron. His looming presence ate up the doorway, and how the heck he knew she was there she had no idea. But judging by the heat emanating from behind him, and the fresh sheen of sweat at his brow, he'd already been hard at work. And it wasn't even that late in the morning.

And there she was, so proud of herself for remembering to put her colonial underwear on underneath her outfit. Boy, did she have a sense of misplaced pride. She would never have been cut out for the Army, with their whole slogan of doing more before nine a.m. than most would do all day, but apparently, Mr. Brannigan would be.

"Miss McCrary." He nodded once, that angular chin stopping to point directly at her, as if to highlight his disapproval and her otherness in one shot. Though his expression was stern, Beth got the impression that was his standard look. As if, kneeing him in the balls aside, he wouldn't have smiled at her, or anyone, or acted jovially under normal circumstances. His two-word clipped greeting said it all.

Good morning. I'm busy. I appreciate your boss's business, but not you. And you smell.

That last thought trickled through at the same moment the sweat dripped down her underclothes. God, she was *so* not built for this.

"Welcome." He turned his back to her and walked farther into his shop, all but implying that she should follow.

"I've reviewed Mr. Richmond's requests, along with the supplies available to me." His back remained to her as he rummaged through a cupboard in the corner of his shop next to a stack of unfinished bayonets. "Iron and pewter I can get straight away, but the bronze shall take longer. At least a fortnight's delay, perhaps beyond, especially if your employer insists on the additional embellishments." Mr. Brannigan walked back to Beth, papers in hand, though he never looked up.

"The base metals for all the rigging are available, and that's about all I have on hand at the moment. The rest I must inquire after. I do know of an anchor smith, however, who can work on the anchors . . . unless Mr. Richmond has already contracted for one? And who is the shipwright overseeing the project? I failed to see names of the other tradesmen noted in the ledgers you left."

The questions lingered like smog in the stale air over Beth's head, choking and seizing all possible responses. What the heck did she know about colonial shipbuilding?

"I . . . I don't know. He didn't say."

Mr. Brannigan halted in his rustling, then raised his head to her. "Pardon. Your employer didn't say what?" The words were slow and laced with irritated confusion.

Beth shuffled a step or two back under the guise of shifting her weight. "He didn't share that information with me."

Her eyes darted around the shop. Anything, literally *anything*, would be better to stare at than the questioning hazel eyes of the towering colonial blacksmith before her. Off at the edge of the ceiling to the right, where it met the wall, was a rather elaborate cobweb. That would do quite nicely.

Dammit, why did he unnerve her so much? Yes, she had been in a permanent state of nail-biting panic and paranoia for the past few days, but with others she'd met, she could still string sentences together. She had managed to hold her own with Mrs. Potter and Annabelle. Heck, she'd even survived her brief introduction to Mr. Richmond. But this guy? Her insides were a quivering mass of rubber bands around him, some too loose to function and others too tense to be flexible. She had to get her head back in the game around him. She could already tell he was smart and intuitive, and he'd seen her ax. How long before he figured out something was off about her?

Crap! Did they still do witch trials in this time?

"Miss McCrary?"

"Yes?" Beth's eyes were still locked on that cobweb. And, oh hey, look, more cobwebs dusted the rafters toward the back of his shop, too.

"Three months."

The abrupt phrase snapped her eyes back to his. He was facing her, though his gaze surreptitiously danced over her mouth before returning to meet her eyes.

"Three months?"

"Yes. If there are any unexpected delays, I shall inform Mr. Richmond immediately, but three months is reasonable for completion of his requests. Now, if you'll give me a moment, I'll draft up my terms." And with that, he walked past her and sat at the small worktable next to the door. Behind her, a quill scratched and tapped quickly against paper. Beth took the time to look around the forge.

The fire in the corner was the immediate draw, and without the blacksmith's scrutinizing gaze following her around, Beth's panic eased slightly. For a few precious moments, she allowed herself to become a tourist. Tucked into the corner of his shop was a large red-brick fireplace at waist height, twice the size of any fireplace she'd seen. Within it, and toward the back, sat a pile of lit coals. The fire was active, though banked, as if it hadn't been fed its Wheaties yet, but was anxiously lying in wait. Various tongs and picks hung over the edge of the hearth.

"That's a lot of coal," she said more to herself. The scribbling behind her continued. Content to give herself a tour, she reached up above the hearth and grabbed a long wooden beam. When she pulled it down, large bellows off to her left expanded with air. When she raised the beam again, the bellows contracted. A great puff of air was fed into the flames, causing them to glow more brightly.

"Amazing." This was so much better than churning butter in elementary school. As she continued to stoke the flames with the bellows, the increased light from the fire illuminated a small table tucked into the corner. If it wasn't for her position and proximity, she'd never know it was there. Or anyone, for that matter. It was totally hidden from view otherwise.

Beth returned the beam to its original position and knelt in front of the small table, which was no bigger than a stool. "Wow."

Hidden away from the light and caked in thin layers of dust and ash were fanciful boxes, decorative molds, and a baby rattle. The boxes were small and were perhaps meant for jewelry or other precious trinkets. Ornate trimmings and metals decorated the pieces. The molds, likewise, were so detailed. There were about half a dozen, all in different animal shapes. She immediately recognized a bear, a horse, and a wolf. Children's toys, she surmised.

59

Then there was the baby rattle. Babies were something she knew a thing or two about. Beth carefully lifted the rattle from the table and wiped the dust off it with her apron. It was silver, or at least silver in color, and had a bronze stripe going through the center of the orb. The rattle was so small, and judging by how Mr. Brannigan worked, with the resources available in this time, anything with that much detail would have taken forever.

Beth cradled the rattle in her apron as she rose to her feet and walked over to the blacksmith. Once the dust was gone, she transferred it to her hands. The metal was awfully cold for being so close to the forge. As she walked, the rattle's soft tinkling added harmony to the fire's dull roar.

"This is beautiful."

Beth settled right behind Mr. Brannigan. When she shook the rattle, his shoulders bunched and his quill stopped moving. Tension rolled off the man in waves. She didn't need her misstep spelled out for her. There was a whole lot of *do not touch* being fired her way.

"Oh, I'm sorry. I noticed it when I was at the forge." Beth turned to walk back and return the rattle.

"No need to apologize." The blacksmith's deep voice stopped her in her tracks.

When she looked back, his shoulders, a moment ago so tense and rigid, had sagged greatly. His head hung lower over the paper, and even from where Beth stood, it seemed he gripped the quill so tight it threatened to snap under his fist's onslaught.

"You made this."

"Yes."

Beth slowly walked back over to him and stood next to his table. Her backside leaned against it while he sat in a chair facing the wall. It was as close to a face-to-face conversation as they could manage. He dropped the quill, though his eyes never left the desk.

And then her heart squeezed as tight as the compressed bellows. Because she'd seen that look before, and how she wished she'd never have to see it again. But she always did. The haunted eyes, the tense muscles. A person's whole being hanging on by a thread, ready to unravel at a moment's notice.

The blacksmith had lost a child.

Of all the damn things in his forge Miss McCrary had to rummage through, why did it have to be the rattle? Devil take it, even if she had picked up one of Emily's keepsake boxes, the wound wouldn't have been as raw. But the rattle? His son had been all of three months when he passed, and the weight of the thing until then had proven too hefty for his little fingers. Thomas had meant to make a new rattle, lighter in weight and thicker about the handle, while Emily and Elliot were off visiting her sister. That was, until they returned. And a sennight after their arrival, Elliot had spiked a fever, then an angry red rash bloomed on his temple. Emily's fever followed, and then . . .

"What was your child's name?"

A delicate voice broke through his memories and altered the path of his thoughts. A soft savior as it were, for his mind was a moment away from traveling down darker roads. Without realizing it, he turned his head to the right to face the voice. Miss McCrary was a mere foot next to him, leaning back against his worktable, cradling the rattle. The proximity felt too close, too intimate, yet she was there doing no more than acting on behalf of her employer. But when he met her eyes, her sad request remained in the air.

"Elliot." His son's name rose up unbidden, though his throat struggled to get the word out. As if his voice had been a protective gatekeeper of his son's memory, but his soul was desperate to set him free. It had been five years since he'd spoken the name aloud to anyone.

A warm hand landed like a blanket over his clenched fist. Thomas peered down and took in Miss McCrary's pale skin enveloping his own. The contrast was stark, with his hand carrying the tones of his trade. Ashes and bits of iron filings speckled the landscape of his skin. He was about to remove his marred presence from her own clean hand lest he dirty her as well. But when he tugged, she tugged harder, as if to cage him there until she was good and ready to free him.

"That's a beautiful name. I'd love to hear about Elliot, if you'd like to share." Miss McCrary just stood there, leaning against his worktable, talking as if she was making no more of a mention than the weather or the rising tide. Not as if she had just summoned the name of his dead son, a name he hadn't managed to speak aloud in the privacy of his own forge.

After he had worked so hard to bury the agony.

And dammit all to hell if he would unearth those feelings again.

He pulled his fist out of the soft cocoon of her hand and handed her the paper with his terms, plucking the rattle from her grasp. Miss McCrary accepted the trade, though the sadness in her eyes and tightness of her lips were not lost on him.

She's trying to help you, ingrate. Have a care.

Thomas shook the thought away quickly and addressed the paper he'd handed her. "Take that to Mr. Richmond. I trust he'll find things suitable, as most is standard form. However, there is one addendum I have notated at the bottom. My trade is in the midst of a labor shortage, with more able-bodied men choosing to join militias than learn a skill. As such, I am without an apprentice."

Thomas rose from his chair and stood in front of Miss McCrary. He did not wish to be intimidating, but it appeared she hardly felt so regardless. Her slouching against the table had yet to change, though her gaze did track his body as he rose. The look she cast heated his blood, after she had set it to freeze with talk of his son. The sensation unnerved him, though he curiously didn't mind the disturbance. The woman intrigued him.

"I sent word to Mr. Richmond's household yesterday, notifying him of my lack of apprentice and its impacts on his ship's progress. Mrs. Potter replied early this morning and had a most agreeable solution. She mentioned you can read and write, and as such can assist me with bookkeeping relating to your employer's shipbuilding order. I haven't the time or resources to manage the orders and books while still meeting Mr. Richmond's demands."

Miss McCrary stood straight up at that. The rush of her movement nearly led her hip to knock over the inkwell on the table. "What do you mean? I don't know anything about shipbuilding orders."

"But you *can* read and write, and that is more than enough. I shall teach you the rest."

"But you said you're short an apprentice. A blacksmithing apprentice, which I am not. I don't know the first thing about iron or metal."

"Again, there is no need for that. I can manage the labor, but your assistance in managing the ledgers will be vital. Three months, Miss McCrary."

"You keep saying that. Why?"

"Because that is how long it shall take to fill Mr. Richmond's orders *with* your help. That is what I promised him, and that is what I have attested to in my terms." Thomas nodded toward the paper she held in her hand. "If you refuse, the timeline shall be extended and I shall lose the business. Not to mention what sort of favor that might land you in with your employer."

Her hands flew to her hips. "Is the blacksmith . . . blackmailing me? Are you really doing that?"

"No." Thomas lowered his voice and inched closer to her. The air around him grew hotter, though he couldn't detect its source. Was it her fiery temper, his heating blood, or the forge at his back? Whatever it was, it enlivened him in ways he hadn't felt in years. "I'm merely returning the favor. I believe you issued the first blow when we met in the street."

They stood there in a standoff, absorbed in the tension, their combined silence speaking volumes. Until he had the good graces to end it.

"Return my terms to Mr. Richmond, if you please. Once I have his signature, we shall begin straight away. You are to report here at this time each morning. You may go now."

After a prolonged hesitation, Miss McCrary slowly turned toward the door before Thomas remembered his original request of her.

"And leave your ax."

She whirled around to face him. "What? No!"

"I am a blacksmith, Miss McCrary. I shall care for it greatly, you have my word. But I asked after it because I have a sense, despite what you say, that metalworking intrigues you as it does me. I wish to learn from it, as you will from me."

She shook her head fiercely, and the panic in the gesture tugged at what little compassion he still had. He casually stepped toward her and let all the spite stemming from their arrangement flee into the chimney.

He gripped her hands in his. He expected her to rip them away, but she accepted his touch, though she eyed him wildly still. "When you return tomorrow, it shall be sitting on my worktable by the door, I promise. It will be as you left it. I merely wish to study its intricacies, that is all. Consider it a symbol of trust. You'll return for your ax tomorrow with my signed terms, and in exchange I'll offer you a bit more security than what you had when I first met you, I dare say."

"Mr. Brannigan, I—"

"Thomas. You may call me Thomas, if we are to work so closely together."

She eyed him sternly, then cast a glance down at the ground. The look was familiar to him and would be to anyone attempting to swallow their pride.

"Beth, then. Beth is fine as well." She nodded her certainty at allowing him the use of her given name.

He was glad for it, though he didn't know why. But he had three months to figure it out.

CHAPTER 10

Thomas, as it turned out, was a big fat liar. Oh, he had returned her ax to her as he promised, but it was not as she'd left it.

It was a million times better.

When Beth arrived the following morning at Thomas's forge, she let herself in immediately. Propriety could go piss on a car battery. She was so irritated and anxious, she nearly tripped over her skirts as she walked to the table. The entire afternoon the day before had all been too much. The heavy chores, lifting laundry baskets up and down stairs, washing pans in the stuffy kitchen. She was just done. After a brief respite of some bread and chicken was thrown her way, she'd been back at it, lugging a bucket of water and mop around the townhouse and chasing dust bunnies in stairwells.

Even after being off her feet for however many hours of sleep she'd managed to snatch, she was still restless and sore. Things were spinning out of control, and fast. So the last thing she had energy for was wrestling her only source of protection away from a professional weapons maker.

But as she approached the worktable, there lay her baby ax front and center, nestled in a swath of linen. And to her great amazement, the thing was even more beautiful than before. She picked up the ax and let the weight settle in her hands for a brief moment while she examined it. The small patches of rust and metal pitting had been filed away. The handle, by far her favorite part with all its engravings, had been polished to a high shine. Each carved vine stood out in stark contrast to its high-gloss backdrop, as if it were shellacked on. And when Beth ran the pad of her finger along the blade, the metal had been honed to a razor-thin edge. Only the slightest bit of pressure and it would have bitten her skin . . .

The bang of the shop's door startled her. The ax slid from her hold, nicking the inside of her wrist on its way to the ground.

"Shit!" Beth doubled over and gripped her wrist, immediately applying pressure. A dull thud sounded by the door before feet shuffled over to her.

"Here, let me see it."

Warm hands grabbed hold of her wrist, all but shooing her other hand away from the scene of the crime. Towering over her like a great grizzly bear was Thomas. His brows were cast down, and his shoulders hunched around her forearm. Those hazel eyes were glued to her wrist. The door behind him was still ajar, and on the floor by the door was a small satchel. Her eyes glanced back to his hands as he pushed up her jacket sleeve away from the cut.

"It's just a small scratch. I'm fine, really."

But he didn't say anything. He just gripped her wrist more tightly and pulled her behind him as he hurried to the back of his shop. With one hand, he rummaged through a cupboard of various glass bottles, cotton swaths, and a whole lot of tiny metal tools. When he found the one he wanted, he uncorked it with his teeth—*hot*—and poured a generous glug onto a nearby cotton rag. Without any warning or preamble, he pressed the fabric to her wrist, and she braced for impact.

But the sting never came. Her scratch had been just that—a scratch, with very little blood welling up at all. No more than what she'd expect from the slip of a knife while cooking. But it was definitely large enough to have a wince factor of at least a seven on a scale of one to ten.

What gives?

Curious, she leaned forward and sniffed. Sharp, astringent fumes wafted up to her nose, but not the kind one would set a match to. No, this was subtler, yet still potent . . . and immediately recognizable, though not from her medical training.

Vinegar.

Beth wrinkled her nose and gently pried away the cloth, along with Thomas's hand. The cut had already stopped bleeding. Some clean gauze and kling, or whatever passed for that in this time, would do the simple trick and be far more productive than turning her into a base for salad dressing. But before she could inquire, a shadow crept over the pale skin of her arm, blocking out the meager light let in by the open door.

"I'll call for a doctor."

Wait, what?

"It's just a scratch," Beth said as she held up her wrist for Thomas's inspection. "And it's already stopped bleeding. It's hardly in need of a bandage, let alone a doctor. I'd honestly even feel bad about wasting a piece of cloth to keep it wrapped, but given the soot in here, it's not a bad idea."

Thomas gripped her wrist in both hands as he examined the scratch further, though Beth hardly gave a fig about her grandiose paper cut anymore. Because Thomas looked about as convinced as a mom believing their teenager when they insisted they didn't have any homework.

Beth had no idea why Thomas was so riled up about a simple cut, but the longer they were skin to skin, the more unsettled she became. And when the pad of his thumb began to slowly stroke the inside of her wrist, the sensation kept climbing, extending far beyond where his thumb ended. With each back and forth of his touch, the rest of her skin lit up. Every push and slide was like a series of dominoes cascading all over her body. And when she looked up at Thomas, he was no longer staring down at her wrist.

His hazel eyes were locked on hers.

Beth ripped her arm out of his grasp and grabbed another dry rag from the cupboard. "I'll just wrap it. It's fine."

And Beth did just that, though it was looser than she'd prefer. But, fortunately, she pulled the sleeve of her jacket down and that held the cotton in place adequately.

"Fine. Good." Thomas cleared his throat and walked back to close the door before leaning down to pick up the satchel he'd dropped. "I thought you might be hungry." With one hand, he held out the satchel to Beth, while the other hand was folded behind his back. As if he, too, needed to reset and minimize their touching.

Who knew a simple scrape could cause so much agita?

Grateful for the out of having to avoid the gropey elephant in the room and for addressing the fact that she was actually hungry, Beth accepted it. When she pried the fabric open, aromas of yeast and butter rose up to greet her.

"Sit. Eat. Then we shall begin." Thomas gestured over to the table, under which her ax still lay, and then walked to the back of his shop.

Beth sat down and began to pick off chunks of the warm bread. As she popped a fluffy bite into her mouth, she glanced back at Thomas, who was rolling up his sleeves to his elbows. Beth took in the sights of his tanned, toned forearms as he removed his apron from a nearby hook before putting it on.

What the hell had gotten into her? She may as well have been one of the coals in Thomas's forge, for how easy it was to get her lit. All he had to do was breathe in her direction and her body lit up like a Christmas tree.

Beth shook her head, pushed the bread away on the table, and silently cursed Kyle for the number he'd done on her self-esteem. She'd never had a problem with her figure. Heck, most of the time she was covered up in scrubs so what did it matter? But even off the clock, she appreciated her body for what it was, even if her hips made shopping for jeans a bit of a chore. Hello, scrubs and their elastic waistbands!

But when Kyle came into the picture, her perception had changed, and she hated him for it. Over the months they were together, her curves had seemed too curvy for the up-and-coming hot doc, and not in a good way. The pressure to match his picture perfection, to slim down for the wedding photos (at his family's urging), had invaded her psyche like a slow-growing bacteria. She was the pure white shower curtain that, over time, had been overrun with a creeping pink mold along its edges. Still acceptable from the ankles up, but it was only a matter of time before she was due for a replacement.

Her replacement had been Stephanie.

Beth glanced back at Thomas as he leaned over by his forge sorting his tools. As she watched him get organized, she was acutely aware of the soft mound of her belly resting lightly on the tops of her thighs. Of how her hips were just slightly wider than the seat of the chair.

She reminded herself that she was to be his record keeper, and most importantly, that was her ticket to security for the time being. Her value to him extended only to her ability to read and write. Nothing more.

And that was just fine by her. The plan was mutually beneficial.

So that flutter in her chest whenever he was close by? She needed to squash it right quick.

Beth muttered a soft curse as the ink dribbled across the page she was tallying. Her hands anxiously covered the mess as she slowly turned to look over her shoulder at Thomas. The last thing she needed was a hulking boss who made weapons for a living realizing that his newest employee was a big fat liar. But to her pleasant surprise, he appeared to notice no such thing.

She exhaled in relief when she spied Thomas wrapping an order of bayonets in cloth before tying off each one with twine and moving on to the next. His movements were methodical, almost as if his hands needed to perform the same repetitive action lest they fall off due to uselessness. When the last bayonet of the order was wrapped and placed in the pile with the rest, Thomas rose and scanned the items on his wall. Though what he was searching for she couldn't tell.

But she was pretty darn certain nothing had changed since the last two minutes he'd stared at the wares.

Talk about idle hands being the Devil's work.

Beth shook her head and turned her attention back to the giant splotch of ink on the page before her. Damn. And she had been doing so well the last day or so. But, granted, most of the tasks Thomas had her occupied with were more organizational in nature, less pen to paper—or quill to paper, as it were. But, hey, at least she'd been able to sort through his back catalog of the last three years. Once she'd gotten the hang of reading the cursive and shorthand, she successfully managed to create an organized ledger of suppliers, sorted by type and then region, and another for recently completed orders, separated out by those still awaiting payment.

But this stupid ink spot was a literal mar on her progress, not to mention her security in this position. If she could maybe—

"Paper is in the desk drawer."

Beth's shoulders froze as Thomas's words slammed into her from behind. *Crap. How had he seen?*

She turned in her chair to face him and wasn't at all surprised to see a rag in his hand, slick with oil, as he wiped down his tools. But what did surprise her was his gaze, which didn't rest on the ink stain before her.

No. Those hazel eyes burned right into her own, like a giant stare down, except the challenger hardly cared who blinked first.

A sharp chill fluttered up Beth's spine as she turned back and opened the drawer in front of her.

"Thank you," she said softly. Her cheeks flamed hot in her face, but she couldn't tell whether it was from embarrassment or something else.

Definitely embarrassment. Without question.

Beth grabbed a sheet of paper and set it on top of the desk before closing the drawer.

"I gather you are not used to writing lengthy compositions." Thomas's words had quieted, yet Beth's ears picked up on every nuance of his deep voice and softly accented English. The sound was a slow rumble over her skin.

"That is true . . . but I'm certainly capable. I just . . . bumped into the inkwell, that's all."

"Of course. There was no slight implied." His footsteps drew closer as he walked over to the quench basin directly to the right of Beth.

She expected him to cap it, but instead, he merely leaned against the barrel and stared at her, his corded forearms painted with patches of dark ash.

Beth was doing much better when he was behind her and well out of sight. She didn't need the temptation of him hulking so near. Not that there was any temptation to be had.

That part of her had been locked up good and tight. No freaking way would she put herself through the wringer again, even if it did just mean stealing a look at a gorgeous blacksmith here and there.

The pain wasn't worth it. Her own reflection was enough of a reminder of that lesson learned.

Thomas cleared his throat. "The truth of the matter is, despite the origin of our circumstances, you have been a godsend."

Beth whipped her head around to him in confusion. "Excuse me?"

"I have been . . . ill-equipped for quite some time to manage all aspects of my affairs. I used to have more . . . help. But I find your presence here not as intrusive as I first thought it might be. No. In truth, you have set right more problems in a day or two than I could manage in a year." Thomas's words were stilted, as if his statements were only fragments of a whole story. But as he cut his words short and briefly nodded before turning from her to cap the barrel, confusion and uncertainty were left in their wake.

Sometimes a lot could be said in a few words or no words at all. Lucky for Beth, Thomas had painted a crystal clear picture, despite his lack of articulation. He was more than happy to have her clean up his mess and was even happier that he didn't have to notice her while she did it.

Kyle's contagion of self-doubt and inadequacy had the uncanny ability to travel across centuries, apparently. Lucky her.

Beth bit her lip and dipped the quill into the inkwell before bringing it over to the blank page. Like hell she'd let a man wound her so deeply again. Her self-worth was more than her dress size or how useful she could be.

But even as she gave herself the much-needed pep talk she'd recited a hundred times in the past few days, the voice in the back of her mind was more than happy to call her out on how, deep down, she didn't really believe it.

Because pain was pain, regardless of how big a bandage you put over the wound. Beth could turn a blind eye to it all she wanted, but sooner or later, her injuries would either heal or fester.

CHAPTER 11

Thomas wiped the sweat from his brow as the morning heat did its best to compete with the fires he was used to tending daily. His boots scraped against the cobblestones as he quickened his pace back to his shop. The morning deliveries had been uneventful and routine. After he had worked quickly through the week to finish up the two orders, he was eager to offload them to their owners. And just as eager to collect payment and move on to the next mundane weapons order awaiting him on his desk.

He tried to convince himself that the prospect was inspiring, motivating. After all, his business was flourishing. He had the literal good fortune of a good fortune.

Then why did the idea of picking up right where he left off rankle him? Metalworking had always brought him joy. Yet ever since Emily passed on, depression had served as a more constant companion.

Thomas sighed as he rounded the corner and walked up to his forge. His boot hit the top step leading up to the door . . . and then he stopped.

From this angle and where the afternoon sun was in the sky, the light shone into his shop just right so that he had a clear view of Beth through the front window. She was stacking ledgers up on the shelf, making a "workflow," as she called it, where new orders, in-process orders, and completed orders were placed into distinct piles. He faltered on the step and let his hand drop away from the door latch for a moment.

It was her red hair that caught his eye first, the strands of her locks glistening in the early afternoon rays. Earlier in the week, she had worn her hair in a bonnet, yet never kept it as tidy as was fashionable. Then, yesterday, she had worn it free, secured in just a single loose plait down her back.

Emily had often worn her hair in a similar fashion.

Thomas clenched his fist and slashed it down at his side. He stepped back a bit and leaned against the outer brick of his shop, being sure to stay out of sight so Beth wouldn't notice him.

All week, he hadn't been able to look at Beth without guilt weighing him down. Of course, the logic of the attraction was simple and straightforward. Beth was stunning. An absolute vision, with her brilliant smile, sensual figure, and thrilling laugh (on the occasion or two he'd elicited it from her). And he wasn't a fool. It was not uncommon for men to depart their grieving station as widower and take another lover. Often another wife.

It had been five years since Emily had succumbed to smallpox. Surely, enough time had passed that his urges would be understandable, expected even in polite society.

Then why did the very idea of looking at another woman with anything other than propriety feel like a bitter betrayal to the vow he took on his wedding day?

Thomas banged the back of his head against the building in aggravation. His eyes slammed shut with each subsequent knock against the stone.

And that was where the problem got worse. For behind closed eyes, images of Beth in his shop paraded freely before him, with no one to see or judge him for his thoughts. Beth had taken it upon herself to reorganize many items on his shelves, from his jars of solvents and solutions to his measuring rods and assorted hammers. Many of the items had been high up and quite out of her reach.

Yet rather than offer to help her like a gentleman, he remained at his anvil and merely watched under hooded eyes like the true cad he was, apparently. He subtly leered, intrigued as Beth had stacked two empty crates on top of each other and used them as a step stool. The maneuver was quick and efficient, and when Beth continued to climb up and down the crates, bending and drooping, reaching and stretching, his heart pumped in time with her own exertion. And for the first time in recent memory, he wanted to chase that feeling.

He had not been stirred like that since Emily.

Thomas swallowed down the images and opened his eyes. When his memories of Beth faded, guilt flooded in to fill their places. He had not been able to protect his wife from illness. He had not upheld his sacred vow to protect her in sickness. No, he was a shell of the man he once was. Second chances were for fairy tales and women's gossip. Life was crueler, harsher. And what kind of a man would he be to stomp over the memories of his good wife with the thoughts of another woman? He had only his reputation. And in that pursuit, he was stalwart.

A loud thud came from inside his shop. He glanced back toward the window to see Beth juggling a mess of bound ledgers in her arms, one of which had clearly fallen to the floor. Even among the privacy of his own thoughts, Beth still managed to break through.

He shook his head slightly as he gripped the door latch. He needed a change of scenery. *They* needed a change of scenery. They had worked tirelessly together all week in finishing these orders. Now that the orders were finally done and delivered, perhaps a lunchtime walk along the harbor would be welcome. Thomas knew Beth was not from Boston, so he was content to play a bit of tour guide, spewing facts about the city in structured responses. All very safe and appropriate.

As the latch depressed and Thomas opened the door to his forge, he promised himself their relationship was in business only.

For his heart had already been shattered once, the pieces incinerated and left for dust on the wind. The hull that remained was cold and rigid, like a vital limb long severed from its body.

Any hope for healing had been buried long ago with his dead wife.

The seagulls flying overhead in the harbor provided a welcome musical accompaniment to the sounds of the bustling dock. And they were far more pleasant than the shouts of dockworkers hollering as they unloaded barrels of freight from ships. The hard wood of the railing bit into Thomas's forearms as he leaned over slightly, the briny sea air causing a brief sting in his eyes that he quickly batted away.

At least those reflexes were cooperating, adhering to simple commands. For when it came to the woman at his side, apparently, all sense left him.

Thomas glanced over at Beth, who was tossing bits of bread to the seagulls gathering around her ankles. He caught glimpses of her brilliant smile as she twirled around, ensuring each fattened bird received even more indulgence.

His hair tickled the back of his neck as he shook his head, a smile threatening to surface. The care she extended to those blasted birds was no less than what she showed him in his forge throughout the morning. As they spent hours poring over his ledgers, with him showing her the ins and outs of his recordkeeping, he hadn't been prepared for how vulnerable the activity made him. The last person he'd shared his business accounting with was Emily, and bless her soul, she had seen to his organization and accuracy. Not that he didn't have a head for sums and figures. Far from it. But his time had always been better spent at the anvil or the grindstone.

So when he bared his business to Beth, with all of his folded orders and from-memory inventories, it was not without a bit of trepidation.

And to his great relief and astonishment, she took it in stride. Oh, there had been a few odd occurrences. Her clumsiness with the quill at first had been the most surprising since he knew she could write. But after several practice strokes, her skill began to take root. And she flourished from there. A quick study if ever he'd seen one.

And the questions she asked. Though blacksmithing had not been her industry, her interest in it had him preening like a green lad chasing a young girl around a maypole. Her curiosity about pig iron, the location of the nearest foundry, and the various molds needed for the ship rigging sang true to his heart. They soon fell into easy conversation, and to his great surprise again, for she was full of them, he marveled at the effortlessness of their rapport. Her interest in his livelihood made him jovial.

Again, he had not experienced such lightheartedness since his Emily had been alive.

"A doctor! I say, is a doctor about?"

Frantic, rushed calls drew Thomas's and Beth's attention toward the midday crowd in the street. A man was running from person to person, gripping each sleeve and elbow. When his shouts were met with only confusion and shock, he moved on to the next person.

"Hands to yourself, lad, before I lop them off." Isaac Hunterdon, a militia officer Thomas recognized, shrugged the poor man off him, nearly causing the lad to tumble to the ground.

Thomas glared at the assault. There was no love lost between himself and Hunterdon. The man had a reputation as a zealot and was a staunch opponent of the crown. Thomas could hardly fault a man for clinging to one's morals, and he certainly had no preference on what causes his patrons supported, yet it was Hunterdon's methods that painted the man in ill light. Despite Hunterdon's cause and wishes, business did not automatically flow freely and cheaply toward them. The man was broke, and rallying an army on overdue credit and broken promises held none of Thomas's interest or respect. He'd had enough.

"Oy! What's the trouble?" Thomas hollered at the man, who immediately looked up and dashed over.

"What's happening?" Beth abandoned her birds and crept closer to Thomas's side.

"We shall find out momentarily."

"Please, sir. I must find a doctor." The poor lad scrambled closer, his chest heaving, and gripped Thomas's shirt sleeves so tightly he nearly tore the shoulder seams. He looked a few years younger than Thomas and still wore his baker's hat and apron. Bits of flour smudged the man's cheeks and forehead.

"What's the matter?"

"My wife needs a doctor. She is in labor with our first child. A son, no doubt, given how strong his fight is. But he is not coming, and she has been straining for hours. My mother is by her side and just sent word to me at the bakery to find a doctor urgently."

"I can help."

Both men turned toward Beth. The sound of her voice was a shock to Thomas's system he did not expect. Her expression was anxious, yet determined. Dammit to hell, she was all but bouncing on her feet at the news.

"What? Miss, how?" The man turned his body to face Beth more fully, but his white-knuckled grip never left Thomas's sleeves.

"I'm a midwife."

Thomas took in the woman before him. Her stern expression brooked no nonsense, with her squared shoulders and clenched fists adding to her resolve. He hadn't a doubt in her mind she spoke truly and marveled at what she had, up until this point, chosen to keep private.

"Please, come with me. Quickly! It is not far." Beth gripped her skirts and ran after the man, the seagulls taking flight as she made haste.

Thomas followed, wondering what else he had yet to learn about Miss Beth McCrary.

CHAPTER 12

A woman's guttural screams told Beth everything she needed to know about the direction she was heading. As she scrambled up the narrow stairs of the two-story garden apartment building, though she doubted that was what they called it, one thing was crystal clear.

Someone was definitely in labor.

The young man and presumed father-to-be, who Beth had learned was named Francis, had screeched to a halt on the landing at the top of the stairs. Screams, which from the base of the stairwell had been pronounced yet still muted by the brick walls, all but raged behind the door Francis stood in front of. His hands were clumsy with the key ring as he finally found the correct piece of iron and slid it home in the lock.

"How long has she been in labor?" Beth pressed as she and Francis all but tumbled through the narrow door. Heavy footfalls behind her informed her of Thomas's presence in the room, though he stayed way back near the door once he closed them all in.

Natch.

"I do not know. When I left this morning before dawn to prepare the ovens, she was still asleep. Theodora!"

Francis burst into a bedroom located off the main common area of the small dwelling. If Beth thought her postcollege studio apartment above a pizzeria was small, this place had nothing on hers. The apartment's door opened into a combined living room/kitchen area, with various pots and pans hanging over a brick fireplace mantel in the center of the space. A few pieces of furniture were strewn about, but Beth hardly had eyes for any of it. Because as she rounded a corner into the only other room in the home, she got an eyeful of the source of the screams.

Francis nearly slid on the worn rug as he ran over and dropped to his knees at the side of the bed. "Theodora. It's all right, my love. I've brought help."

Francis gripped the sweaty hand of his wife and peppered kisses across her knuckles. Beth didn't have the heart to tell the guy that, given how hard his wife's breathing was and how tightly she was gripping the bedding, he may have wanted to get out of the range of her fist.

Because his angel of a wife was half a heartbeat away from decking him in the teeth. It was usually around this time in labor when the soon-to-be mom, especially if it was their first child, came to two realizations.

The first: *Oh my God, I have several more hours of this hell!* And the second: *Oh my God, this is all his fault!*

Sure enough, Theodora, in all her dark-haired, sweat-slicked glory, regripped her fingers around Francis's nearby wrist and squeeeezed. Even from where Beth stood at the end of the bed, she got a load of the long nails digging into poor Francis's skin. As the contraction took over Theodora's body, the mom-to-be took over her husband's arm and yanked down with the same force as the roar leaving her lungs. Francis's wails rivaled his wife's, and Beth took pity on the man.

Okay, enough was enough.

"Thomas, please take Francis out of the room for a bit." When Beth glanced back, she had to crane her neck and call out to Thomas again before his large presence poked around the doorjamb. His body was as rigid as an oak tree. The life-affirming color in his normally bronzed skin had receded under the cravat around his neck. His eyes did a wonderful job of focusing on anything in the room except the woman abed screaming her lungs out.

Beth walked over to Thomas and took his hands. The slight trembles were hardly noticeable and immediately stilled when she applied a little pressure and cocooned them within her own. "Take Francis out of here. Outside for some fresh air might be best. I'll be down in a few minutes with some information."

A brief, shaky nod was all she got before Thomas threw his shoulders back and exhaled. A moment later, a green-around-the gills Francis was being escorted by Thomas out of the apartment.

Once Beth heard the door shut, she turned to her patient. "Miss, I'm Beth. Your husband said you've been in labor since the morning."

Frantic nodding preceded a wince and a groan as a contraction washed over her.

"She didn't eat breakfast, the poor dear. Had hardly a bite or two of toast before the babe started making himself known. But I say, how can you help, Miss . . . Beth?"

Beth hadn't even noticed the older woman sitting by the window. She was dressed in a beige gown, with her gray hair poking out underneath the rim of the lace cap. Her apron was pristine, however, and her hands fidgeted with a soft-pink cotton handkerchief. Though the woman's eyes focused on Beth, her hands slowly skimmed each edge of the handkerchief. When her fingers reached a corner, she rotated the fabric and began skimming again. Beth recognized the nervous tick for what it was.

Helplessness.

"You're Francis's mother, is that correct?"

"Yes, I am," the old woman said softly, clearly attempting to fight down the warble in her voice. "You may call me Regina. And I'm mortified to admit it, but I fear I cannot help Theodora in the ways I should." Glassy gray eyes met Beth's. "I have only ever brought my Francis into the world, and that was quite some time ago. I am not . . . equipped . . ."

"Shhh. Don't worry." Beth gripped the woman's hands as she knelt at her feet. "I'm a midwife and a pretty darn good one. I'm not going anywhere."

81

If the woman was shocked by Beth's frankness, she didn't show it. And that was a relief. Because Beth didn't have the mental capacity to play lost time traveler *and* a midwife intent on delivering a baby in the eighteenth century. Her medical skills were the only things propelling her forward. She could either woman up and git 'r done or cower in a corner while Francis kept frantically searching for an available doctor.

When she assessed the two options side by side, there was hardly a choice in the matter.

Beth stood up and walked over to Theodora, who lay back against a pillow with her eyes closed. The woman's chest rose and fell steadily, along with her prominent baby bump. A calm respite in between storms. The woman needed her strength. Since Francis said this was her first child, there was most likely a long haul ahead of her. First labors could be brutal.

Good thing she was an expert at empowering new mamas.

Beth grabbed a small stool and pulled it over to the bedside, then grabbed the woman's hand. Her pulse was rapid but steady. A positive sign, as well as her normalized respirations.

"Theodora, I'm here to help deliver your baby."

"Push!"

Predawn light was beginning to trickle in through the small bedroom window as Theodora gritted her teeth through the next wave of pain. Beth was kneeling at the foot of the bed, focused on the baby's crowning head. She only peered up at Theodora to confirm that, yes, the woman's stomach was tightening up when the pain hit.

"Push with those contractions. You can do this. I see the head. You're almost there!"

"Gruhhh!"

The frail bed frame creaked as Theodora bent forward, eyes clamped shut, teeth clenched, and bared down like hell. To Beth's great relief, and she bet Theodora's as well, the push was productive. A mass of dark hair covering a less-than-spherical head made its way through the birth canal to Beth's waiting hands.

Don't worry, kid. We all start out as coneheads.

Shoulders would be next, but when Beth glanced up at Theodora, her head lay back against the sopping pillow. Eyes closed, mouth open, chest heaving. The mama was spent. Her body had downshifted to accommodating base needs only after almost twenty-four hours of labor.

"Theodora, c'mon. One more push." Beth had to fight to keep her voice steady. Exhaustion was dragging her down as well. She usually had support staff with her: nurses, medical assistants, or at least another midwife available on call to take over when the labor lasted beyond a twelve-hour shift. But here? A whole lot of nada. She would have been grateful for even some fumes to run on at this point.

Theodora's stomach contracted again, and the pain unpleasantly revitalized the exhausted woman. Good thing because Beth held the baby's head in her hands and couldn't do anything until the shoulders pushed through.

A silent heave was all Theodora could manage, as her voice had gone hoarse hours ago. But it was more than enough. A shoulder popped through, which was all Beth needed as she grabbed under the baby's arm and pulled the rest of its body free. With quick hands, she brought the baby up to lie on the new mama's chest, the umbilical cord still attached and draping like a tether across Theodora's baby-free bump.

"Here's your son. Congratulations, Mama. You were amazing."

As Beth opened up the collar of Theodora's shift to expose more of her skin, the new mama's shaky arms slowly rose and wrapped around the wriggling baby. Skin to skin and heart to heart, mama and baby settled in while Beth stepped back and grabbed the two pieces of cotton string she had asked Regina to boil and lay out to dry.

Once the cord stopped pulsing, Beth tied it off with the string pieces spaced several inches apart. A cleaned, borrowed knife from Thomas did the job as she sliced through the cord.

"What's his name?"

"Jeremy . . . Jeremy Alexander Molnar," Theodora whispered, her glassy eyes still glued to her son, who had begun to root around on her chest.

"He's perfect. I'll get your husband." Beth smiled as she turned to leave the room.

"Miss Beth?"

"Hmm?" She halted and looked back.

"Thank you. You are an angel. I thank God Francis found you."

"I'm just happy to help. Now, let me get your husband."

A short while later, after the happy family was reunited and everyone appeared healthy and well, Beth retired from the apartment building and stood outside the building's entrance alone. Damn, she was exhausted. She was willing to bet that even her under-eye bags had under-eye bags. Beth pushed her hands into the small of her back and stretched out her spine. The dull soreness didn't abate, but only spread out more thoroughly to the rest of her lower back.

Wonderful.

And judging by the slowly brightening sky and the lack of anyone in the street, it was barely dawn yet. Regina had left hours ago, and Francis had passed out in a chair in the common room while Theodora was in labor. Beth had been so preoccupied with the family, she'd lost track of Thomas. Where had he gone? Probably back home, given the hour.

A pang of disappointment struck her. Of course he'd go home. Did she expect him to stay by her side all hours of the night while she helped with a labor that, newsflash, didn't exactly have a predetermined end time?

No, she didn't.

All right, maybe she did . . . but just a little.

As she dropped her chin, Beth got an eyeful of her clothes. Jesus Christ, she looked like an extra from *Sweeney Todd*. What she wouldn't give for a spare set of hospital scrubs and a gallon of hydrogen peroxide. Too bad none of that was coming her way in ye olde Beantown.

How the heck was she going to get back to Mr. Richmond's house with her clothes coated in blood and afterbirth? Ain't no birthing gowns or personal protective equipment around here. And what would Mrs. Potter say when she noticed Beth's absence? Because she most definitely *would* notice her absence. Would she lose her living arrangements? Be found out for the liar she was? Would the authorities believe—

"Is it a boy, then?"

Deep, soft-spoken words floated through the early morning air and halted Beth's what-if train. She whipped her head around to the left. In the barely there rising light, Thomas stood leaning against a nearby wrought iron fence in front of a row of houses. His right shoulder was cushioned between the slats while his arms were crossed over his chest. Boots were clasped at the ankles, as if he were pausing on a casual stroll about town. Before the sun was even up.

"Have you been here this whole time?" Beth turned and walked toward him, flabbergasted at him still being there. The shock was helpful because it ensured her legs continued their forward movement regardless of their utter exhaustion.

He shrugged and glanced at his boots, then returned his gaze to her. "A boy?"

Beth nodded as confusion and fatigue warred for what remaining energy she had left.

"Is he well? And the mother?"

"Both fine." She nodded slowly again.

Thomas's lips thinned as he nodded his agreement before unhooking his ankles and pushing off from the fence. "Good. Now, come." He gestured with his head to follow as he turned to walk down the street behind him.

"Excuse me? I'm not just going to—"

"I've sent word to Mrs. Potter about your aid to the young family. All is secure there, so worry not. Now, please. My home is not far. I can provide you with clean clothes and ablutions before you return to Mr. Richmond's household."

Beth blinked once. Twice. Two more times, and then hustled her tired and aching butt to catch up with Thomas.

She didn't know why her heart was double-timing it as well and whether it was because of adrenaline or something else.

CHAPTER 13

The worn leather of Thomas's boots did a terrible job of keeping his feet dry against the morning dew sprinkling the grass. His soles had long been in need of mending. And it wasn't until he was sliding his key into the lock of his home that the thought occurred to him.

When had he last been to see the cobbler? Or for that matter, when had he last taken any care for anything that wasn't related to iron production? He glanced back at Beth. Bedraggled would have been a kind word to describe her appearance. Her clothes were soiled beyond recognition, tendrils of her vibrant red hair had sprung free from her plait, and her ashen complexion only appeared more so as the rising sun illuminated her drawn features.

Thomas's heart squeezed at the sight. For he had not had the opportunity or interest to care for another in quite some time, including himself, apparently. Though the urge damn well struck him now.

"Please, make yourself at home." As he crossed the threshold and stepped aside for Beth to enter, he got a good look at the place in the early morning light. And earnestly wished he'd had the foresight to tidy up.

Ash and soot coated the floor surrounding the hearth. Tools were strewn about the mantel, with very few in their appropriate spots. His small table sat in the center of his common room with its chair still pulled out and his plate and cup still resting on top where he'd left them. From whenever he'd had a meal there last. Hell if he could remember, as most of his hours were spent at his forge.

When had he let his home settle into such an unkempt state?

Loud creaking called his attention to the far side of the room.

"Oh, this is nice. Wonderful, actually."

Beth had relaxed into the rocking chair. As she pushed the balls of her feet gently off the floor, the wooden seat began its steady back-and-forth motion. Her eyes drifted closed as her head fell back against the neck of the chair. Unconsciously, it seemed, her fingers rose to the tie at the base of her plait and pulled it free. Gently, slowly, they separated each rope of tendrils until all her locks were free to cascade about her shoulders.

Thomas tensed instantly. His feet turned him around fully, all but preparing to launch him at the chair. Offer Beth another place to sit. Preserve it. Relocate it. Do anything that might separate Beth from the memories he had of Emily in that chair, rocking his son to sleep.

But then the most surprising thing occurred.

He was about halfway across the room when his stride screeched to a halt. His body was still, and the only sound was the creaking of the rocker on the wooden floor. Well, that wasn't entirely true. His heart tapped out a rhythm in his chest so loud, he couldn't be sure a carriage wasn't rumbling outside on the street.

Because as he took in Beth's resting form, he prepared for the guilt and anguish to slam into him. But they never came. Instead, his body hummed with intrigue and, dare he say, amazement.

Unbidden, he slowly walked toward Beth, who still lay back in the chair with her eyes closed. He was utterly mesmerized and in awe of the woman before him. She had just delivered a babe safely into the world and had pushed her body to run strong for hours on end. And what wondrous feat had his skills so readily accomplished of late? Another few dozen nails and a handful more bayonets to add to his tally.

Thomas's breeches scraped against the scratchy wood floor in front of Beth's feet as he knelt before her. Soft breaths had begun to float out between her slightly opened lips. The deep rise and fall of her chest settled into a steady rhythm. Her eyelids no longer fluttered in their fight to remain open but rested heavily, her lashes fanning out on the crests of her pale cheeks.

Sleep had claimed her, and all he wanted for the world was to allow her to resume her respite. Because, yes, she desperately needed the rest, but also he desperately desired to observe her longer, cad that he was. The woman, for all her fervor and curiosities, was nothing if not lush. Every glimpse of creamy skin or enticing curve tugged harder at his dormant, basal interest. An innocent poke at a very starved bear.

"Beth." His whisper was a half-hearted attempt to rouse her, and he damn well knew it. After a mental slap on his wrist, he tried in earnest . . . more so.

"Beth, wake up." Louder, yet still nothing.

Thomas curled his lips in and shook his head in frustration. She needed to get clean and back home, and he needed to get off the floor and not be at eye level with her skirts. Hesitantly, he rested his palm on her knee and jostled it lightly. "It is time to wake. Beth . . ."

Her eyes shot open as she sucked in a deep breath, startled. Her hand went to her knee, the very one covered by Thomas's hand. By God, he hadn't had the strength to remove himself from her yet. Confusion painted her expression as she glanced down at where their hands mingled.

Thomas cleared his throat. "You sleep like the dead, though you have more than enough reason to do so. You were slow to rouse."

"Oh, yes. I've been told that before."

Unease settled in Thomas's gut at her confession, and the sentiment was as foreign as wearing women's clothes. Was that . . . jealousy?

"Thanks for waking me, though."

"Of course." Their hands remained as they were. To Thomas's surprised delight, she did not retreat. "You are unlike any woman I've ever met," he whispered before shaking his head and remembering his place. "I mean, admittedly, I did not know much of your background before making arrangements for your aid, but—"

"You were surprised that I could deliver a baby? Why? Do you not have midwives here? Lord knows it's a profession that's been around since the flood." The questions she threw at him were surprising, more so because of her defensive tone.

"No, not at all. I merely—"

"Didn't expect me."

Thomas paused and stared into Beth's blue eyes. Eyes that locked on him and brooked no nonsense, despite her obvious exhaustion. He couldn't fib to her if he wanted to. So he didn't.

"No," he said flatly as he squeezed her knee. "There is nothing about you I could have expected. And I am grateful all the more for it."

Beth closed her mouth and blinked a time or two. A smirk crept along Thomas's face. He was content in his ability to shock the unflappable woman before him.

As her features softened slightly, her warm fingers squeezed his back.

Thomas slyly smiled and gave one quick pulse to her hand before he removed himself and stood to his full height. "Let us see if we can't get you cleaned up before I return you to Mrs. Potter."

———

If Beth could recommend one thing about colonial dress, it was the adjustability. Especially for a curvier woman. In her own time, there would have been no way Beth could have reliably crammed her booty into another woman's clothes. But here? The lack of definitive measurements and zip button flies was a major bonus. Everything she wore was fastened with ties and pins and, boy, did that make things easier when borrowing duds.

Especially when one had to borrow women's clothes from a presumably single man who lived alone and, oh yeah, really shouldn't have women's clothes on hand. Add to it the fact that said man was a walking enigma who also happened to be a steamy dreamsicle with the yummiest cleft chin she'd ever seen. Seriously, she just wanted to nibble on the darn thing.

Yet as Beth walked next to Thomas, about a block away from Mr. Richmond's house, her mind couldn't help but knock around other things about the man. Specifically, what he'd said to her.

You are unlike any woman I've ever met.

There is nothing about you I could have expected. And I am grateful all the more for it.

He appreciated her. Honest to God appreciated her, and not because of anything other than who she was. The concept was so heady and foreign that processing it was proving difficult.

Beth glanced at the man at her side. Her fingers were tucked around the curve of his biceps as he escorted her back to the house. Even though the linen of his shirt sleeves was on the rougher side, it was thin enough that she could enjoy every curve and contour of his toned arm. Slight heat radiated through the fabric, though she couldn't tell whether it was June's early morning sun or something more. Even though her mind had enough to worry about, and it was probably due more to exhaustion than anything else, Beth reveled in the feel of him. Offering a woman one's arm was a chivalrous gesture long since lost in her own time, and certainly one that never occurred to Kyle. She was surprised at how much she enjoyed it.

Yet Thomas had offered his arm to her freely. No, not offered, insisted, as she was still very tired and he stated his regret that, due to the early hour, she'd have to walk back.

"So tell me, whose clothes am I wearing?"

Thomas briefly stiffened in her hold, yet his step didn't falter. "Her name was Emily."

Beth's stomach dropped like a stone. "Was?"

"Emily was my wife." Thomas raised his chin higher, as though keeping his chin and neck at a ninety-degree angle would somehow help him get the words out.

"I'm sorry. Did she . . . ?"

"Yes. She and my son—"

"Elliot."

Thomas glanced at Beth and drew his lips into a thin line. "Yes,

Elliot." He paused to clear his throat. "They died five years ago. Smallpox."

Beth looked down at the lavender jacket and dark gray skirt she wore. The apron was pale blue, similar in color to her old jacket. The clothes had been stiff and a bit musty when he had handed them to her at his home. That explained why.

"I'm sorry." Beth softly spoke her apology again, though she hated apologizing for something that wasn't her fault. It still didn't change the guilt or her wish that things were different. "How long—"

"Your skills as a midwife are impressive. Admittedly, I was disinclined to help the lad when he was first calling for help. I thought perhaps he had been burgled or his horse slipped a shoe. Yet I was glad you were there to offer aid. Doctors are in short supply around here, and available ones are tending to the growing needs of the local militias or employed by private families. How long did you apprentice?"

"Well, after college . . . uh . . ." Crap. How did she explain postgraduate studies? Wait, Harvard was already established, wasn't it? But doubtful women had any access to it then. "I studied medical instruction for four years after my initial schooling, then I worked at mastering the specifics of midwifery for two more years. I've been in practice ever since."

Beth prayed she sounded convincing, but she couldn't bring herself to ignore her training outright. Though, judging by the deep furrow of his brow, she'd just stepped in it big time. When he didn't respond immediately, she racked her brain for another plausible explanation she could offer.

Before she was able to pull something out of her hat, Thomas interjected. "Ten years."

"What?"

"I had served as an apprentice blacksmith for ten years before I was given the rank of journeyman blacksmith."

"What does that mean?"

Thomas looked at her questioningly but obliged. "I had proficiently learned the skills of my trade and was recognized by a master blacksmith, under whom I trained since I was a young lad. He gave me my title and the good wishes that I may travel wherever my profession needed me."

"Ah, I see. Well, ten years is certainly a long time. How old are you anyway, if you don't mind my asking?"

"I do not mind it, though your forwardness about the question is refreshing." He chuckled slightly. "I am thirty-three. And you, if I may inquire?"

"Twenty-seven."

Thomas's hand covered Beth's own as it lay nestled in the crook of his elbow. "A woman wise beyond her years."

The compliment made her smile. Another glimmer of appreciation thrown her way, which she wasn't used to receiving so readily back home. It was something she'd miss from this time, for sure.

But then the reminder that she wasn't on a colonial vacation hit her like a gut punch. There wouldn't be anything for her to miss unless she figured out how she'd landed here in the first place. Her distractions of the past few days had skewed her focus. She wouldn't allow herself to get sidetracked again. She couldn't. The eighteenth century was no place for a modern woman.

"Here we are."

Beth hadn't even realized they'd arrived at the backyard of Mr. Richmond's property. Talk about distractions.

"Well, thank you for walking me back." Beth slipped her hand free of his arm as she reached for the latch on the back gate.

"Rest well today. Tomorrow morning, we shall resume with the ledgers."

If the exhaustion hadn't made itself known before, it sure as heck decided to make up for lost time. Despite every urge not to, Beth's mouth stretched wide in a monumental yawn. The tension around her lips was so great she was sure she must have sucked in all the surrounding oxygen from a city block. And did she remember to cover her mouth in front of her pseudo-employer/business part-ner/guy who gave her his dead wife's clothes to wear because she'd ruined hers while helping bring life into the world?

Nope, nope, nope-er-rooni. Beth yawned with all the couth of a gorilla. Right in front of Thomas's face. Yay.

As Beth's jaw returned to normal hinge capacity, Thomas chuckled. The low rumble of his laugh resonated through her like the vibration from a passing train.

"Let me lift the latch—"

"I'll just unstick the lever—"

When Thomas bent down to open the gate's fastening, Beth's hand was already on the latch. She turned back toward him to affirm she had it well in hand and was met with his mouth two inches from her own.

Thomas sucked in a sharp breath as recognition of their proximity made itself known. And then that same breath slowly left those lips and danced across her nose and cheeks, tickling her skin and perking up her senses. Flecks of light brown floated in the amber pools of his eyes . . . eyes that had suddenly been trained on her own before dropping lower to focus on her lips.

Because Beth's rational thought had apparently not made the cross-century trip along with her, her brain was merely along for the ride. Off duty, as it were. That was never more obvious than when Beth leaned in close to the blacksmith, the tops of her breasts slightly compressing against the pads of his chest, and kissed him.

The shock was apparent on both ends, yet only briefly. Though she'd made the first move, it took only a few seconds for Thomas's lips to move against hers. The softness of his mouth mixed with the abrasiveness of his morning stubble caused tingles in all kinds of places. Places she hadn't focused on for a long time.

And he tasted *good*. Like smoke and coffee, with the sweetest of bitter tones, the edgiest of dark beer. Like bittersweet chocolate and a stout pint.

Damn if she didn't want more, but she forced herself to pull away. The house would be stirring already, and she wasn't up to snuff on the rules of propriety of the time, but she was pretty sure this constituted a big no-no. PDAs and all that.

"I should go." She said the words to Thomas's still-closed eyes, and the blissful, stunned expression on his face was adorable. Then he opened them. The hazel gaze that floated her way was fuzzy, yet the lift of his mouth was anything but.

He hadn't hated the kiss.

"Good night. I mean, good morning. No, that's not right. I mean, I guess it is? Anyway, I'll see you tomorrow."

Shut up shut up shut up.

Beth turned before Thomas could comment on her inability to put words together and bolted through the gate and into the back door.

How the heck was she ever going to rest now?

CHAPTER 14

Visions of a hard, angled jaw speckled with morning scruff painted Beth's feverish dreamscape. Her lips parted and her breath puffed in short bursts as memories of Thomas's warm mouth pressed against her own rose to the surface. The hot, tacky skin on her legs clung to the bedsheet. She kicked, her eyes still closed, until the toes of one foot, then the other were kissed by only slightly cooler air from her bedroom. The roughness of the sheets enlivened her, drew her back into the dream. The starchy cotton and the uneven stitching scraped against her calves, and she recalled the delicious rasp of Thomas's stubble against her skin. Beth's tongue poked out and slowly traced the rim of her lower lip, her heart rising with each breath. Salty perspiration lined her lips. Despite the heat, her skin prickled as goose bumps rose along her neck and across her shoulders. The hardness of Thomas's chest pressed briefly against hers ignited more fire, more images, more—

Soft, yet firm knocking at Beth's door dragged her the last lap home to being fully awake. And sweating, apparently, with her legs kicked over the edge of the bed and the sheets tangled in a mess. Her shift had risen way up, and she couldn't shake her post-REM sleep dream fog. Though, as thoughts of what she had just been dreaming about solidified, she wasn't sure she minded the early morning discombobulation.

"Beth, are you still abed?" Annabelle's singsong voice followed the knocking.

Crap.

"Uh . . . just a moment!"

Beth kicked off the sheet and flung herself out of bed. Her shift settled on its own and she raced to the corner to grab the pile of borrowed clothes from the day before and winced.

Despite the ease of adjustability compared to modern button flies, as she wore the duds throughout the day, the size difference definitely made itself known. The jacket, which she *thought* she'd managed to pin closed adequately, kept pulling across her chest. And when she had to fold linens, stretching her arms wide to hold the larger items, two pins had popped free. Blessedly, she'd been by herself at the time. And the ties at her waist, while at first had plenty of slack, kept unraveling with all the bending she did lifting laundry baskets. The threadbare nature of the ties didn't help the cause, and when she tried to bind them tighter, the threads had snapped. She had been forced to keep her skirt up with a piece of kitchen twine instead.

The experience was enlightening, though. She figured she had a pretty good idea of what a holiday ham endured each season and had no desire to repeat the experience.

Hesitantly, as she was unsure how Annabelle would take to her in her manner of undress, she cracked open the door and poked her head around. "Hi there."

Annabelle's wide eyes fell on Beth's frizzy hair, shift-clad shoulder and bare forearm snaking out around the door. The poor woman's shock was so apparent, Beth very well could have had a porcupine sitting on her head (heck, it probably looked like she did), and Annabelle couldn't have been more shocked.

The loudest cackle Beth had ever heard erupted out of Annabelle. The formerly quiet, mild-mannered girl leaned back, arms braced over her midsection, and let the laughter fly.

"My goodness, Beth, you are a sight." Annabelle's shoulders still shook with residual giggles once the initial wave of hysterics passed, though her expression changed from bafflement to concern when Beth didn't move from her perch. "What is it? Are you ill?"

"No, not at all. I, uh . . . had a mishap with my clothes from yesterday."

"A . . . mishap, you say."

"Yes. Nothing a good washing and some needle and thread can't fix." The nerves were coming out hard and fast. God, she was a terrible liar. Her guilt was only made worse by how sweet Annabelle was. Why couldn't the woman be a mean girl instead? Beth had no problem lying to nasties.

"Look, I hate to ask this of you, especially since you've been more than generous with me for the last week. But would you, or another one of the women on staff, happen to have some extra clothes?"

Annabelle planted her hands on her hips, confusion painting her expression. "I've never met a grown woman with so many troubles dressing herself."

Beth braced for the worst, though the idea of Annabelle condemning anyone was a joke in and of itself. The sweet girl practically sneezed rainbows.

"All right," she said with a sigh. "I'll be back in a moment. The linens I have in mind may be in need of some mending as well, but nothing you couldn't manage."

"Thank you! Yes, absolutely. I shall mend away."

Annabelle's side-eye was anything but subtle as she turned away, then stopped. "Oh, Beth. That brings to mind a conversation I had with Mrs. Potter yesterday. It seems your trunks have not yet arrived from your uncle's estate."

Crap.

"Oh, no? Really?" Crap crap crap. Play dumb. Escape. Evade. Lie. No, wait, nothing had changed in the last thirty seconds. She still sucked at lying. Ugh.

"Truly. No word has come through the post either. Have you written to him at all? Perhaps an inquiry?"

"You know, I haven't. But I will do that today. Yes." She nodded like a bobblehead. A *lying* bobblehead.

"Good, I am glad to hear it." Annabelle's words came out slowly, almost cautiously. For the first time in the past week, Beth detected something in the young woman that didn't quite sit well. The bitterness at her realization was pervasive and saddening. Annabelle no longer trusted her. And dammit, didn't she have Kyle to thank for being able to sniff out that particular trait this time around?

A short time later, Beth donned her new clothes and ran down the hall, in a hurry to get to Thomas's forge. Better to focus on happy thoughts than unsettling ones, at any rate. Her heels clicked against the wood as her feet two-timed it, though she couldn't help scratching up a storm around her collar. The new gown brought out all sorts of itchies, and if she couldn't stop herself from scratching like an animal, people were sure to think she had fleas. Or what would they call them? *Vermin.* Ick.

Beth slowed in front of the hallway mirror, lit softly by two sconces burning low because that part of the manor didn't receive sunlight during the day, despite the early hour. She pulled aside the ruffled lace collar of the tawny gown, expecting to see an angry red rash from all her scratching.

But red was not the color reflected back at her. Or her normal, pale complexion, for that matter.

"What the hell?"

Her entire right shoulder and collarbone were green. A pale, mellow green that was in no way anything closely related to her skin tone.

Beth's bottom lip quivered as she poked along her shoulder, scraping her fingernail along her green skin as if it was coated in makeup that could be removed. All seemed right, except what didn't . . . which was right in front of her. Yet as her brain came up empty with any logical explanations as to what she was seeing, it did remind her of one thing she had been too distracted of late to focus on: she wasn't supposed to exist in this time.

When the mind was panicked and grasping at straws, it could surely take one to peculiar places. For Beth, that place was strangely Commonwealth General, where there had always been a wall calendar displaying various inspirational quotes each month at the nurse's station. The one that came to mind, as she stared in horror at the inexplicable, had been attributed to Buddha and was turning out to be the ultimate I-told-you-so. As Beth traced her shaking fingers along the slope of her shoulder, where the line of demarcation from normal to green stood out like a razor's bite, those quoted words were the only things knocking around in her terrified mind.

The trouble is, you think you have time.

Thomas dipped his quill into the inkwell for the third time since he had sat down. The intention was straightforward: write up the bill of sale for the bayonets he'd finished assembling. It was as simple a task as there was. The language was the same as it always had been, with only the quantities and costs changing. Nothing he hadn't done a thousand times over in his profession.

Yet he had let his quill run dry twice, without even making a mark on the pages because his mind had been driven to distraction with thoughts of Beth.

Groaning, he dropped the quill on the desk and let his head fall into his hands. His skull was heavier somehow. Likely due to all the rocks taking up residence where his good sense ought to have been. Because Thomas had not managed to get that woman off his mind or the taste of her off his lips. And, Lord, her forwardness! Others would label it unbecoming, but he could not have admired her more for it. Refreshing and enticing. She was not a coy, timid girl who would pass him in the market, admire him for his size and stature, only to giggle and blush before averting eye contact. In truth, he'd never had an interest in another aside from his Emily. What would have been the point?

Beth was different, however. She had command of a profession, and it was breathtaking to watch her take charge. She was confident, mature, and damn luscious. A deep chuckle rumbled through him as his mind wandered back to the kiss and how unbalanced she'd seemed. The falter in her words, the way her eyes danced about to anything other than him. It was charming, almost thrilling, even, to see her act in a manner other than the confident woman he'd known these past few days.

How long had it been since he had even tasted a woman? Again, not since Emily. And what did it say about him that the one woman who had outwardly shown an intimate affection toward him was wearing his dead wife's clothes?

The legs of Thomas's chair screeched against the floor as he scooted back and turned around. Beyond the anvil, on the small table in the corner, were the trinkets of his past. Trinkets Beth had cleverly found, though he'd never intended to show another soul. And yet, when she inquired about them—hell, even spoke his son's name—the grief he'd known as a bedfellow these five years had been familiar, though slightly . . . less. Less crushing, less weighty.

Loud bangs resounded against the wooden door of Thomas's forge. Curious, as Beth never knocked and she was the only one he expected. Thomas sighed as the banging persisted. Frustrated, he abandoned his long-neglected bill of sale and walked toward the door.

"Brannigan. Do you leave all your customers to wallow in the heat before allowing them entry or just those loyal to our new republic?"

Isaac Hunterdon, a trader and militia officer, stood before Thomas. Though slightly smaller in stature than the blacksmith, his scowl more than made up for any lack of physical prowess, along with the sword at his hip. Thomas internally rolled his eyes at the weapon, for what need could the man possibly have for it in the early morning trading hours? Had he intended to lop off a casket's cork with the blade merely to begin his day's drinking with showmanship? It was woefully arrogant, highly inefficient, and more than likely an extension of the man's lacking endowment.

Thomas stepped back and allowed Hunterdon to enter the forge. He was in no mood to entertain a political debate with the man. Hunterdon's arrogance was just as prolific as his choice of weapon, and Thomas had no intention of engaging with either.

"You have need of a smith?"

"Well, I certainly wouldn't seek out your services to mend my shoes, would I?" Hunterdon took in Thomas's shop, circling around with his arms braced behind his back, until his gaze landed on the bundled pile of bayonets Thomas had just completed.

"Speak your business, Hunterdon. I am a busy man."

"Clearly, as I can see you've just finished another arms order. I am in need of weapons as well. Tell me, though." Hunterdon nodded his head toward the pile. "Would those bayonets be used against your fellow loyalists? Or are they a lovely gift for the British to send them back where they came from?"

"My customers are no concern of yours."

"Oh, I believe they are. You see, we are in the midst of a war—"

"There is no war, just men killing each other."

"Men killing each other for a cause."

"Whatever their causes, they are not mine. I am not involved."

"Oh, I'd say you are." Hunterdon walked over toward Thomas, the brim of the trader's tricornered hat threatening to invade the blacksmith's personal space. "I know you sold muskets to those redcoats last month."

"I sell muskets to everyone. It is hardly a crime."

"It is when those are used against your own people! Fellow Bostonians, traders, merchants, sons of mothers, and husbands of wives."

"I sell to loyalists and British alike. And if a musket ball I molded leaves your weapon and lodges into the heart of a British officer, is that man not also a son? A husband?"

"British filth have no souls," Hunterdon spat out. "They tax us without—"

"They have money," Thomas grounded out, "which is more than can be said for you and your fellow Sons of Liberty. The British pay in cash, while you all pay in credit. So, will I take their hard payment over your word of profound promise? Yes, because I, like you, serve the needs of the people . . . people who are willing to pay for a hard day's labor, regardless of whether those people are loyalist or British. I care not. Now, as I said, I am not involved in your higher calling. However, if you wish to employ my services, I suggest you come up with the blunt first. Good day."

Thomas held the door wide. His fist gripped the door handle so tightly he doubted the old bolts would hold before the imbecile finally took his leave.

Hunterdon walked toward the door, his grip likewise firm on the hilt of his sword. The tension added to the already rising heat of the forge as the banked coals slowly caught more flames from the open door's air. "Careful, Brannigan."

"Always."

As Hunterdon turned from Thomas and exited the forge, Thomas was about to slam the door . . . until a sharp yelp outside caught his attention.

"Apologies, miss."

Hunterdon's voice had turned from a viper's venom to sweet as sugar. When Thomas looked out the doorway, Beth was frantically untangling a loose apron string from Brannigan's sword hilt.

"No, it was all my fault. I should have watched where I was going. I was a bit distracted."

"The distraction, miss, is mine entirely. Here, allow me." Hunterdon's fingers brushed against Beth's own as he unlooped a final strap before freeing it from his sword. "There," he said, lightly patting the back of her hand. "No harm done."

"Miss McCrary." Thomas's booming voice brought her head up.

Hunterdon looked back and forth between the two. The serpent's grin soured Thomas's stomach as he silently cursed the encounter.

"Coming!"

Blessedly, the woman had the good sense to abandon Hunterdon and follow Thomas into the forge.

The door to his shop had a deadbolt mechanism, in addition to the standard door lock. He had never in his time there bothered with the bolt.

Once Beth was safely shuttled inside, he slammed the door and slid the bolt home.

CHAPTER 15

The soles of Beth's shoes shuffled along the cobblestones as she headed home from the forge later that evening, with Thomas as her escort. The *scrape-slide-scrape* rhythm of her feet was the only thing that kept her on track as she walked in the best straight line she could manage while her muscles moved on autopilot.

"Is everything all right?"

"Hmm?" Beth murmured at the sound, though her answer to the speaker was more automatic than genuine.

"I have addressed you several times, with no response."

"Hmm." Beth nodded at the sound as she stared down at her shoes. The fogginess of her distracted mind registered the noise around her as Thomas's voice. A polite, noncommittal nod was all she could manage, however, as they strolled along the street. She was somewhat disappointed to be heading back home, as the seemingly endless bills of sale and inventory records she'd completed that day had kept her mind off things she didn't want to think about.

Like her urge to reach for the collar of her dress every five seconds to see whether she'd advanced from pale seafoam green to full-blown Kermit the Frog.

As if ignoring my troubles will make them disappear.

It was later than usual when she had left the shop. Thomas has been so engrossed in his work and she in hers that neither one had noticed the sun had already set. Briefly, she wondered whether Mrs. Potter would be annoyed with her for coming back so late. Then she shook off the thought. Like any of it mattered. Regardless of her morbid thoughts, Thomas, obviously unaware of her circumstances, still insisted on walking her home.

Home. There was that word again. It had turned into more of a joke than a destination. Because home most certainly wasn't here, in 1770, where her clothes were held together by pins and strings and dodging horse poop was more urgent than dodging potholes. Her real home was in a single-family house she owned, minus the family, and in a profession where she wore scrubs every day and her standard conversations with hospital colleagues involved her defending her career choice.

When she compared the two like that, what she'd left behind didn't sound so great either. *Hello, rock and a hard place.*

" . . . ax?"

Huh?

The strangely placed word dragged her out of her morose thoughts. Beth looked up at Thomas. The flickering light from the streetlamps did more to shadow than illuminate. Though in the low light, his firm jaw and stern gaze were effective reminders of why she had been distracted from her woes for a while.

And also reminded her of how terribly she had been receiving his generosity.

"I'm sorry. I'm a bit out of sorts. I didn't hear what you said."

"I merely inquired whether you still carry your ax with you."

"Oh. Yes, I do. I kind of feel a bit lost without it, oddly. Why do you ask?"

Thomas looked away, then shrugged. "In truth, I was just trying to get your attention. You've responded to nothing else I've said."

"I haven't? I guess I've got a lot on my mind. Sorry if I was rude."

Thomas dismissed her apology with a shake of his head. Silence descended between the pair once more. Scratches of heels on cobblestones and the clopping of horses' hooves went from background music to center stage as they walked on.

"Beth, have I offended you with my . . . attentions?"

"I'm not sure I understand what you mean. There hasn't been anything you've done that's offended me."

Thomas cleared his throat and nervously tugged at the cravat around his neck. The fabric was pulled free just enough for Beth to pick up on the bob of his Adam's apple. "The morning after you delivered the baby. When I walked you home—"

"As you're doing now?" Beth crooked an eyebrow his way.

"Yes." He laughed briefly. "As I am doing now. That morning, outside the garden gate, when we . . . kissed. Was it . . . ?"

"Unwanted?" Beth shrugged a shoulder as she offered up the word.

"Yes," Thomas breathed out. "Was it unwanted?"

"No. Not in the least." Beth smiled at him, the first genuine smile she'd given in days.

The words, however, flew out of her mouth before she could censor them, scan for historical appropriateness, or, heck, at least take a crack at playing a little hard to get. But nope. Her brain decided to lay her desperation out for all to see. Well, maybe not all. Just one hulking blacksmith who had taken to standing sentry at her side while walking her home.

Home.

"That is good to hear." Thomas stopped walking and cupped Beth's elbow, urging her to stop as well. When she turned to face him, Thomas didn't remove his hand. Instead, he raised it higher up her forearm. Neither of them pulled away. They just stood there as the stale humid air thickened between them.

Beth didn't know what to do or think, but the fluttering in her stomach was more than enough action to convince her nerves something was going on. Should she lean in again? Would he step closer?

As if hearing her, he lowered his head slightly, so his lips were aligned with hers. Was that an invitation? Or did he . . . ?

"Well," Thomas breathed out abruptly before straightening and unnecessarily adjusting his vest. "Let me get you back to Mrs. Potter. The hour is late. I know a quicker way. There are fewer lamps, but the moon is bright tonight. This way."

Talk about letting air out of a balloon.

He scurried them down a block she'd never noticed before, though it seemingly ran parallel to her normal route. As they maneuvered around the parked horse carts and stacked barrels along the sides, they passed another road perpendicular to theirs, though the buildings along each side of it partly obstructed its view due to the ornate pillars of the architecture. Before Beth and Thomas cleared the first pillar, soft moans echoed through the dark shadows of the partially hidden road.

Beth stopped, then Thomas, slightly ahead of her, perked up his ears and slowly backtracked until he was at her back. Well hidden by shadow, Beth scanned the darkness for the sounds. Was someone injured? She squinted harder until the obscure outline of two bodies became apparent.

Writhing bodies.

In the dark, Beth made out the curvaceous outline of a woman who was braced against the brick wall, enveloped in the arms of a man. The two were squirming and panting as they kissed each other with unruly abandon. The woman brought up one of her legs and hooked it around the man's waist, trapping him to her.

From Beth's vantage point, she could both see everything and make out nothing. A hidden obscurity that painted the most vivid picture. And as those soft moans escalated to deep grunts and louder pants, Beth had a harder time looking away.

Just as she thought she should run, leave the couple to their private moment, she hesitated.

But not before backing into the warmth of Thomas's broad chest, hot and magnetic behind her.

Of all the places a gentleman would take a lady, regardless of station or stature, a moonlit back alley mere blocks from the loud and coarse harbor was not one of them. Bottom of the list, in fact. And certainly not when that lady happened upon a couple indulging in a private moment while the lovers were backed against a wall and barely hidden by an apple cart.

A gentleman would remove her from the situation. Carefully take her by the elbow and hurry her off to see her safely home. Shield her from man's basal urges. Protect her from exposure.

Yet Thomas did not. The sight before him, and the woman at his side, did well to scramble his senses.

Beth hesitated briefly before stepping back a pace or two and colliding into his chest. The jarring motion was swift, abrupt. She had entered his space, though the intrusion was anything but unwanted. Her head, uncapped and tucked beneath his chin, taunted him. He was of the mind to move back, step away from her and allow her more space.

He could not.

Thomas loosely curled his hands around Beth's shoulders as she looked on at the couple. She didn't move, though his fingers were only loosely draped over her, giving her more than enough slack to flee. Push off. Smack him across the chin before running away to denounce him as a scoundrel to Mr. Richmond and the like.

Beth did none of those things. Instead of retreating, she slowly let her head fall against his chest. Thomas froze in place as the weight of her body melted against him. Gently, hesitantly, he lowered his fingertips more firmly over the caps of her shoulders, decidedly clamping her to him. They stood like that for a full minute, back to front fused together, and said nothing. Beth just watched on as the woman against the wall moaned louder, the lady's fingers digging into the sleeves of her eager lover. And then the man returned the favor.

The woman's gown had already been loosened, and the tops of her breasts were fully illuminated under the moon's glow. Thomas glanced down. Beth's chest, though still bound by her gown and stays, rose and fell with the same pace as the woman across the way. With each breath she took, her creamy mounds rose slightly higher. All Thomas had to do was bend down a minuscule amount and brush his lips against them. Lick and taste the tempting offering before him. His cock, hard and needy, throbbed at the thought. He attempted to turn, adjust his hips so his offending member would not glance against her sumptuous body.

But then she laid her hand against his own and held him secure in his position against her. His fingers stilled. The kiss they shared earlier had been a surprise, though a delectable one. A shock to the system in the best of ways, a coy uncertainty that invited the thrill of the chase.

But this was different. He was not a voyeur by nature, but he couldn't ignore the need, pure and simple. Though it had been an eternity since he'd experienced the craving, it had not been lost for lack of use. Merely banked, like simmering coals awaiting a burst of air so they could flame to life.

He should stand down. Take her hand and rush her away from there.

Have a damn care, Thomas. You are playing with fire.

Then Beth's hot breaths fluttered over his forearm, raising the hairs in excitement. Thomas bit down on his bottom lip hard as he dropped his head lower. His eyes stared in ravenous hunger as his fingertips curled underneath the rim of her bodice. Soft skin kissed the backs of his nails as his fingers nestled farther in. A hair's breadth away from his lips was the barely visible column of Beth's throat, given that the handkerchief she wore was draped solidly around her neck and shoulders. As her eyes slid closed, Thomas touched his parched lips to her jawline. Her mouth widened on a gentle moan, so he chased the sound, kissing and licking up her skin to the soft crook of her neck behind her ear until her mewling grew fevered in pitch.

More.

Heat and urgency took up residence where his good sense left him. His mind was no longer captaining his ship. Beth's soft sounds of acceptance had seen to that.

She wants this. She wants you.

Thomas's other arm snaked around Beth's waist. Every dip and curve of her frame cushioned his arm, welcoming him like a warm bed to a weary soul. The sensation was comforting and arousing, one his body had not known in ages. He was like a beast long starved.

Harried, frantic grunts grew louder across the way. He feathered his lips across Beth's cheek, tempting and kissing as the scene before them reached its pinnacle. Thomas glanced around briefly. Yes, they were well hidden behind the pillar and out of the direct moonlight. If

Beth had doubts or any reservations about passersby, there would be no one to spy them.

Then Beth turned her head and kissed him. Hard.

The match had been struck.

Their kiss was a duel of lips and tongues, need and passion. All urge to sip and savor had vanished. Thomas took and gave and devoured all he could of the woman in his arms. No confusion, no words, no hesitancy. Just desire and bliss.

Barely muffled groans rose up from the couple beyond the pillar, but Thomas could hardly register them, let alone his own heartbeat. His only concern was for Beth. Tasting her. Holding her.

Beth's bold hands moved to the front of his stomach, lightly grazing, hesitant against the fabric. His abdominal muscles twitched with each barely felt caress. The toying and teasing were agony and ecstasy. So when he took a small step closer and forced her arms to fully clasp him around his middle, the relief at the contact only fueled his need for more.

Thomas cradled Beth's delicate face in his hands as his mouth plundered hers. They were nearly chest to chest, and the proximity was heady. She was everywhere. On his tongue, in his senses, in his mind, on his skin. Nary a moment had gone by the past few days where she had not consumed him in some way. But now that he had her in his arms, he realized just how starved for her he was.

And how much more he craved her.

The muffled sounds of the couple in the alley had turned to silence. Though his body was more than content to chase and kiss her delectable mouth until his legs gave out, concern for her safety won over. He embraced her more tightly to him—out of a need to protect her, he told himself—and broke away with a final brush of his lips against hers. When he opened his eyes, hers were still closed. Soft pants left her kiss-swollen lips, and for a brief moment, he envisioned a life where he woke to that image every day, Beth in his arms, flushed and heated from his attentions.

Damn, if she didn't look perfect.

"You, Beth, are unlike any woman I've ever met," he whispered before dragging her farther behind the pillar as the couple they'd been observing walked by.

"You . . . you said that already," Beth panted. Her hands remained around him, with her body nearly curled to his.

"It warranted the repetition."

Her response was an ear-to-ear smile that rivaled the moon's glow. "Thomas, I don't want you to think that I'm—"

"All I'm thinking of now is how I should get you home . . ."

Her face fell and her body immediately began to tense before he spoke again.

"So that I can eagerly anticipate your company tomorrow."

CHAPTER 16

Beth's skirts swirled about her ankles as she made another turn at the end of the hallway, doubling back on her route. The oil painting of Mr. Richmond, in his powdered wig and high collared jacket, hung on the wall she paced in front of. Beth nibbled her fingernail while she convinced herself that, no, Mr. Richmond's pale gray eyes were not *actually* watching her. Judging her. Accusing her of being a wanton woman who dallied in voyeurism and making out with gorgeous men in dark alleys.

Correction: man. A singular gorgeous man.

Gah!

Her pacing continued up and down the hallway. Again, the shelf holding candlesticks rushed past her. Again, the gilded frame of the mirror blurred by. Beth met the window at the end of the hall before she turned to continue wearing a hole in the floor. That was the extent of her productivity. Because her mind was still in that alley, snuggly tucked away behind a pillar. Leaning back against Thomas's broad chest. Feeling his heartbeat drum out a pounding war cry against her body.

In her line of work, there were symptoms and there were signs. Symptoms were subjective: a patient feeling nauseous, complaining of a backache, experiencing fatigue. All things Beth took at face value while considering the source. Likewise, symptoms had been prevalent in her relationship with Kyle. Taking her out to dinner, sharing movie popcorn, giving the same cash equivalent in gift cards for every present-giving occasion. No, they weren't subjective, because they actually happened, but these were acts she definitely took at face value.

Signs, however, were different. Signs couldn't be faked with determination or change of whim. Rising blood pressure, blown blood vessels, vomiting. Good luck faking any of that.

The same, again, could be said for her relationship. Beth's pulse not quickening whenever Kyle would touch her, the dryness that plagued her when they'd have sex . . .

His soft cock that would rest against the inside of her leg—while she was fully naked under him.

Beth bit down on her bottom lip as she recalled the seemingly endless amount of time she'd spent on foreplay with Kyle. The stroking, kissing, and massaging she did just to get him to a point where they could even have sex, let alone any enjoyment for her in the act. Just a lot of determination and a boatload of lube.

Her heels dug into the floor as she stopped in front of the hallway mirror. Pain, sharp and fresh, bloomed from her palms as she dug her fingernails into them. Dammit, how could she have not noticed the signs sooner? Or perhaps she'd noticed them but hadn't been all that eager on making a change. Kyle was the hot new allergist who oozed confidence and had influential colleagues flock to him like flies to shit.

Including Stephanie.

Had she been just another fly? Or had he genuinely seen anything in her worthy of more?

Beth examined herself in the mirror. Freckles dotted the bridge of her nose. Slight laugh lines were beginning to show at the corners of her mouth and eyes. And it was those bright blue eyes, which had always been commented on by others as stunning or breathtaking, that stared back at her as she pondered her reflection. That, however, was usually where the compliments ended.

Yet she had stolen Thomas's breath with her eyes closed in a dark alley under the shadow of a pillar, all while the hard length of him caressed her backside. A definitive sign of the man's arousal.

For her.

Not a symptom, but a concrete sign. And all through layers of fabric and overwhelmed senses.

Then Beth's eyes landed on the glaring swathe of pale green skin she struggled to hide under the handkerchief wrapped around her shoulders. A thought bubbled up inside her. *Perhaps I should tell him.*

"Elizabeth! There you are." Mrs. Potter turned the corner, paused in surprise, then nearly charged at Beth as if she were wearing a red cape and the housekeeper was an enraged bull.

Beth quickly grasped the handkerchief's ties at her throat. To her surprise, a note appeared beneath Beth's nose as Mrs. Potter held out her arm.

"You are to go to the square downtown and collect these items right away."

Beth took the list and squinted down at it before raising her head to the woman. "I was just about to leave for Mr. Brannigan's shop. We're nearly done with the inventory order for Mr. Richmond's ship."

"No, no, no, there is no time," the housekeeper tsked, shaking her head. "Mr. Richmond's private physician has been called away to New York."

"What does that have to do with me going to the blacksmith?"

"Are you daft, girl?" Mrs. Potter's shock was so apparent, Beth hardly had time to figure out where she had floundered.

What am I missing?

"No?"

The housekeeper threw her hands in the air and sighed. "Well, I shall hope, for your sake, that you'll be spared any ailments that may fall upon this house. The rest of the staff, historically, have not always been so fortunate. Need I remind you of poor John? We are aiding him as best we can, but it is at great expense. And even then, he is slow to heal."

"Oh, the valet, right?"

"The valet, she says. Yes, of course, Mr. Richmond's *valet*. The very man whose duties you're fulfilling while he's nursing a broken leg.

Oh!" she said, raising her hand to her forehead, "My blood. You've gone and got my blood up." The woman squeezed her eyes shut tightly.

The mood had shifted, and Beth quickly cut down on the back talk. Despite her best efforts, all she could think about was Mrs. Potter blowing her top like Mrs. Potts losing the top of her tea kettle when Chip would aggravate her.

Beth also knew the signs of high blood pressure when she saw it, having worked with enough preeclampsia patients. Gently, she took the old woman by the elbow and ushered her to a chair in the nearby sitting room. "Sit, please. I didn't mean to aggravate you. But try to focus on your breathing and slowing your heart rate down."

After a few moments of calm, with Beth directing the woman to exhale fully every third tick of the hallway's pendulum clock, the situation settled. So much so that the persistent Mrs. Potter jammed the piece of paper back into Beth's hand and closed her fingers around it, but not before holding Beth with a solemn stare.

"We serve Mr. Richmond with great devotion, and he has always cared for us well. But these are troubling times." The old woman glanced away and worried her bottom lip. "He is away on business, and his physician has left. When his resources are gone, how do you think the rest of us manage?"

And then it hit home.

Mr. Richmond had access to healthcare because of his money and status. But that didn't automatically extend to his staff. Not even his most loyal ones, despite their high blood pressure and broken bones.

Beth gripped the list tighter and swallowed down another hard truth about the time she found herself in. Money and medicine were two sides of the same coin . . . a coin only certain members of society were able to afford.

Which meant everyone else got left behind.

───────

Shouts and grunts up ahead echoed against the tall buildings and mixed with the sounds of jostling jars in the satchel at Beth's side. Her errands were finished for the day, and the noises drew her attention like a house fire.

Men's voices. And cries of pain.

Beth's heart hammered in her chest as her feet sped up, carrying her to the sounds up ahead. Her foolish curiosity overpowered her sense of self-preservation.

"Now that's a nice shade of red dripping from your nose, lad. It matches the redcoats your master loves so dearly."

"Hurry this up, Will. All the squirm has left him, and my belly is roaring. You've sent the message."

Grunts and cheers rose up around the corner as Beth finally took in the scene and halted at the sight before her. The heavy satchel slung across her chest settled at her hip. Its contents, jars and bottles from the apothecary, rattled as they slammed into her hip bone.

On the ground in the square lay a young man, though it was a stretch if he was even out of his late teens, crumpled in on himself. Four men circled around him. Two had their arms crossed over their chests and stood slightly back, one with a more bored expression than the other. A third man had the butt of his musket angled against the young man's neck, while the fourth slammed the toe of his boot home into the man's stomach. A choked cough sputtered out of the victim. Even from Beth's distance, she couldn't ignore the deep red trail of blood that painted his face and the cobblestones beneath his cheek.

"Enough, Will. He's been taught his lesson. Let us go." The man with the musket grabbed Will by the collar and pulled him back, but not before a final kick was delivered under the young man's chin. Beth winced at the impact. Then the man, Will, knelt in front of the victim's bloodied face. His fingers gripped the matted hair as he leaned in.

"Tell your master, the haberdasher, we know he's been removing our papers from around the city. I've seen him rip down our postings in front of his shop." Will spat on the man's thigh, the fabric of which was soaked through with all manner of mess. "One might suspect he supports the throne if he goes about tearing down public meeting information from the opposition. A dangerous stance, truly."

The man's eyes were swollen shut. All he could do was shake and softly mumble. And no one stopped to help. The few people who did turn down that road quickly doubled back after seeing the altercation. Shop owners had closed their doors and shutters to the melee in the street. She alone stood as witness to the beating.

And that was when Beth saw red herself.

"Hey! Leave him alone!"

Will glanced up from his squatted position and stared at Beth. The other three men did the same.

"This is no concern of yours, miss. Off with you now." Will shooed her away as he rose and turned to the others.

"You can't do that. You can't throw your weight around and hurt people like that." Beth's blood was boiling, yet in the back of her mind, she was piling up the consequences for running her mouth.

The men looked curiously at each other, then back to her.

"And what weight are you referring to? Unless you're talking about your weighty arse. I could throw that around easily, despite its size. Is that what you're offering?" The wicked grin that stretched across the man's face made Beth's stomach sour. Almost as much as his rotten teeth, the extent of which became clearer as he walked closer to her.

Shit. Didn't think this one through.

"I'm not offering anything."

Before she could figure out what to do next, the young man got to his feet and scurried away. No one chased him, thankfully, but Beth's relief was mixed with worry. She had hoped to try and help him, clean his wounds or reduce the swelling. Something.

"Will, come on. You always have much better luck with women who actually *want* you," one of the other men called out, laughing.

Up close, Will was far more disgusting. The grime in his tied-back hair was so thick, it clumped patches of strands together, offering clear views of his thinning scalp. His waistcoat was unbuttoned, and blood smattered his vest and breeches in the same manner salad dressing might splatter the button-down shirt of a messy eater.

But he was bigger than her by at least a head. And regardless of what she wanted to believe, in this situation, size definitely mattered.

"You've got a mouth on you, girl."

Beth gripped the strap to her satchel more tightly.

"Are you joining us or not, Will? Tabitha's working at Billy's Tavern tonight. She tolerates your shit better than anyone." His friend laughed at the gibe.

For the love of chocolate chip pancakes, please listen to your friends. Beth tried to hunker down, make herself appear smaller in stature. Or, at the very least, less interesting.

Will sawed his jaw back and forth. His eyes raked over her serving girl's uniform. Her heart beat in her ears as the wordless showdown stretched on. Finally, Will spat at the ground and broke the silence.

"Piss off," he muttered before turning to join his friends, who walked down the street out of sight.

Beth stood there, stock still, until she was damn sure they weren't going to return. Warm rain started to fall, dotting the cobblestones with big fat drops. Her shoulders, satchel, and hair all absorbed the water as the rain trickled down with increasing intensity. Still, she stood there, unsure what to do next. Part fear, part trauma soaked through her bones, paralyzing her, mingling with the rapidly drenching rain.

If things had gotten worse, if Will hadn't left, what could she have possibly done? There was no police, no 911 to call, no onlookers willing to offer aid. Her head spun with how out of control her life had become.

"Your ax." A deep, firm voice broke through her panic.

Beth spun around. Thomas stood before her, legs braced and arms clenched at his sides. His fists were balled, and his jaw was unmoving. Unbound dark hair fell drenched on his shoulders as rain cascaded off the tip of his nose. He appeared as a statue, still and strong, while the world around him wreaked havoc and flapped wildly.

Then his words sank in. *My ax. Of course!*

Beth scrambled around in her pocket and pulled out the ax, which, in her panic, she'd forgotten about.

Thomas stalked forward until he was right in front of her. He laid his hands on the sides of her upper arms as he met her eyes. "Use it. If ever you feel threatened and I am not around, never hesitate to protect yourself."

"But how did you know I was here?"

"I received a missive from Mrs. Potter this morning stating you'd not be assisting me today. She provided no other explanation, no reason for the change in our agreement. The communication left me . . . unsatisfied, so I sought you out. When I inquired after you at Mr. Richmond's house, the housekeeper's assistant said you were sent to the apothecary, though she neglected to mention which one."

"Oh."

His hands, warm against the chill of the rain, gently squeezed her arms as he pulled her slightly closer to him. "So I visited them all."

"Wait, what?" Had he really spent all morning looking for her?

"Mr. Walters was the last shop of the four I knew in the city." Thomas jerked his chin toward where Beth had purchased the items for Mrs. Potter. "And I am grateful I came when I did." Thomas's warm breath fanned her eyelashes, causing drops of rain to cascade off and land on her cheeks. "Beth. If you see those men again, don't engage them. They want a fight, and it matters not from whom they get it."

"Yes." Beth nodded before glancing down at the ground, slightly ashamed for her pride getting in the way of her common sense.

But before she could wallow further, Thomas placed his curled finger under her chin and urged her head to rise. "And don't forget," he whispered before the corner of his lip rose in a smirk. "If need be, always go for the cods."

CHAPTER 17

The afternoon's rain continued into a late-night deluge. The final dregs of patrons at the tavern crawled out the door as the dim lantern lights did their best to illuminate the way. Thomas stood settled within an alley that offered a perfect view of the tavern's front entrance. Every stitch of fabric on him had been soaked through, yet he paid it no mind. Except for a slight nose twitch whenever a drop of water landed on his face, his body was frozen in its purpose as he waited.

The additional weight of the knives he'd strapped to him had instantly been absorbed into his frame. His legs, hips, and chest had gladly accepted the hidden holsters, with the freshly honed blades all pointing down and ready to be called into action at a moment's notice. Despite his trade, Thomas didn't own a gun himself. He had made enough of them to know his preference for arms. Blades had been his forte, and he never sold an edged weapon he had not personally tested and trained with himself. Guns were for the untrained soldier with an abundance of misplaced confidence. Blades were for ruthless and skilled warriors. Intentional. Lethal.

He closed his eyes and breathed deeply to calm his senses. Despite the elements, no chill reached him. No hesitation hampered him. He was as primed as any predator determined to protect their own.

When Thomas had stumbled upon Beth in the market square, inches away from one of Hunterdon's men, for Thomas had faintly recognized him, fear had gripped Thomas like a vice. For a brief moment, visions had flashed of him losing Beth, of a giant chasm of despair opening up and swallowing him whole again. What if that man threatened her, touched her, *harmed her* . . . ?

Thomas had been too far away and never would have made it to Beth in time if something happened. And if the man saw Thomas running to Beth's aid, would he hurt her out of spite or self-preservation? Thomas's distance away was his downfall. And though Thomas was an impeccable marksman with his knives, he couldn't even risk throwing a blade at the villain lest Beth be injured as well. Once again, Thomas had been helpless.

Until now.

A rough grunt preceded a loud curse as a man stumbled out of the tavern. The street was pitch black. Most of the candles in the street lanterns had burned down. The glow of the half-moon, coupled with the dim candlelight, was all the man had to go on as he shuffled down the street with a pronounced wobble to his stride. Once he turned down a side road, Thomas pushed off the wall he was waiting against and followed the man into the night, staying out of sight.

When his prey passed the milliner's storefront, the man paused and looked back in the direction of the tavern as faint murmurs of a few more patrons departing carried through the air.

When the man turned back around, Thomas struck. He grabbed the man by the collar and flung him against the brick wall of the shop. Thomas smirked in satisfaction as he smashed the man's head into the abrasive surface. Blood trickled from the drunkard's mouth.

Thomas took care to remain in darkness. His arms were wound taut with aggression as they caged the man against the wall. The fool's legs, which had barely managed to hobble his drunk arse away from the tavern, had given out from under him. Yet he still remained upright.

Thomas gripped the man's slimy jacket more tightly and lifted. Inch by inch, his heels left the ground. All purchase was taken from him.

"What's going on? Who the fuck are you?" the fool spat out, though the words were more garbled than menacing. Spittle and raindrops flung from his lips and landed on Thomas's shoulder.

"I shall only say this once." The words rumbled deeply from Thomas's chest, as if his inner warrior had a message of his own to deliver. "Stay away from Miss McCrary."

The man sputtered and cursed in confusion. "I don't know what you're talking about. I've never heard of a McCrary."

Thomas dropped him. The fool's legs sank into a pile of uselessness as he fell to the ground. Though some predators relished the cat and mouse game, he had no interest. No, he was here to send a message. And he would not leave until he ensured its swift delivery.

Thomas squatted down in front of the man. The creak of his boot leather strained against his calves, and Thomas welcomed the tightness, the tension. Then he flipped the simpering man onto his back. Between one breath and the next, Thomas grabbed a blade from his ankle holster and held it to the man's neck. The thin, razor edge poked through the stubble under his chin. The skin offered little resistance, and a thin trickle of blood dribbled down onto the man's dingy cravat.

"The woman in the square. With the red hair," Thomas clarified for the fool's benefit.

The drunkard squirmed as he tried to push Thomas off him. But Thomas wouldn't budge. It was like a fly trying to move a lion by merely fluttering its wings. Then, amid the panic, a glimmer of recollection seemed to pass through the man's eyes.

"The woman with the satchel?" he choked out. "With the . . . haberdasher's assistant . . ."

"That'd be the one."

"I never touched her. God's honest! I swear!" The man whimpered against the sharpened blade as piss soaked through his breeches.

"Good. I shall know if you do."

Then Thomas sheathed his knife, rose, and turned to leave. The man hissed and winced behind him as the shallow slice at his neck was exposed to the night air. Thomas kept his back to the simpering fool as he left. He should have been content with his delivery. He hadn't seriously harmed the man, only sent a message to stay away from Beth. He hadn't hidden his identity specifically, though the rain and darkness certainty helped shield him. Yet for some reason, once he had walked about twenty paces away, he stopped and looked down and back toward the man before leaving for good.

Would he be recognized? Perhaps.

Would his revenge be any less severe if the man knew it was Thomas who delivered it, instead of an unknown man in the night?

Never.

If it wasn't for the fact that she hadn't had sex in at least six months, Beth would have been sure she had morning sickness. Except it wasn't the morning. Or the afternoon. It was nearly midnight and she hadn't eaten anything since she came home that afternoon from the square. She hadn't had much of an appetite.

No, that wasn't entirely true either. She hadn't had much of an appetite *for food*. A certain blacksmith, on the other hand, may have fit the bill. But she couldn't even think of cracking a sexual innuendo.

Her stomach was revolting. Literally turning into its own black hole of destruction. The pangs came in inconsistent waves. Some lasted a few seconds, some lasted a few minutes. Like contractions.

Hello, irony.

Beth lay in bed, exhaling after the latest round of stomach cramps subsided, and debated. In her futile quest for sleep, the tossing and turning had presented her with another piece of regretful information. Her rash, which had been confined to her shoulder area, had expanded. It now cast a pale green pall along her arm, ending just past her elbow, and painted the expanse of her cleavage.

Fear at what it all meant had been clawing at her. With every new inch of tinted skin, every wave of pain, she had fewer answers and more worries. Her delusional, sleepless mind continued to flash the same solution over and over again.

The blacksmith. Should she tell him?

She was pretty certain that him knowing about her time travel wouldn't change whatever was happening to her. But there was more to it than that.

Beth was flat-out scared. Terrified. But less so for what the implications were, because like hell if she knew, but more because she didn't want to go through it alone.

In the short week and a half or so since she found herself in this mess, it had been made brighter by Thomas. Her time watching him work, helping him with his ledgers, being held by him, protected, even if only in her mind. And especially the admiration he had toward her work. Her profession. He never belittled, only acclaimed. The praise was new and wondrous. Losing it would be agonizing.

Losing Thomas would be agonizing.

Determination wormed its way into Beth's mind, rooting into her iron will. If she had everything to lose anyway, why not add to the pile?

Beth shot out of bed and ran to the small desk in the corner of her room. She took out a quill and some paper. She didn't even bother to sit down as the ink flowed from the tip onto the page.

She wrote about everything. From Kyle to the antique shop to the ax to Mrs. Potter and Annabelle. Every turn in her journey, every hard landing along the way. Then she sealed it and grabbed her clothes.

Mr. Richmond's house was quiet and Thomas's forge would be empty. If she could leave now, let herself into his shop, and place the note on his worktable, he'd see it in the morning. Then the ball would be in his court. If he labeled her crazy and called for the militia, or whatever passed for police these days, she'd run. Take her ax and figure out her next steps.

But if he didn't dismiss her and stayed by her side, she'd have a partner. An ally against whatever she was fighting.

Maybe more than a partner?

Beth threw her feet in shoes, grabbed the note, and scurried out of the house before she could change her mind.

The afternoon's light rain had turned into the evening's heavy showers. She hadn't bothered with her cap and didn't have a coat or cloak. So she picked up the pace, nearly jogging through the streets. The rain and wind slapped her face. Her hair licked across her eyes as the wind picked up when she turned corners. The fabric of her gown logged water like a sponge, yet she pushed through. Her thigh muscles strained against the wet weight. Her note, however, was tucked safely in her pocket. Next to her ax. That was all she cared about.

Beth's steps slowed as she reached Thomas's forge. She pulled out the key he'd given her and let herself in, checking the door closed with her hip and nearly falling against it in the process. Once the elements were sealed out, the silence of the forge descending on her loud thoughts, she turned.

Thomas stood in front of the fire, naked from the waist up. Rain dripped off the ends of his hair and the tip of his nose. His hands held his linen shirt, which he was wringing out onto the floor. Every muscle on his chest was illuminated. Every dip and edge's shadow was accented by the flicker of the flames. Raindrops still kissed the dark hairs on his chest.

"Beth? What are you doing here? Are you all right?" He dropped the shirt on the anvil and rushed toward her. His eyes fell on every inch of her while his hands hovered about her without aim. He was frantic, wild, as if looking for an enemy he couldn't see.

She grabbed his hands softly, brought them together in her own, and smiled. "I'm all right."

She intended to rub circles into his hands, to calm and soothe, yet he immediately reversed their positions. His hands—his much larger, fire-warmed hands—now covered hers. Without hesitation, he began to rub away the chill.

It was just what she needed.

"I came here to tell you something." The softness of her own voice was unusual and took her by surprise. Because her mind was no longer in control. Her body, and all its exhausted put-through-the-ringer instincts, was in the driver's seat.

Beth stared at Thomas. His eyes were laced with concern. His upturned brows and tight-lipped expression pleaded with her to speak. Thomas was a man of action, a man who molded metal to his whims. Yet here he stood before her, struggling with his inaction, itching to offer aid. He waited for her answer, for any information on which he could act.

And without a single word, he had given her the answer to her question.

He would be her ally.

All she had to do was ask.

CHAPTER 18

Thomas's forge had never been so cold. Or perhaps it was the icy fear rooted in his gut at the sight of a nearly drenched Beth before him. The hour was beyond late, and no good news ever came unannounced at that hour.

His thoughts immediately wandered to the soldier he had just come from warning off. But how would the man have gotten to Beth so quickly? His eyes widened as he took stock of the woman before him. Every curl out of place, every disheveled piece of fabric turned into blazing signals of potential terrors. He had just finished examining her elbow, eyeing a piece of thread hanging loose, when her chilly palm cupped his cheek.

"I don't know how else to tell you I'm fine . . . but something tells me you wouldn't believe me even if I shouted it from the rooftops."

"Did he touch you?" Thomas breathed out. He couldn't keep the ragged desperation out of his voice.

Shock and confusion met his accusation. She dropped her hand from his face and slid her other hand from his own. "What on earth are you talking about?"

"The man from the square. The one who threatened you." He reached out and cupped her shoulder. He was relieved when she allowed it.

"Why would he touch me? I only ever saw him that one time."

"Good." Thomas nodded. "That is good."

Beth cocked her head. "Why are you asking about him?"

Thomas inhaled deeply and raised his chin higher. Like hell he'd be missish for seeing to her safety. "I sought him out at a tavern I know militia soldiers frequent. I told him to stay away from you. No, that's not quite right." He glanced at the floor a moment before grasping both of her shoulders and holding her gaze. "I held my blade to his throat as he pissed fear all over the ground. I assured him I would know the moment his presence ever darkened your door again . . . and advised against it."

Thomas didn't know where the possessiveness came from, nor why he even told her to begin with. He certainly had no intention of bringing her into any potential foray. Yet when he finally found her in the square after searching every damn apothecary in the south side of Boston, the scene he had stumbled upon froze him. Not because she was standing up for a badly beaten victim, or because she was unafraid to square off alone against an armed man.

It was the sheer paralyzing thought that, despite all the hell he had been through, Thomas would not come through whole if Beth were harmed. The realization had been so shocking, so foreign, he couldn't identify it at first. Yet that was the precise root of it.

No, *she* was the precise root of it. And it all began when this woman, a stranger, spoke his son's name out loud. She hadn't tried to replace the memories of his family but, instead, attempted to preserve them.

Beth stood there, silenced. Her bottom lip, which was slightly larger than the top, hung open. Her eyes, wide as blue moons, welled with tears. One rebellious drop broke free and fell, cascading down the pale slope of her round cheek. Thomas's thumb was there and caught it before it landed on her gown. The pad of his finger absorbed the slight wetness before sliding over to caress the swell of her lower lip. It was petal soft and warmer than her cheek.

Then her lithe tongue danced across the tip of his finger. Slowly, gently. The sensation surprised him, until those gorgeous lips closed against his thumb and pressed upon him the sweetest kiss he'd ever been blessed with. Beth's eyes had closed. Another tear fell down the other cheek before she opened her eyes to him.

"You have no idea how much I needed to hear that." Her voice was soft, though he suspected it was intentional to hide any unwanted warble. Endearing, yet unnecessary. She could croak like a bullfrog and he'd still think of her voice as a songbird's.

"It is no more than the truth."

Rustling near his waist drew his eyes down. Beth had untied her pocket, which he knew held her ax, and turned to quickly lay it on his worktable.

When she turned back around, the icy fear he harbored earlier had thawed.

One look from Beth, and he had been lit aflame.

Beth had underestimated how powerful it was to have someone in her corner. To have someone look out for her well-being without her even knowing she needed it. She wasn't used to the consideration, the care. It was exhilarating.

Thomas was exhilarating.

Beth's fingers trembled slightly as she took a step closer to Thomas and laid her palms on his bare chest. His skin was a furnace beneath her fingertips. It rivaled the rising heat in her cheeks, but just barely. When he didn't move, she explored further. The course tickles of his chest hair beneath her palms sent tingles dancing down her spine. She was desperate to chase the sensation and dug her nails into his chest slightly as her body warmed. Her hot breath dusted across the backs of her hands.

And then he closed the distance.

Thomas's hot mouth was on Beth's in an instant. Their bodies met in a frantic collision of haste and desire. His chest and arms, bare and scorching, quickly consumed Beth's senses. She should have been cold. Should have been shivering in her wet garments.

She was anything but.

Thomas's kisses were persistent. For every nip and lick she

offered, he matched her movements and gave her more. Their dance quickly turned into a negotiation. At times, she'd playfully pull back and entice him to follow her. He'd match her game by backing her into the worktable so she couldn't retreat. And then he'd take what was owed. A searing kiss, a palmful of her breast. He was ravenous.

She could relate.

Beth brushed the backs of her fingers down his rigid stomach. His muscles jumped under her touch. She smiled against his lips, until his strong hands snaked around her back. His pinky finger looped into the fastening of her gown. The tug was soft, inviting. A question, not a request.

Beth broke the kiss and grabbed his hands from behind her back. Crap. Her skin! How the hell was she going to hide her rash from him?

At her hesitation, Thomas stilled. Crappity crap crap.

Her mind spun to produce a solution. Was she self-conscious about her figure? Sometimes. Around Kyle, she definitely had more of those moments. But with Thomas? She hadn't thought of her weight once. Still, should she use that as a reason for him not to see her undressed?

" . . . a vision of my dreams." Thomas had spoken, but the words hadn't registered.

"Huh?"

Thomas held her face in his hands, leaned his forehead against hers, and closed his eyes. "I know I shouldn't speak so boldly, but you have been a vision of my dreams."

What?

"Those long hours you'd assist me at this table. The times you'd stand and bend to organize the orders. Every time, I was at the anvil and distracted to insanity. Distracted by visions of holding your delectable arse against my cock. Imagining the feel of your gorgeous breasts in my palms, overflowing my hands. Do you have any idea how many nails I hammered crooked while eyeing your skirts? How many blades I ruined because I was too engrossed in the fullness of your lips as you worried them while doing sums of supplies? I would have had more success using my cock as the hammer. The iron I was forging wouldn't have known the difference in hardness, I assure you."

Holy shit.

"Thomas . . ."

He leaned back. The expression on his face was pleading, almost painful. Yet his hands never left her face. He didn't bring them lower to cop a feel. Nor did he grab her hand and place it on the very noticeable bulge in his breeches. Because, obviously, he really, really, really wanted to resume their activities. But no. He just stood there and allowed her to decide their fate. And there wasn't a doubt in her mind that, if she stopped it right there, he'd be just fine with it. No apologies, no excuses.

He trusted her on how they should move forward.

As a partner.

The thought of trust gnawed at her. Absurdly, she recalled all those stupid trust exercises she'd been forced to do at summer camp, where a friend blindfolded her and shouted directions on how to get to the end of the obstacle course. Or those trust falls, where—again, blindfolded—Beth would have to fall back into someone's waiting arms, trusting they'd be there to support her.

And then the idea came to her.

"Turn around."

Thomas cocked his head to the side at the order. "Pardon?"

Beth ran over to some nearby shelves and returned with a clean folded cloth. Thomas had them stacked to the side to wipe off bits of iron shavings that may land on his worktable. When she returned, she unfurled the cloth and refolded it in three layers.

The perfect width for shielding one's eyes.

Not a moment too soon, Thomas realized what Beth was planning. And thank God he didn't question it. Didn't think her pervy or improper. Because let's be honest here. Wasn't everything they were about to do improper?

Thomas flashed her a crooked, knowing smile before he slowly turned away from her. Beth had to stand on her tippy-toes to wrap the cloth fully around his eyes. Once the knot was secured at the back of his head, he whipped back around.

Anything left to say took a hike as the two of them slammed into each other. Beth gave her brain permission to shut the heck up as she trailed her tongue across Thomas's lips, over the stubble of his angled chin, and down the column of his neck. The soft pants and whimpers of the giant man before her were damn sexy and empowering. With him having no sight, she could do what she liked, and everything would be a giant surprise cake coated with a thick layer of anticipation frosting.

Beth kissed down the front of Thomas's broad chest. Her hands, mouth, everything couldn't get enough. She had begun to curse her plan of not having to remove her clothes to be with Thomas. The fabric hung heavily off her shoulders and chest, constricting her movement and dulling the sensations. The rough fibers of the damp fabric were so scratchy, it was as if her nipples and breasts were rubbing against steel wool. Talk about chafing. Likewise, the ache between her legs felt too distant to be relieved, like the last runner in a race pining for the water station at the finish line. But all that changed when her fingernail scraped over Thomas's nipple.

A guttural groan ripped from the man as his hands cupped her ass and lifted her as if she weighed nothing, wet skirts and all. His mouth was on hers as his powerful arms settled her on top of the worktable. Metal files and clamps skittered to the floor as he leaned Beth back against the wooden tabletop. With one arm securing her, Thomas reached down with the other and hurriedly lifted the folds of her skirts.

"Speak, Beth. If you don't want this, speak." The blindfold was doing a heck of a job of blinding her newfound beast. With no visuals, Thomas's senses must have wound him too tightly. He was a cork about to burst. His hand rested on the buttons at the fall of his breeches, just waiting for a word, a breath, a kiss. Anything.

"I want this."

She placed her hand on top of his and helped him undo the fastenings. His cock sprang free of the fabric. Beth's fingers shooed his own away and took over running her palm up and down his great length. Each pump had them breathing and moaning into each other's open mouths. Until finally, Thomas nestled closer in between Beth's legs.

With his arm still encircled around her waist, he clutched her closer to him and positioned his cock at her entrance. Beth closed her eyes as he slid the head up and down her opening once, twice, a third time, until he was well coated in her arousal. Then he settled in and rocked his hips forward.

The invasion was sudden and glorious. Beth inhaled greatly as Thomas stretched her wide. He was thicker than Kyle, longer than Kyle, and immediately hit spots that, for a physician, Kyle had been woefully ignorant of. Thomas was attentive, mesmerizing. With each hard thrust, he slightly swiveled his hips on the retreat. The sensation was spellbinding. Each joining rocked Beth higher and higher, yet he wasn't fast or without care.

Quite the opposite.

"Beth . . ." he breathed into the crook of her neck as he pumped into her.

Some strokes were hard and deep, while others were slow and seductive. The back of her head nearly rocked against the wall as his maneuvers began their increased pace. She hooked her heels around his ass and pressed him even more, urging him on. She met each thrust with a sharper moan. His name echoed into the cavern of his empty forge. Then she squeezed her eyes shut tightly as he lifted her again.

And held her close to his chest as he pumped furiously into her.

Without her feet on the ground or her ass on the table, he had stolen one of her senses. Just like she had taken one of his. The act was tortuous and incredible. Thomas thrust into her one final time. Her orgasm took hold, blasting through her body from the inside out. Like a supernova erupting from within. As she rode the wave of ecstasy, her pussy pulsed around his cock. He roared his release at the ceiling as hot spurts jetted from him. His hold around her body tightened, but not in a restrictive way. Thomas's grip both decreased in intensity and increased in compassion. Beth sighed into his comfort and strength, for that was all her body had in her. Thomas exhaled. His chest, glistening with sweat, rose and fell in more controlled measures.

Then she was moving again. Her hair was whipped around as

Thomas carried her to the far corner of his forge, near the table with the trinkets from his deceased wife and son. Firm padding touched her back as he laid her down on a small bedroll. How had she not noticed that before? Once she was settled, he removed the blindfold.

"Let me guess," Beth panted as she brushed his sweaty hair out of his eyes. "That was not what you expected."

Thomas smiled and kissed Beth tenderly before standing and adjusting himself. He couldn't hide his happiness any more than she could. "On the contrary. You have made me realize that my expectations are in need of reexamination."

"I'm so glad I could enlighten you."

"I am as well." He flashed that gorgeous smile again as he reached for his shirt. "Rest here tonight. I shall head to my house for a few things to see to your comfort. I'm afraid I don't have much to offer here."

Postcoital bliss descended over Beth. She didn't have it in her to argue with the man. After all, it was past midnight. Though the bedroll she was on left much to be desired, she hardly cared.

Because everything she desired in that moment was currently putting on his boots and angling for the door.

Sleep came fast and furious for Beth. Her body and mind were beyond grateful for the respite. So grateful, in fact, that she was too satiated to notice Thomas cleaning up the worktable's items strewn about the floor.

Or him leaning over her note. The one she intended to leave for him while she wasn't there.

The one detailing how she was from the future.

CHAPTER 19

The tension at the front of Thomas's mind worsened again. He pinched the bridge of his nose and squeezed his eyes shut. The predawn sun did its best to leak through the small windows of his forge. Sleep had been knocking at his door. His limbs had grown tired under the weight of his exhaustion.

He had not slept a wink. Not since discovering Beth's note with his name on it. His hindquarters, however, had long ago fallen asleep as he sat with his legs sprawled out in front of him and his back rigid against the stone wall. Bleary eyes looked down at the trembling paper in his hand and read the words for the thirtieth time that night and soon-to-be morning.

Thomas, it will not be easy for you to understand what you're about to read, but please try. I <u>need</u> you to try. Because though I don't know how yet exactly, I need your help . . .

I am not from Salem. I am from Boston, but a future Boston. The day before I met you was June 19, 2022. The following morning, I ran into an antique shop . . .

His mind read through the date again. And again. For it was surely folly. How could she expect him to believe such nonsense? He was not an academic, true, but a tradesman, and a very successful one at that.

Did she intend to poke fun at him? Imply him too dim not to know the year in which they lived?

Thomas glanced up at the source of his agitation. Beth was still curled up in the corner, asleep on his lumpy bedroll. How the woman slept like the dead on that thing was a marvel. He would keep it rolled up in the corner and use it when his work kept him late into the night and the trek home was too bothersome. Hot iron hardly cared whether one's body was exhausted. Still, the sad lump of fabric offered little in the way of comfort.

Despite the tale she wrote, he still worried for her comfort, dammit. Beth's damp clothes had dried, and her body was covered in two wool blankets Thomas kept with his bedroll. It had been the best he could offer her, as he'd never left the forge once he read her note.

Thomas put down the note, only to pick up Beth's ax again.

I was holding the ax in the antique shop when it all started. There was a pale green residue on the weapon. When I touched it, the surrounding dust in the shop caused me to sneeze. I covered my mouth with my hand. My head spun right after. I had never been so dizzy in my life. I passed out on the shop's floor . . . and woke up on the street, in the shadow of a covered wagon. Around people who didn't dress like me, who didn't speak like me.

Because I wasn't from their time.

"You read it."

Thomas looked up. Beth sat on top of the bedroll with her legs crossed. How had he not even heard her rustling? Her face was solemn and paler than he would have preferred. Her lips, which had been so plump and delectable the night before, were pressed together in a thin, worried line.

"Yes, I read it."

Beth nodded her head slightly. Then more silence descended on them. The morning had not yet fully begun. It was the hazy twilight of the dawn when all was still. Crickets had ceased their chirping, yet the birds had not yet arisen with their song.

The blasted silence was too damn loud.

"Do you have any questions?" Beth stood, smoothed down her skirts, and walked a few steps toward him.

He chuckled. "She asks if I have questions."

"I'm sure it's a shock."

"You don't speak as they do from Salem."

Beth paused her advances.

"Your speech is different from the locals here, of course. But I have known travelers from Salem. Even they do not speak as you do. Your dialect is foreign." Thomas gripped the note and willed his legs to get him upright. "You are not from Salem."

"No." She shook her head. "I'm from Boston. Everything I wrote in that note is true. I just hadn't intended for you to read it so soon."

"But you expect me to believe you are from a Boston that is more than two hundred years in the future."

Beth nodded. Then the rage took hold.

"What else have you lied about? Have you stolen from me? Fabricated my ledgers?" Thomas's finger shook as he pointed to the papers at his desk.

"What? No! Never! Thomas, I'm not a liar or a thief. I know it's far-fetched, but please . . ."

"Does Mr. Richmond know? Mrs. Potter?"

"No. No, they don't," Beth murmured. "I took a chance in trusting you."

"Why? Why me?"

"Because you trusted me enough to be your partner."

"In business, yes! You had a much-needed skill and labor was in short supply." Thomas backed away and turned to glare out the window. His hands were fisted at his hips yet, inexplicably, he still held her note with care.

"No!" It was Beth's turn to rage.

He turned around and gawked at the elevation in her voice.

"Don't act like we are just business partners. Business partners sure as hell don't do what we did last night."

"Beth, you are asking me to believe in madness." His words came out in a pleading breath of exasperation.

"Remember back to when we first met. What was I wearing?"

"A smock of some kind."

"A smock," she said dryly. "Is that really what you thought of my clothing?"

Thomas thought back to when she ran into him in the street. She had worn a crisp shirt and breeches, both of which were dyed a horrendous dark blue. No gown, no stays, no bonnet. Her shoes, likewise, had been odd. White and rigid, with a generously rounded toe that surprisingly hurt when she stepped on his boot by accident.

He had been so fixated on the surprise of her, and then the weapon in her hand, that he had forgotten. He had never seen clothes like that before, let alone a woman dressed in them.

"All sorts of fashions come through the city. I am hardly up on the latest trends."

Beth rolled her eyes and nibbled her finger as she paced in front of him. Then she stopped abruptly and turned back to him. "Other than my ax and clothes, I don't have anything from my time to prove my point. Except my knowledge of the past. Or your present, as it were."

Thomas shook his head in confusion. His lack of sleep and her persistence in her tale were weighing on him.

Beth walked to the worktable behind Thomas and grabbed her ax. "This was sitting on the table in the antique shop I walked into the morning I traveled here. It was included in an array of other items devoted to the Revolutionary War."

"What war? I have never heard of such a war."

"That's because it won't happen for another six years." She sighed before nailing him with pleading eyes.

"The table had iron nails, musket balls, tin soldiers, all from this time period. It even had a map of Paul Revere's Boston."

Thomas's stomach bottomed out at the name that left Beth's lips. "You know Revere? How?"

"I know *of* Paul Revere. Nearly every American does in my time."

His head spun with details that made no sense. "He's a well-known silversmith." Thomas dismissed it with a wave of his hand. "It's not surprising he's made a name for himself. I've worked with him several times."

"No. He's more than that. We know him for his midnight ride."

Thomas stared at her, baffled.

"As part of the events leading up to the start of the Revolutionary War—America's war for independence against the British—he warned the colonial militia that the British troops were approaching. It was kind of a big deal."

"You're mad, woman." He shook his head. "Out of my shop! Now!"

"No! Please, listen to me. You *must* hear me." Beth ran toward him and grasped the collar of his open shirt. Her eyes were wild. Tears, stormy and persistent, rimmed her eyes despite her efforts to fight them back. Yet her grip remained firm as she rattled on. "Revere was also a member of the Sons of Liberty, along with Samuel Adams and John Hancock. His house is in the North End of Boston and, in my time, is the oldest building in the city . . . 19 North Square, I believe, is the address. It's a very popular tourist destination. I've been there at least three times on school field trips."

"Revere . . . is in the North End," Thomas whispered and nodded. "No, I won't hear of it!" Exhaustion, shock, confusion, and care for the woman before him warred for residence in his mind. It was too much.

"His mark!" Beth raised a hand to her forehead. "You've worked with him, you've said."

Thomas nodded reluctantly.

"Docents at his house giving the tours always talked about his marks. He has a maker's mark on all his silver pieces. Sometimes he'd engrave his initials 'PR' in ornate letters on the handles of spoons and things. But for other items, larger items especially, he'd stamp his last name. 'REVERE' in all capital letters, outlined in a rectangular block. You must have seen his mark, Thomas. Please, tell me I'm not making this up and you believe me."

Thomas wrenched out of her grasp, though even in his anger he gently pushed her to the side. Heavy boots carried him to the small table in the corner where Beth had first noticed his son's rattle. Beneath the rattle was a drawer. A locked drawer, and one Thomas had not opened in many years. With his back obscuring Beth's vision, he reached for a key hidden in a ceramic pot and unlocked the drawer. Inside sat a keepsake box for Emily's trinkets she'd collected when they traveled.

A box he had commissioned from Revere and his other silversmiths. A box hidden in a drawer Beth had no previous access to.

Of course a mark would be there. Every tradesman marked his

work. One was a fool not to. Yet, in truth, he hadn't had cause to ever look at the mark. He'd paid good coin for the purchase and his relationship with other smiths in the city made it so he never worried for lack of quality or value from other tradesmen.

The silver was cold in his palm as Thomas turned the box upside down. There, in the middle of the four feet, was a rectangular stamped maker's mark.

REVERE.

It did not make any sense why a serving girl employed in a whaler's household, especially a serving girl who just arrived in the city, would know so much about the silversmith. A chill trickled across Thomas's skin. Gooseflesh pebbled his forearms as he ran through her proclamations. Things he couldn't explain how she knew.

Revere was a member of the Sons of Liberty, which Thomas suspected but hadn't yet confirmed.

Revere was a silversmith. And she described his mark in perfect detail without having seen the trinket box.

Revere lived in the North End. Yes, Thomas knew that to be true.

The other things she mentioned—this Revolutionary War, Revere warning the militia of advancing British soldiers—made little sense. Yet she said they hadn't happened yet.

Is she really speaking true?

Thomas slowly turned to Beth. The silver box never left his palm.

"I'm going to go." Beth had already made her way to the door. Her hand rested on the handle. "Please think things over, Thomas. I'm not lying. I'm not trying to swindle you out of money or anything like that. I'm just . . . lost." Beth's last word broke as she said it. Her voice had lost its zeal. Even amid his confusion, his heart squeezed at her despair. "And I need help."

A moment later, the door to his shop closed with a thud. Beth had left him alone.

Yet her presence around him had never been more prevalent.

CHAPTER 20

R un.
The word was a blaring beacon in Beth's mind as she turned the corner and jogged the final block to Mr. Richmond's house. The sun was coming up more fully. Rays of gold peeked through alleys and around carts as she ran down the street.

Her conversation with Thomas turned over in her head. *He didn't believe me.* Beth's iron-willed determination sank like a stone. There was only so much talking up one could do. If the other party wasn't on board, it was game over. And that hurt.

Because she really didn't want it to be game over with Thomas. Not because she needed help, but because she needed . . . him.

Her feet slowed their pace as the front of Mr. Richmond's home came into view. The carriage outside the front entrance made her stop. *What's a carriage doing out in front at this hour?*

As if summoned by Beth's thought, Mrs. Potter opened the front door and hobbled down the steps to greet the driver. Beth ducked behind a nearby bush. She hadn't intended to be caught doing the walk of shame back from Thomas's forge. And certainly not by her boss.

"I say, what is the meaning of such an early call?" Mrs. Potter's shrill voice, still unused from sleep, carried across the way.

"Apologies, ma'am." The driver jumped off the back of the carriage and groaned as he unloaded a large trunk. "We encountered a delay or two over the past few weeks. Damn carriage wheel fell in a ditch right as we left Salem. Pardon my language." The driver dipped his head low before standing to full attention. "Had to get that repaired. Then one of the horses took ill. The poor thing had shit coming out of both ends. I thought he'd nearly explode from the effort. Lord knows I would. Oh, apologies, ma'am." Another dip at the waist. "Thought I'd have to return back for another beast to make the trip, but he came around. Didn't you, old boy."

The driver walked over to one of the two black horses and started petting his mane before turning back to Mrs. Potter. "We were all set to venture out again, until poor Miss McCrary here got the runs while staying at an inn along the way. I warned her to keep clear of the mutton. Smelled off and had a gray tinge to it, but the young miss dove headfirst into the bowl and—"

"Albert, enough! Get my trunk and be off with you. You are no longer needed."

The door to the carriage opened. A booted heel kicked down a set of small stairs. Beth stretched her neck out from her hiding spot to get a better glimpse.

A young woman in modest clothing stepped out of the carriage. She held a book in one hand, a fan in the other, and a whole lot of attitude shoved up her skirts, apparently. The woman's nose was so high in the air, she was liable to pass out. But that wasn't as shocking as her most defining feature: her long red hair.

"Miss McCrary?" Mrs. Potter looked at the woman in confusion.

"Yes, that's me. I say, you have anything to eat in there? Or at least show me to my room where I can lie down properly?" The young woman put her hands on the small of her back and pushed out a stretch.

"Elizabeth McCrary," Mrs. Potter deadpanned. "Sent by your uncle?"

"Yes, have we not determined this already? My, I know you city folk think us simple, but you aren't exactly doing yourselves any favors here. My uncle, absurd man that he is, thought some time in service to a household would improve my character. Hence why I've been shipped off here for a time. But he promised it'll all be in my favor. For the price of a summer spent mopping floors and washing pots, I've been guaranteed a new autumn wardrobe." Her expression turned smug, as if she were a rider who had just bartered a child's pony for a barn full of thoroughbreds.

Beth craned her neck to see further. But as she stretched, a sharp tremor rippled through her thigh. Fatigue, sudden and heavy, deadened her leg. Her weight dropped to the ground. Beth cried out as her kneecap slammed into the cobblestones. The tremor pulsed for several more seconds before subsiding. Once relief radiated through her and the fatigue passed, Beth hoisted herself off the ground and looked up.

To three pairs of questioning eyes. The most curious look came from Mrs. Potter. However, the curiosity quickly fell away as recognition and indignation took its place.

It was the look of someone who just realized they had been duped.

There are things less conspicuous than running away from the scene of the crime. Beth had watched at least a dozen heist movies and knew the moves that got the jewels safely into the caravan and away from the pursuing security. Calm, a seemingly outward disregard for what was happening around them, and a damn good decoy.

Beth had none of those things when she bolted from Mrs. Potter and the newly established Miss McCrary. The look on Mrs. Potter's fallen face gutted Beth, though. She liked the woman and had come to really admire her. There was something to be said for someone who worked hard, took pride in her performance, yet knew the way of the world wouldn't ever see her advancing beyond her station. To still give your all pridefully, without the prospect of advancement, was definitely a foreign concept in Beth's and Kyle's circles.

It was kind of refreshing to take the status out of it and just be content to exist while doing your best at something that suits you. Kind of like how midwifery was for her.

The pang of loss at running from Mrs. Potter, knowing Beth had to steer clear of the woman going forward and figure out a new plan, still burned, however. It didn't make her retreat any easier.

Bright golden rays peered over the water's edge as Beth neared the harbor. The streets had become more familiar. No, they didn't resemble the city grid of her time, but they had slowly turned into the shape of a neighborhood Beth was getting more comfortable with. The knowledge was soothing as she scanned the empty street, searching for where to go next.

A low rumble rose up in the distance behind her. A methodical clomping quickly followed. Carriage wheels and horses.

"Shit! Where to go? Where to go?"

It didn't take a crystal ball to figure out that the carriage heading her way was most likely the same one at Mr. Richmond's house. There were hardly any other people out at that hour. A few dockworkers had begun to stir, sure, but certainly no carriages yet.

Crap. Did they intend to arrest her for impersonating the real Miss McCrary? Criminal justice in this time left a lot to be desired, for sure.

A loud grunt off to her left spooked her. The door to the bakery was open. A young baker was piling up large sacks of flour to keep the door from closing. After dropping his second sack of flour, he turned to go back inside. But not before he spied Beth staring at him.

"Miss Beth! What are you doing out so early in the morning?" Francis, the young father whose son she helped deliver, eyed her with surprise and delight as he rested his fists on his waist.

Bingo.

Beth ran over to Francis. The poor guy hardly had enough time to step aside before she barreled through the front door and ducked out of the street's view.

"Are you all right?" Francis walked in after her and leaned a hip against the wooden counter. "I'm not used to seeing others at this hour. It's usually just me and the seagulls."

"Yes, I'm fine."

No, you're not. You're a criminal and a fugitive stuck in the past who lost

143

the only person you could trust and, oh yeah, you just kissed your living arrangements goodbye, too. And you're green.

Your move, Gumby.

"Actually, no. I'm not fine. I'm pretty darn far from fine. Mind if I sit for a moment?"

Francis nodded profusely as he grabbed a stool and brought it over to her. Her aching leg muscles welcomed the rest.

"You know, I can never thank you enough for all your help with Theodora and our son. I was beyond scared, though I'm sure you noticed." Francis's matter-of-fact mention of his family slowly drew Beth out of her panic. She looked up to see him scooping out a slightly bubbly paste onto a well-floured counter. He added more scoops of flour to the paste and began mixing it all together with his hands as he talked.

"But you just had this way with everyone. Calmed us all down right quick, I'll say. And little Jeremy is pudging up quite nicely. I would, too, if I had my wife's offerings." He smiled as he gently pushed the heel of his palm into the amassed dough before turning it over and repeating the maneuver.

"I'm glad to hear they're well. Perhaps I can pay them a visit if they're up for it. New moms should always be checked on. I usually follow up six weeks after the birth, but . . ." *I don't think I'll be around that long.*

"Oh, Thea would love that! We've been so long in this city without a midwife willing to tend to us. You're a breath of fresh air, Miss Beth."

The statement shocked her. "Who helps with the births now? Or the prenatal care? Surely you have doctors or surgeons, someone to . . ."

"Surgeons? My goodness, they must do things quite differently where you're from. No, none of that, I'm afraid. Unless you have the funds to procure private care, you rely on the services of a midwife. But . . ." Thomas shaped the loaf he was working on, set it aside, and scooped out some more paste to mix with flour. "Maddy left. She was our midwife and helped all the working-class folk get by. But when her housing could no longer be offered freely, as is the custom here in exchange for a midwife's services, she picked up and went elsewhere. Too many British and militia members moving into the city. Not enough lodgings to go around. We've been without a midwife for about a year now."

Beth swallowed down her frustration. There was nothing like a crude history lesson to jar one awake. Childbirth at this time was dangerous. Pregnancy at this time was dangerous. Children living beyond infancy was not always a guarantee. But to go through it without the benefit of even basic midwifery care? One of the oldest professions in the world? She couldn't fathom.

So her next move didn't surprise her at all.

"Are Thea and Jeremy still at your place? Would you mind terribly if I go pay a call there right now? I'd love to help in any way I can."

Francis's smile calmed every previously jittery nerve in her body. With that single smile, her anxiety had retreated to the recesses of her mind. Her disappointment over losing Thomas, her sadness at lying to Mrs. Potter, her worry about her skin and what these new painful symptoms meant—they all lessened, and her board-certified nurse-midwife hat sat more firmly on her head.

She jumped off the stool. Her previously unsteady legs held her strongly. Because if she needed to hide out for a bit, doing so with Theodora, Francis, and a newborn was as safe a place as any. Especially since her plan to tell Thomas had backfired majorly.

With her next step figured out, she brushed off her skirts and smiled back at Francis.

Let's do this.

CHAPTER 21

Thomas slammed his fist against Mr. Richmond's door for the second time. Patience had never been his strong suit. Especially when he was desperate. He jockeyed his weight from one leg to the other and pumped his fists as he waited.

The last time such desperation had consumed him was when he held the lifeless body of his son. And then his wife.

The sun was past the high point in the sky. After Beth left him that morning, he had been so confused. He was grateful his body acted graciously where his mind could not. Exhaustion had won the hour and his shaky legs had eventually brought him to his bedroll, where he finally succumbed to sleep.

On top of blankets that smelled like Beth. That some of her warmth still clung to.

As he slept, dreams took hold. They were memories at first, the worst of his life. Images of Emily and Elliot dying. Even though they were dreams, Thomas remembered the physical details. The weight of Elliot's lifeless body, the width of the shovel handle in his palms as he scooped more dirt into the graves. The loud thud as he heaved his last pack into the back of the cart as he prepared to leave.

Yet those dreams, those memories, didn't linger long. As Thomas tossed and turned, new images rose to the surface of his mind. Beth's wavy, red hair slipping in and out of his fingers in the alley. Her bright, sunny laugh as she teased him about his lack of assembly in his ledgers, muttering something about organized chaos.

Her kind, compassionate blue eyes as she spoke Elliot's name for the first time. How meaningful it was to hear it again, especially from someone else's lips, after years of Thomas never speaking his own son's name. Never being brave enough to, for fear doing so would anger the wound that had never solidly healed.

And then another vision appeared in his dream. Thomas was at his anvil, drawing out another damn bayonet. A weapon he had done so often he could create it in his sleep. His focus was split, however. At the worktable, Beth sat scribbling notes. Yet by her side was a white specter.

Emily.

She looked not a day older than when she'd left him. Her long auburn hair hung loosely about her shoulders. Her simple brown gown had been the one she'd worn home from visiting her sister in the countryside.

The very day her fever started to show.

White vapors floated all around her. In the dream, Thomas couldn't take his sight off her. His hands continued to work the metal, thankfully, despite his distraction. Emily was staring down at Beth, who was oblivious to the spirit next to her. Thomas smiled at Beth's deep concentration. The tip of her pink tongue curled over the edge of her top lip.

Then Emily looked at him directly, smiled, and floated toward him. Once she got near, however, she turned past his anvil and went straight to the shelves with her trinket boxes, Elliot's rattle, and all of his previous ornaments and specialty wares. Items that had once given him great joy to create.

Wisps floated around her as she leaned over, yet her back was to him so he could not see immediately what she selected. When she stood up, she turned and hovered over to him. Her feet seemed firmly on the ground, yet her head never bobbed with her stride. Her glide was effortless.

His wife, who he had not laid eyes on in five years, stood before him in spirit form. In her hands was her silver trinket box. The one he'd had commissioned by Revere.

Her slight hands turned the box over and revealed the smith's maker's mark. Revere's last name, bold and stated, stared back at him. The mark was as he knew it to appear, yet confusion glazed his vision.

Until he looked up.

His Emily held up the box to him. Her eyes were encouraging, her smile brilliant. No fear, no sadness. Thomas was assaulted from all sides with happiness and encouragement. It emanated out of Emily's spirit and slammed into him like a gale-force wind. He had no choice but to stand there and take it. Then Emily's hand reached up and cupped the side of his face. Her presence was visible but not tangible. Yet just seeing her outstretched arm in front of him was reassuring.

Then she looked back at Beth, who had stopped her scribbling and stood up. She turned to face him, yet didn't move. She just rested her hands in front of her and grinned slightly. Her eyes were full of compassion.

To his great surprise, the bayonet in his hand had been completed. Quenched, filed, and assembled in the span of mere moments. While he hadn't moved an inch.

But Emily had. She'd stepped back from him and wandered over to stand behind Beth's shoulder. Left in Thomas's other hand was the silver trinket box, with Revere's mark facing up.

When he had woken from his dreams, confusion still warred with sense. Yet it was more like a disagreement than a battle. A disagreement left room for one to change minds, an opportunity to coax the other to their way of thought, whereas a battle left room for pain and suffering . . . and losses on both sides. He was no longer equipped to manage pain and suffering.

That left one option.

Thomas's fist hit the door again. "Open!"

After the third try, Mrs. Potter finally answered the door. She was panting, and Thomas immediately regretted his impatience and aggression. The poor woman didn't need or deserve his fury.

"Mr. Brannigan. Apologies! I was engaged on the other side of the property. To what do I owe the visit?"

"Miss McCrary. I must speak with her."

"Oh, I'm afraid I must tell you some troubling news and apologize profusely as a result. We had been lied to, sir." She gripped her hands and looked up and down the street. "The woman who previously represented herself to us as Miss McCrary was a fraud. An imposter."

Thomas had only fallen asleep for a few hours since Beth left his forge. It was only the afternoon. Had she told others of her secret as well? "Explain, please."

"Certainly, sir. The real Miss McCrary arrived at Mr. Richmond's homestead in the predawn hours. Traveling delays, you see. Both girls share a resemblance in hair color, which was the only attribute Mr. McCrary had provided to me when he said he'd be sending his niece to aid in maintaining the house. I mistook the two. Yet when I saw the imposter this morning in the street, no doubt attempting to creep back into the house, her ruse was found out. And she fled. I know not where to. The driver tried to follow her and track her down, but to no avail. Sir, I do apologize profusely. I had no idea—"

"I must go." Thomas hurried away from Mrs. Potter. He had to find Beth. Had apologies to make himself.

His legs pumped hard as his feet ate up the cobblestones beneath him. His exact destination was a mystery, but he had faith. He trusted he would find her.

For she had trusted him with so much more.

There was something about a newborn baby's smell that was instantly calming. As Beth sat on the edge of Theodora's bed, cradling baby Jeremy in her arms, she realized the scented candle industry had missed out on a huge commodity. Vanilla and lavender were nice and all, but inhaling a newborn's scent was instant bliss. Even with Beth's nerves as jumbled as they were, Jeremy's nearness did wonders to her state of mind.

Because newborns were newborns. Nothing changing there. They were still as soft, squirmy, and cutely predictable as they had always been. Or as they would always be.

"Thank you for stopping by and watching him. The rest was glorious." Theodora folded a small blanket and sat down in the rocking chair across from Beth.

"Of course. You know, people always tell you to sleep when the baby sleeps, but honestly? That's a load of crap and is usually preached by either men or women who have lots of help. The truth is, with newborns, all bets are off. You do what works for you."

"I must say, your speech is both uncommon and refreshing. Where did you say you were from again?"

"It doesn't matter," Beth whispered down into Jeremy's scrunched-up sleeping face. The weight of the swaddled baby in her arms was comforting and right. Her body, her makeup, took to the position like a fish to water. Beth shut her eyes and silently reveled in the familiar. For she couldn't anticipate when, if ever, she'd have that feeling again.

"So, that clump of blood was normal, you say?"

"Oh, yes." Beth opened her eyes and looked at Theodora. Even though the new mom was lying back in the rocking chair, her body still radiated tension and concern. The poor chair's arms were taking the brunt of the woman's stress. Her fingernails were curling in against the wood.

"Blood clots can be normal in the few weeks after birth. I had a patient . . . I mean, mother who had passed a blood clot the size of a potato about four weeks after her baby was born. Scared her big time, but she was fine. However, it was a symptom of her overdoing it. She would sit for hours on end and moved very little. All that sitting interfered with her healing and limited blood flow. And then . . . boom! She went to pee and popped out a potato. I mean, a ball of blood the size of a potato." Beth quickly backtracked. "Not an actual potato."

Smooth.

Theodora's eyes widened. "My goodness. Well, I suppose I should be grateful my bleeding is uneventful. The clump of blood I saw on the cloth this morning was the size of a peanut." She chuckled. "Hardly as interesting."

"You're doing just fine, Mama. After four days, you and baby are doing just fine."

"Thank you." Theodora relaxed in her exhausted relief before she smiled at Beth. "You know, there is another woman with child who lives near the bakery. Annelise, a seamstress. She's perhaps a few months along and is not so heavy yet, but she complains of sharp pains down her leg, especially when she sweeps."

"Sciatica." Beth nodded. "I'd be happy to see whether I can help her, if you think she'd appreciate it."

"Oh, that would be wonderful. Annelise would be thrilled." Theodora beamed.

Beth stood from the bed, leaned over, and handed Jeremy back to his mother. When Beth stood upright, a wave of nausea nearly pitted her forward into Theodora's lap. Her stomach twisted and pinched, like the time she got food poisoning from eating an old egg salad sandwich at the hospital cafeteria.

"Beth, are you all right?"

A cold bite of air slammed into the front of her teeth as she wheezed in a sharp breath. Her hand flew to the side of her waist. Her abdomen tensed.

"I'm fine . . . I'm fine." Beth waved off Theodora's concern. "I think I'm just going to step out for some fresh air, however. I must have eaten something that didn't agree with me."

Beth didn't wait for Theodora to dismiss her. She two-timed it out the door and down the stairs. By the time she got out the front door, her heart was racing. The sun was high in the sky and did a great job of beaming straight down onto her side of the street. The handkerchief tied tightly around her neck was suffocating. Yet there was no way she'd untie it and risk her skin being noticed. But the heat and tightness were killing her.

Everything is killing you.

"Calm down. C'mon. Deep breath in . . . Deep breath out . . ."

Beth closed her eyes and slowly expanded her lungs. Each full breath she took pushed down the anxiety about her symptoms. The pangs were still there, along with the nausea and slight tremors, but her breathing she could control.

And she desperately needed to control something.

A slight breeze floated through, carrying with it the briny scent of the ocean. Then her gut twisted again, but not from the earlier pain.

No, this new assault was sparked by a recent memory of the last time she'd been near the harbor. With Thomas.

Beth's legs slowly carried her down the street to where the end of the road opened out near the wharf. Seagulls cawed and circled overhead. The birds made her smile, even through her discomfort, as she recalled feeding them with Thomas a few days ago. Well, she had pretended to be focused on feeding them. In actuality, she was tossing bread their way, true, but she was mostly sneaking glances at Thomas.

And marveling at how good being with him felt. How good *she* felt just sharing a simple act with him. No pressure to perform, no doubts about how she measured up. No insecurities about her body, no pain of rejection. Just her existing in a sphere where she was happy. And dammit if a lot of that happiness wasn't directly attributed to her blacksmith.

But he isn't yours, is he?

The reminder stung, and the realization that she was alone again, grappling with whatever the heck was happening to her, was nothing short of terrifying.

Beth shuffled along the cobblestones until she could hear the hollering of the dockworkers. Loud bangs of casks and crates warred with lapping waves and crunching carriage tires.

Would this ever feel like home? And what if I don't have a choice in the matter?

"Oh, sorry, miss!"

Two teenage boys bolted past Beth, with one knocking into her, nearly throwing her off balance. Once she righted herself, she looked up to see who had jostled her . . .

And got an eyeful of Thomas, with his back against the railing that faced the water. His thighs were wide, arms straight at his sides, fists clenched. His eyes were laser-focused on her. He looked like a great defender, or a terrifying menace.

Neither mattered as she ran toward him. Because good, bad, or indifferent, her entire body hummed with electricity when he was nearby.

So, yes, she would always run toward him. She just hoped he wouldn't run in the other direction.

CHAPTER 22

Thomas had never been more tightly coiled in his life. He was pretty sure that, as soon as his boots sprang off the ground, he'd demolish anything in his way of reaching Beth. His lips quirked at the thought of reducing a horse cart to splinters. Or even plowing through those two careless lads who'd bumped into her. Either one would do.

He pushed off the railing, and in an instant, his arms were around her waist. His hand cupped the back of her head to his shoulder as he held her there. Breathing her in. Rememorizing the feel of her against him.

Damn, it was glorious. And right. Immediately, his anxiety settled. He had found her.

"What does this mean?" Beth whispered against his chest as she shook her head with uncertainty. "Do you—"

He wasted no time kissing her. His haste, however, was his only outward show of aggression. He took his time feeling, exploring, reliving everything about her sweet mouth. The soft mewls she made, the way she went slightly lax in his arms. He ate it all up, cherished every sensation, and mentally kicked himself for letting her run out of his forge before he'd had a chance to tell her he believed her.

Because believe her he did, as fantastical as it sounded.

Only when he was finally content enough in his attentions did he pull back, but just enough to look upon her clearly. Like hell he'd risk letting her run away again.

"I believe you."

Beth stilled in his arms and eyed him with confusion, so he said the words again. Louder. Stronger. With no regrets or hesitation.

"I believe you. I am sorry I ever gave you cause to run from me. I would sooner cut off my hand than see that disappointment in your eyes again. Especially knowing I was the cause of it."

"You really believe me, then?" Her smile, bright and brilliant, was tempered, however, by her furrowed brow.

She still has doubts. Show her more. Show her she can trust you.

Thomas took her hand, snaked it through his arm, and cupped her elbow as he guided her along the wharf. "I'll admit, it is quite a tale. And it did take me time to absorb all you told me. When I woke up following my troubled sleep, things became . . . clearer."

"Sleep can do that," Beth murmured. "What changed your mind? I mean, I'm grateful to have you as an ally, but—"

"We are far more than allies." Thomas stopped walking and smiled down at her. "And I shall strive to prove that to you for as long as I need to." When Beth smiled back at him, he was content that his message got through, and they resumed walking.

"I could not fathom how you knew of Revere's mark, let alone his residence and"—he lowered his voice—"his association with the Sons of Liberty. The silver box, your ax . . . As wondrous as it sounds, I trust you."

"You have no idea how happy that makes me."

"Judging by your tightening grip on my arm, I have some idea." He chuckled. "Now, tell me, what happened with Mrs. Potter? I went to call on you and was met with a rather flustered housekeeper denouncing you as an imposter and a fraud."

Beth winced. "Yeah, about that. When I arrived here, she saw me outside Mr. Richmond's house and mistook me for someone else, someone with red hair who she sent for to work in the residence. I was alone and desperate, not to mention confused as all get out, so I didn't exactly correct her assumption. It was going just fine until the real person showed up this morning."

"Ah. That explains things. Where did you go? I had only begun my search by the harbor when good fortune sent me to you."

"Francis."

The name of another man was hardly what Thomas expected to hear. "Who?"

"The baker. I helped his wife deliver her baby, remember?"

"Ah, yes."

"The sun was just coming up when I had run away from the residence after being found out. I came down here, to the water. I had no idea where to go or what to do. Francis was just opening up the bakery and noticed me."

Thomas's frustration at himself churned his insides. Hearing her panic, her aimlessness as a result of his actions toward her in the morning, was despicable, unforgivable. Yet she had forgiven him wholeheartedly, even though he did not deserve it. He had much to atone for.

" . . . and it was fortunate he found me because Theodora had been struggling a bit postpregnancy."

Talk of her as a midwife drew his attention away from his self-loathing.

"Theodora and Francis told me how the former midwife for the community left. Something about lack of free housing. So the working-class women have been on their own for the last year or so. No one to oversee their health during pregnancy, no one to assist in the deliveries, no follow-up. It was heart-wrenching."

"Unless you choose to fight for crown or country, you are stuck in the middle of a war not of your design. Merchants, tradesmen, and everyone striving to earn an honest living are no exception." Thomas slowed his stride as a thought occurred. "I will say, your skills would be widely valuable here. There are many who would benefit. Now that your residence in Mr. Richmond's household is no longer viable, you shall stay with me."

"The thought of being helpful here is so exciting— Wait, what?" It was Beth's turn to halt their walk.

"Stay." Thomas turned and took her hands in his. "With me. In my home. You will be safe there."

Beth's silence was endearing and slightly unnerving, for he was not meek in his offer. He had not the patience to mince words or play coy. He wanted her. In his home. In his city. In his bed. In his heart.

"I know not all that you left behind in your time. But here, there is much I can offer you. Much the people of Boston need from you."

Her silence ticked on a moment longer. Every damn sound around them magnified to eruptive levels. He wished to hear the sound of her saying yes, the sweet chime of her voice agreeing to his demand. Instead, she stayed silent while the city assaulted him with dock-workers cursing after women and dogs growling over scraps of meat.

At last, her voice filtered through the din of the raucous harbor, but even louder than that was her smile.

"Thank you." Her body rose up against his. Her arms flung around his neck. "You are the best life preserver I have ever asked for."

"I'm unfamiliar with that phrase, but I'm happy to be whatever you need me to be."

Bliss had eluded Thomas for so long. He would be damned if he'd let it out of his iron grip again.

Isaac Hunterdon leaned back against the alley wall. His left leg was bent at a ninety-degree angle, with his foot braced against the building. Around him, soldiers gathered to hear every word from his latest report. As Isaac spoke, he'd pause every few sentences. The anticipation he built for the outcome was another tool in his arsenal. He needed his men beholden to him, lapping up his stories and orders.

Loyalty was priceless. Hard to win and even harder to keep.

Isaac leaned forward slightly. His thigh muscles in his bent leg tightened and flexed. The strain was welcome, almost painful, and fueled his energy. "The New York boys burned the lieutenant gover-nor's effigy to the fucking ground. Had a good, sizable crowd for the display, too, I heard. And they did it right at the start of his day, just as he was walking into his office. It's a shame I could not have been there in person."

Soft murmurs of agreement and confident grins met each word.

Pleased, Isaac continued to regale his men with happenings from the Sons of Liberty New York chapter. Every fire, every ruination, every act of vandalism shown to the British loyalists was fuel for their country's cause. And as news of their band's actions spread through the colonies, hopes ran higher for recognition on a larger scale.

For representation. The ultimate prize of a truly liberated nation.

"I do love a good fire." Will grinned, exposing the gap in his teeth. Isaac's man had never been much to look at, but he served a purpose. In their line of work, brawn was more effective than beauty. And Isaac had enough brains for the lot of them, so no worry there.

"Isaac, any news on the weapons manufacture? The men are clamoring for more arms, especially the new recruits from Harvard." Anthony, Isaac's man responsible for recruiting, folded his arms across his chest and waited for a response. He was a master of persuasion, though damn impatient.

"I know. The blacksmith won't fill my order without proper coin upfront." Isaac sneered at the memory of Brannigan calling his bluff. The truth of the matter was that Isaac's lack of funds was a larger problem for the militia than he would let on. Some of his men might have started to feel the pinch, though most would cut off their hand before saying anything to him. Isaac had promised compensation and had struggled to deliver. It wasn't easy to start an uprising, instill devotion to a cause that had only just taken root. The funds would come, of that he was certain. He just needed to drum up more support. Rally more men to his side.

That was Isaac's problem, though. The lower class was easier to embolden and convince. But the upper class had the funds. It was a delicate negotiation that took skill and time.

"He'll not take our credit?" Will chimed in, though it was more out of solidarity than true concern. The man hardly cared about the whys, only the what-nexts. He was a soldier's soldier: he rarely asked questions and was always up for a fight. And fiercely loyal as well, which made him suited to Isaac's cause.

"Don't concern yourselves with the payments. I have it in hand. I'll get him to fill the order. He'll get his money."

A few of his men shuffled backward. Murmured whispers and not-so-discreet turns of their heads spoke volumes. His time was running out . . . and so was his word.

"Speak of the devil, Isaac. Isn't that Brannigan?"

Anthony's words brought Isaac's head around the alley's corner. Sure enough, Brannigan was there, walking hand in hand with a red-haired woman. The same one Isaac had gotten entangled with outside of the blacksmith's forge. The exchange had been brief and was hardly anything he dwelled on. But he did remember Brannigan's loud insistence that she get inside.

Away from him.

"Oy, it's that bitch from the square," Will growled as the other men around him laughed.

"The one who wouldn't have you. That's right! She came to aid that tailor's boy," Anthony said.

"Tailor? The one we sent the message to about when he removed our bills posted near his shop?" Isaac leaned forward.

"Yes, the same."

Isaac listened to Anthony retell the events as he looked on. The couple continued their walk down the street, oblivious to the predators around them.

Brannigan had money. His successful blacksmithing operation had more than funded British armaments, yet the smith claimed to be ambivalent toward either cause. Horse shit.

"It seems Brannigan is wont to make his loyalties known. And it would appear they do not lie with the good people of this city or this republic." Bubbling, hot anger mixed with the precariousness of Isaac's situation.

And presented him with a solution that would strongly persuade the blacksmith to their cause.

CHAPTER 23

Beth was bone-weary as Thomas shut the door behind her. They had just arrived at his home, and without permission or preamble, she went right over to his rocking chair and parked it. No, that would imply she intentionally placed herself in the chair. It was more like her body saw a seat and collapsed into it. She had very little say in the matter.

This new type of exhaustion was all-consuming. More than the tiredness she felt after a long delivery. More than the stress of finding out your week-old husband had cheated on you. All the events of Beth's world had converged into a single weighted blanket wrapped tightly around her.

So, yeah, like hell she was getting out of that chair anytime soon.

Thomas set his things down and walked over to her, then squatted down at her feet. His hands reached for the hems of her skirts and fumbled around in the fabric.

"Hey, what are you—"

He quickly removed her shoes, held both of her ankles in one hand, and brought over a small nearby stool. He gently laid her feet on the stool.

Then he stood up and walked to the hearth. On the mantel was a pitcher. He grabbed a tin cup next to it and poured. Even though Beth was not in her clear mind, she couldn't help but admire the simple, domestic task. And when he handed her the cup and she sipped the cool water, that weighted blanket suddenly got a whole lot tighter.

"You know, I couldn't remember the last time Kyle brought me a glass of water." She whispered the words into the cup, never intending for Thomas to really hear or comment. She should have known he was more finely attuned to her than that.

"You've mentioned that name before, Kyle. Who was he to you?" Thomas cleared off the small table in the center of the room and sat in the chair next to it. Beth marveled at how such a delicate chair could hold a man of his size without buckling or bending. But, like everything else about Thomas, the chair was steady.

"My ex. Well, technically, we're still married, but—I guess it was a few weeks ago now—I caught him cheating on me. On our wedding day." Recapping the events stung, especially telling them to Thomas.

But he just sat there and didn't say a word. His stern features could cut glass, and he looked as if he was prepared to jump through time to pummel Kyle's ass on her behalf (not a bad idea, honestly), but he was silent. He was giving her the space she needed to tell her story.

And since her last opportunity to do so hadn't gone her way, she was beyond grateful for the gift.

"We had been together for over a year. We worked together, sort of. I was a midwife who did deliveries all over the city, but I also delivered at the hospital where he worked. He was a new doctor when we met. He had terrible jokes, absolutely terrible, but I laughed at them anyway. I wanted to be welcoming, make a good first impression. You see, in my time, midwives aren't held in such high esteem as they are now. Especially not among my colleagues."

Thomas's chin dropped at the news.

"The thing is, though . . ." Beth was gearing up for a rant, but it was no use holding back the flood gates. She had a captive audience and no will whatsoever to hold back anymore. "I love my job. I love everything about it. Empowering women, building a supportive family community, bringing beautiful babies into this world. I love it all. But in my time, medicine is far more advanced. And while there are definitely amazing strides taken in obstetric care, the truth is that the act of helping women give birth isn't bright and shiny. It's hard, long, and messy. It doesn't get you endless degrees on a wall or prime speaking engagements at national conferences. And I know you have no idea what any of that stuff is, but in my time, those things matter. To Kyle, they mattered. More than me. More than my career, more than our relationship, and more than my appearance."

Hot wetness fell down the sides of her cheeks. Crap, she hadn't even realized she was crying. But then Thomas came over and took the cup from her hands, then covered them in his own.

"You are worth so much more than the esteem of others, especially those who do not deserve you. To me, you are breathtaking."

Beth stared down into Thomas's hazel eyes. Determination and strength radiated from them, as if he were pushing his iron will into her. There were no lies, no false sentiments to make her feel better. Only the truth and encouragement.

"I don't know how I got here," she whispered. "But I don't hate it. Not with you nearby."

"I could never hate anything that brought you into my life." Thomas rubbed the rough pads of his thumbs along the backs of her knuckles. The small motion of support was so much bigger than he would know.

It was enough of a push for her to unburden her final weight. Beth sat forward slightly, released her hands from his, and reached into her pocket. She unearthed her ax, small and comforting, from beneath the fabric. And she held that thing as tightly as she could.

"There's something else I need to tell you . . . the only thing I didn't mention in my note. I don't know why it's happening, but something *is* happening. And it's not good, Thomas."

"Show me." He didn't hesitate in the slightest. He had her back before she could hardly finish getting the words out.

She could do this.

Her ax lay in her lap as she raised her hands up to where her handkerchief was tucked into her gown and stays. Trembling fingers pulled out the fabric corners. Thomas's eyes tracked her hands. Confusion painted his features, yet he stayed silent.

"A few days ago, I noticed a change happening to me. I don't know

why or how, but it's shocking and scary, and yeah . . . I'm scared."
Beth's nods turned into jitters. Nervous movements to cover up her
fear.

But then Thomas was there, without hesitation. His fingers went
to the loosened flaps of fabric and peeled the linen off her shoulders.
The sharp intake of his breath was the only sound that broke through
the silence.

Beth glanced down at what she'd been working so hard to ignore.
Pale green covered her shoulders and extended underneath her
sleeves and, she knew, down her arms, though they were still covered.
The color flowed over her skin like watercolor on a canvas. There
were no clearly defined limits or borders. No rhyme or reason to the
shapes and pathways. Just an ever-expanding blanket of green where
one should never see green.

"What is this?" Thomas's hands covered her shoulders, her neck,
her chest. He rubbed firmly, though not harshly, as if his insistence
alone could wipe away the blotches.

"I don't know. A few days ago, I noticed it. The colored area was
small at first and just appeared on my neck. But it's been spreading,
and I can't stop it. I don't know what it is or why it's happening, but
I've been feeling . . . ill."

Thomas's eyes had turned wide. Wild. "Ill . . . ?"

The words ghosted through Thomas's lips. His complexion paled
and his grip around her shoulders tightened. Concerned, Beth placed
her hand against his chest. The rise in his heartbeat was steady and
unsettling. Soft puffs of breath left Thomas in rapid-fire succession
and tickled her nose.

A spike in heart rate. Rapid breathing. Ashen skin.

The textbook symptoms of shock washed over Beth as the man
who had sought to comfort her fell apart quickly in her arms. And
then she remembered . . .

He lost his wife and son to an illness.

Beth closed the distance and threw her arms around his neck. Her
fingers pressed and kneaded rhythmic circles up and down his back as
she made cooing noises into his ear. Anything to divert his brain from
what it was digging up and anchor his senses to the here and now.

"Hey. Shhh. It's okay. I'm fine. See? I'm in your arms, and I'm breathing. I'm not warm or feverish. I am confident that there is absolutely nothing medically wrong with me."

Bit of a stretch there, but not entirely untrue. Let's call this crisis medically adjacent.

Thomas rocked in Beth's arms for a few more moments until his muscles stilled beneath her fingertips. Her arms strained to hold his expanding back as he took in a great breath, then settled and pulled back to look at her.

The image broke Beth's heart. Thomas's hazel eyes were pinched at the corners, and his lips nearly trembled with the effort to stay silent.

"Scream if you need to," Beth urged.

The pain on his face quickly morphed into surprise, and then a quick laugh burst out of him. Not exactly the reaction she had expected, but she'd happily take it over shock any day.

"I . . . Goodness, what a thing to say," he breathed out. "Thank you. I shall be fine."

"No, I'm serious. Scream. Let it all out. No one's close by to hear you, and you'll feel better. It always works for me. I imagine you were thinking about your family, right?" She hesitated to bring it up for fear of causing him to revert back into his pain, but his color had returned. His breathing had leveled out. She took a chance that his storm had passed. Because as selfish as it was, she still needed him for what was to come next.

"Please scream, Thomas," Beth pleaded. "It'll help. Or pet a soft blanket or tap out a tune on your knee. Something."

Thomas's expression grew somber. "I gather those are distraction techniques in your time."

Beth nodded slightly. Then it was his turn to gather her in his arms. His solid, warm body against hers was all the convincing she needed that his thoughts had moved on. At least for now.

"Yes, I was thinking of my family and how I lost them to an illness I was powerless to stop. My body often betrays my good sense. I am calm now, I assure you. Please, tell me what ails you and I shall listen."

Beth nodded slightly against his shoulder and then sat back to speak. "Extreme nausea, fatigue. Tremors in my arms and legs. It all comes and goes, seemingly without cause or reason. But the symptoms are getting worse. I have a hunch they're related to my time travel. But I don't know how to stop them, or get back home, or if the two are even really connected at all."

Thomas took the news in stride and remained calm. Stoic. A gentle listener who only spoke when Beth had finished.

"The blindfold from last night, when we . . ." Thomas cleared his throat. "That is why you covered my eyes. You did not want me to see your body because of your skin."

"Yes." She nodded in resignation.

"You were self-conscious for a different reason than you let on."

"Yes." It didn't matter what century she was in, apparently. She'd always assumed people had a hang-up about her size. And admittedly, despite her occasional inner pep talks, sometimes she did as well.

Warm hands crept up the sides of her neck and gently cradled her head. "Hear me now. You are perfect as you are. Your body, your mind, your calling to bring new life into this world, it is perfect. I will endeavor to show you just how perfect for as many days as you'll let me. I will not allow some unknown pestilence to take you from me. I am through with grief."

Thomas looked down at the floor. Determination was forming in his eyes, swirling behind hazel gates like a fire yearning to break free. And when he raised his gaze to her at last, she froze.

"I shall bring a war against anything that threatens my peace again, even if my enemy is not of this world."

The kiss that came next was aggressive in the best of ways. Intense, commanding, reassuring. He was like a general leading troops into battle. Rallying a war cry against imposing forces. It was heady and uplifting. At once, any fear, doubt, and uncertainty that plagued her flew out the window.

She pulled back from him and inspected her partner. Determination was painted across his features, from the hard set of his jaw to the way his muscles nearly vibrated from inaction. He believed in her. Would fight for her. Help her.

And she would fight along with him, even if she had no idea how. Because she didn't intend on going anywhere.

The red woolen bedgown Beth had on was hot and itchy. It was shorter than the normal gowns she wore, and it crisscrossed in front and went high up to her neck. She was grateful for the coverage but was sweating like a pig. Her apron around the middle cinched everything tight.

All these layers are killing me. Don't they know it's nearly summer?

"It may be uncomfortable near the heat, but the wool is necessary. If a flame sparks on your gown, it will smolder on the wool, not burn through. I had it made for Emily once, but she was never the smithing sort."

"It's fine. It's perfect." *It's a lie, but go with it.*

Thomas glanced back at Beth, who still stood a respectable distance away from the fire. Both had slept fitfully. At one point, Beth must have fallen asleep in the rocking chair, because she recalled the feeling of weightlessness before the soft length of the mattress cushioned her weary body. When she woke that morning, she was tucked into a bed while Thomas had already risen for the day.

They hadn't spoken much after her big reveal. It was obvious they both had too many wheels churning, and time was ominous.

Thomas grabbed an iron billet and threw it in the forge. The fire around the metal glowed bright orange. She understood why he kept everything so dark inside. Staring at that fire all day without protective eyewear did a number on your sight.

"Emily's sister was due to give birth. That was why she and Elliot went to the country to visit. To be with her sister. I had commitments here, so she had to travel without me."

The words were so hushed, Beth almost missed them. His voice was barely audible over the crackle of the fire.

She walked over to Thomas, who just stood there staring into the blaze. He occasionally poked and prodded the iron, but she got the sense it was more to keep his hands busy than anything else.

"A fortnight after her sister had the baby, Emily and Elliot traveled back home. The inn they stayed at on the way was crowded, swarming with travelers from all over. I knew more people had been falling ill. Had heard how smallpox had been spreading. I just never paid much mind to it."

Thomas grabbed his tongs and placed them around the billet. With his other hand, he reached for Beth. "Grip this end in both hands. Once you've got it tight, carry it over to the anvil."

Beth did as instructed.

"Keep both hands on the tongs. I will begin to hammer out the metal. When I say turn, turn the iron a quarter rotation."

Beth nodded as she gripped the tongs more tightly. And then Thomas brought the hammer down. She had heard the clang many times before, but never from this close a distance. The sound rattled her jaw, but the sight of the man next to her threw her even more.

Sweat, ash, and determination speckled his brow and upper chest, where his shirt was open. Every muscle popped with each release of his arm. His legs, those massively strong thighs, were braced wide. She had never seen a more emblematic pillar of strength. Especially not one who radiated power while casually uncorking his depths of despair.

"Turn."

Beth shook her thoughts out and turned over the billet so Thomas could continue.

"Elliot died first," he yelled through the din. "Emily quickly followed. I was powerless to stop the pox from overtaking them. Utterly helpless as their fevers spread . . . Turn."

She did as commanded, though all her attention was on Thomas. Her incredibly strong, magnificent blacksmith was cracking. Flecks of iron flew at him as he hammered, yet he hardly noticed. He had become wild in his actions, stuck in his memories.

Before Thomas hurt himself, Beth took the billet from the iron and placed it back on the mantel right in front of the fire, so it wouldn't cool down so quickly. His hammer landed on the empty anvil. Breaths rushed out of him as he threw down his tool.

She threw her arms around his neck and shushed him the way she would a crying baby. His chest, wide and warm beneath her arms, frantically heaved in gusts of air, yet she held tight, cooing and hugging her giant. Before he dropped the hammer, his eyes had been manic, crazed. His body had been on automatic, pounding at the metal. She understood why, but it gutted her at how long he had been hurting. How the only outlet for his grief was through his work. But it wasn't joyous or meaningful work. Not like this. Instead, it drained him. Sucked him dry. When the poor man had nothing left to give.

Solid, warm arms encircled her waist. His breathing had calmed, though his blood still pulsed wildly beneath her palms.

"You don't enjoy making all the weapons you're asked to forge, do you? The countless muskets . . . the ammunition . . ."

A heavy sigh rasped out of the giant man in her arms. "No, I do not."

Beth thought back to the small shelves of items in the corner. The ornate boxes. His son's rattle. They were so beautiful, so uniquely engraved. She was willing to bet he hadn't made anything like that in a long time. "You enjoy being more creative."

"I do. It was why I was so drawn to your ax when I first met you. It was a breath of fresh air. In truth, I haven't been able to get it, or you, out of my mind since that day." Thomas pulled back. "Since I lost my family, I have been no more than a shell of who I once was. Until you plowed into me in the street." He smiled.

Beth rolled her eyes. "Yeah, don't remind me. Not my most graceful of moments."

He chuckled. "Perhaps not. But I wouldn't have changed our encounter for anything in the world." Then his tone grew serious. "I don't know how to fight this illness or how to return you safely to your time. All I know is my own strength. So I will use it to make you a new weapon, a small dagger. But one uniquely crafted, of my own design."

His offer of a gift took her breath away. "It's perfect."

"But you shall help me make it. If I can tie you to this world, to my world, in some small way, I will."

Thomas pulled Beth against his chest and held her there. The leather of his apron was cool against her cheek, yet his arms around her radiated heat and power. She was protected in the cage of his strong arms. It didn't surprise her that his view on battling her symptoms was more otherworldly. She was in an era when beliefs in God's power and the supernatural were more widely accepted than in her time. His faith in the unseen was apparent, even if he didn't say so explicitly.

But the dagger. That he insisted she help him make it? As a partner? The trust that flowed from him was a tidal wave of encouragement. It was such a heady rush that she was grateful he was holding her. She doubted her ability to stand upright in the moment.

Because she had just found her person. Her other half. Who cared for her as she was and trusted her outright. The notion was so uplifting, so inspiring, so loving.

And so temporary.

The writing was on the wall. One way or the other, she wasn't sticking around. Whether her symptoms got worse and the choice was taken away from her or she miraculously found a way back home. Both options sucked a big fat one.

Beth squeezed her eyes together and nestled against Thomas's chest.

How the hell could she leave him when she'd only just found him?

CHAPTER 24

The vibrations of the grinding stone's rotation thrummed through Thomas's foot as he stepped on the pedal. Rasping, methodical hums filled his forge as he rounded off the small blade's edge. The hilt was simple, yet polished to a high shine. The aggressive rumble in his stomach was the only signal of the passing hours. A quick glance out the window revealed the deepening sun and harsher shadows. The afternoon had progressed into early evening. He hardly cared. His sole focus was on the knife.

It would fit perfectly in Beth's slight hand. All that was left were the engravings.

When the idea came to him, the images had slammed full force into his mind. Clean lines, elegant curves, daring dips, and blazing finishes.

A burning pressure tightened in his chest at the excitement. His eagerness to get started was a blissful crack in the ice of the last five years. A new bud sprouting through winter's frozen terrain.

Thomas ran his thumb along the freshly filed edge. Sharp, yet delicate. Like his Beth.

When the burning inclination to throw a new billet in the fire gripped him earlier, Beth had been huddled against his chest. But when he pulled back from her, the loss had been acute, yet fleeting. "Give me a few hours."

He rubbed his palms up and down her forearms and drifted a light kiss across her temple. The crease on her forehead melted away, as did her palpable tension. Concern and curiosity replaced her worry, however.

"Why? What are you doing?"

"Something I haven't done in ages."

After some more prodding on her part and insistence on his that she go and talk to Theodora about visiting the seamstress who was with child, Beth relented. But not before he took her to the forge again and showed her, from start to finish, how to draw out the metal. She was a quick study and asked pertinent questions at the right moments. Beth never griped at the muscle involved or at the tediousness of the process. She just stayed by his side, hammering and working a piece of metal that, once quenched, would make for a fine weapon—and a token of him to keep with her.

When it was time to file down the blade and work on the finery, Thomas gave Beth leave to visit with Theodora. It was a hard good-bye, but she'd be safe with the baker's family and the like. She agreed to return before nightfall. His files were in his hands a moment after the door closed behind her.

Hours later, he sat on the stool with the newly formed knife in his hand. A knife Beth had helped create, one he would customize for its new owner.

Thomas rose from the grindstone and walked to his worktable. There, under a clean cloth to protect it from ash and metal filings, was Beth's ax. He'd asked her to leave it behind. The shocked expression she threw had coaxed a smile from him. Yes, he preferred she always have a form of protection on her. But for this short time, his need for it was greater.

Because he wished to make a pair of the pattern.

Thomas pulled back the cloth and picked up the ax. Deep creases of vines snaked up and down the handle. They were so intricately woven, so clean and precise that, at first, he was concerned he couldn't match it. That his skills were not honed enough, not artistic enough. He ran his thumbnail along one of the creases and followed its valley from the base of the ax head to the tail of the handle. Neither bump nor ridge snagged his nail along its journey.

Could he match it?

He wasn't certain, but the possibility excited him, damn near tugging his balls up tight at the prospect and what he could give Beth by getting it just right.

Thomas chuckled at the imagery. *Of course the thought of this woman holding a weapon would give me a cockstand.*

Thomas turned the ax over to inspect how the engravings came together on the other side. Amazing. No obvious connection points. The skill was unmatched, truly. His eyes traveled farther up the handle until something unusual caught his attention. At the base of the ax blade, where it was forged to the handle, was a slight divot. It was too high up and too tucked away to be noticed by the wielder's hand. But its presence was immediate and all-consuming. Thomas's heart thrummed in his chest. His quickening pulse radiated through his fingertips as they hovered over the pocket.

For filled in its center was a tiny clump of dust, no bigger than the tip of an awl. And it was bright green.

Words read earlier through a tumble of confusion and panic slammed into him. *Thomas, it will not be easy for you to understand what you're about to read, but please try.*

His finger threatened to touch the menacing divot. "No . . ."

Beth's words rose up from memory. *I was holding the ax in the antique shop when it all started. There was a pale green residue on the weapon. When I touched it . . . and breathed it in . . .*

She hadn't known. This entire time, Beth hadn't known the residue resided in her own pocket. The dust she suspected brought her here.

Thomas threw the ax onto the table like the thing was white-hot and backed up, only stopping when his backside hit the anvil. He slammed his eyes closed. Her final words crept into his brain, his bones. His heart.

. . . and woke up on the street, in the shadow of a covered wagon. Around

people who didn't dress like me, who didn't speak like me. Because I wasn't from their time.

Thomas slid down the base of the anvil until the floor met him. "Dammit all to hell!"

His screams and muttering spiraled into despair at the implication of his finding. His fists clenched his hair tightly as grief rocked his solid frame once more. For surely he'd just discovered the mechanism for her travel here.

The baser beast within wanted to take the ax and throw it in his quench basin. Rid the damn thing of the devilish dust so he could keep Beth here, by his side. In his time. It wouldn't be a hard task. A flick of his wrist and the ax would be clean. And she'd be here.

Would you prefer to be her jailor over her protector?

Just then, Thomas remembered her illness. Her hesitation to tell him about her ailments and how they were worsening with each moment she spent here. With him. What if helping her return to her time cured her of her infections? Restored her health?

Thomas lifted his head and rested it against the cold anvil. His mind pounded from the tension.

And the choice. Though it was hardly a choice at all.

Thomas would save her a thousand times over. He would happily go to his grave with the knowledge she would exist in health in some future time without him. He just needed to swallow down his pride.

Second chances weren't guaranteed just because one was a fool in love.

"You'll never guess what happened!"

Beth walked into the front door of Thomas's home just as the sun was going down. Her stomach preceded her entrance into the living room with the grumble to end all grumbles. Mortified, she locked the door and her hands flew to hide her face.

"Sorry. I didn't realize how hungry I was. I've had a few nibbles here and there, but the day got away from me."

Thomas sat at the small table in the middle of the room. His presence was somber, but as soon as he looked at her, his lips lifted in his trademark smirk of endearment. "What, pray tell, was so exciting that you would forget to eat?"

Beth clapped her hands together and ran over to him. "Twins!"

The smile died on Thomas's face. He cocked his head to the side in confusion as he slowly, hesitantly dropped his eyes to her abdomen.

Beth rolled her eyes. *Men are so dang literal.* "Annelise," Beth deadpanned.

The lightbulb of recognition dawned on Thomas's face.

"Annelise is going to have twins!" Beth squealed.

Thomas bent his head low and whistled. It was the universal calling sign for all men saying, *Better them than me.* "That is quite the news. I knew a pair of twins once as a boy. I thought they looked nothing alike, yet the brothers often played tricks on the old woman who lived nearby. One would pretend to be the other so he could get a second helping of her pies. I can't say I've known any since, though."

"Annelise had no idea. Can you believe that? She's at least six months along in her pregnancy and she had no idea she was carrying twins." Beth's hand flew to her forehead as she shook her head in disbelief.

"But how would the woman know such a thing?" Thomas eyed her with curiosity.

"Oh! Oh, right. Sorry. I'm forgetting myself." Beth walked over to the rocking chair and collapsed. Once she kicked off her shoes, she elaborated. "In my time, we have technology that allows us to detect how many babies will be born and how far along the mother is in her pregnancy."

Thomas stared at her, then blinked. "Technology?"

"Oh, boy. OK, yes, devices. Medical equipment. I know it's hard to wrap your head around, and I don't really know how I can explain it in today's terms to help you understand, but yes, modern medicine has advanced in some profound ways."

"Yet you were able to detect such things now without your modern marvels."

Beth leaned back against the headrest and closed her eyes briefly before opening them. "Yes, I was. I knew what to feel for. When

Annelise let me examine her, it was hard to miss. And she had no idea. No idea whatsoever!" She leaned forward to address him. "Thomas, she thought she was gaining too much weight so she cut back on what she was eating. Can you believe it? I have no way to know her weight for sure, but she's definitely not at a healthy weight for carrying twins. You should have seen Francis when I told him to make sure she receives a delivery of at least two loaves of bread each day. The poor man was beside himself."

She rambled on about Annelise, and Thomas just sat there silently. He never interrupted or cut her off. Never tried to change the subject or pretended to be interested. He just sat there and genuinely listened to her every word. It was as close to a hi-honey-how-are-you moment as she'd ever had. Babies hadn't interested Kyle. Pregnancies, according to him, were common and the treatment boilerplate.

As if treating allergic reactions to bee stings and dog hair wasn't.

Yet Thomas hung on her every word, as if she was about to rattle off the secrets of the Egyptian pharaohs or explain how time travel worked.

Joke's on you about that last one, buddy. I still don't have a frickin' clue.

"She has no one." Beth recalled her time with Annelise and shook her head. "There's no one to oversee her prenatal care. No one to help with her delivery. Giving birth to multiples in my time, with our advancements, can be risky. But here? Infant mortality in this time is too high to stomach, let alone the risk to the mother. I have to figure out how I can best support her. Perhaps there's a book or journal—"

"I thought you said she was six months along."

"Yes." Beth blinked at him.

"You anticipate staying another three months until she gives birth." His tone was not questioning. Merely stating the unspoken elephant in the room.

We both know three months is likely not in the cards.

But damn if that didn't hurt. Annelise needed her! All the working-class expectant mothers in Boston needed her. Resources were so scarce, especially for those who tirelessly supported the city. Conditions were so brutal. If she could help in a small way, in a way that was natural and rewarding to her, how could she ignore the call?

The truth was that, in light of all her symptoms, all of her feelings for Thomas, all of her ups and downs the past few weeks, she loved being a midwife and loved it even more when the people she helped appreciated her.

So, if she had to stay . . .

"I believe I've found a way to send you back home."

The brakes in Beth's mind screeched something fierce. "What?"

Thomas stood and walked over to Beth. Instead of kneeling at her feet, he took her hand and guided her up to stand before him. She was shaky. Her legs were fatigued, and though she tried to hide it, the grim line of his mouth gave away her tell. With one strong arm, he held her steady, throwing a look of remorse her way. In his other hand, he held her ax.

"There is a divot at the connection point where the ax head meets the handle. Look closer and tell me what you see."

Beth narrowed in on where his fingertip was pointing. Then her stomach bottomed out, though Thomas still held her firmly.

A tiny patch of green dust. Nestled safely in a tiny protective crater. At an angle so steep her hand would have never come in contact with it.

"Oh, God." Beth's legs gave out. The metal ax clanged to the floor. She was in Thomas's arms a second later. He never gave her the opportunity to fall. Her head was spinning as he carried her into the bedroom and laid her down on top of the quilt. After a few deep breaths, she managed to gather her wits and sit up. Thomas sat next to her on the bed and gripped her hand tightly. Worry creased his brow.

"Do not ever hide your illness from me, do you understand? It torments me to an extreme to see you in pain. Lean on my strength." His voice softened as he rubbed the backs of her knuckles. "Especially now . . . as I insist you allow me to escort you from this place back to your own time."

Beth was groggy and confused, but she definitely didn't hear that right. "You're going to need to repeat that. What do you mean?"

Thomas closed his eyes and sighed deeply. "I cannot abide your pain, for it is mine. Let me be clear, Beth. I am a selfish man. A very selfish man who wants nothing more than to keep you by my side for the rest of my days. To love this delectable body each night, kiss you each morning, and laugh with you for all the hours in between." His voice cracked, and he tried to clear his throat. "But if staying here worsens your pain . . . no, I cannot allow that. Not when there exists a way to send you back. A way to keep you safe."

The implications of Thomas's words finally sank in. If her symptoms were getting worse the longer she stayed here, there was no telling what would happen. A shiver of the unknown, the unspoken, skittered up her spine.

Or she could go back home.

Home. Where she had indoor plumbing, but a personal life in shambles.

But by staying here, she could continue helping pregnant women desperate for care, while standing beside the man of her dreams. Though for how long, she didn't know.

Thomas's thumb smoothed over her cheekbones as he gripped her head in his hands. "Allow me one last night with you, Beth." He brought his forehead to hers and closed his eyes. "Please."

His plea was heartbreaking. Because he was right. She couldn't stay here and risk hurting him by adding to his grief if she got worse. Beth didn't realize it at first, but his decision on the matter was his own form of protection. Protecting her from having to choose between what was right and what would make her happy. For it was clear she couldn't be both. So she would take what she could while she could.

"Yes," she whispered.

CHAPTER 25

"I have something I'd like to share with you. Something I've kept to myself for quite some time." Thomas leaned in for a quick kiss before jumping off the edge of the bed. He stood before her with his hand outstretched, damn near knightly in his stance. All he was missing was armor and a sword at his hip, and Beth would have pegged him as a dead ringer for a medieval knight. Purpose and pride radiated off the man like heat off newly poured asphalt.

Would he ever stop taking her breath away?

"You have me intrigued, sir knight." She laid her hand in his palm and got up to follow him.

"Sir knight? Am I a hero in a children's tale?" He tried to act indignant, but he could hardly keep the humor out of his voice.

"Well, let's see. You make swords, you save damsels in distress—"

"I'd hardly call yourself a damsel. You seem to save yourself just fine, despite my intentions."

"True." She nodded. "But you're missing the point. You, sir, have all the makings of a knight in shining armor. Or a blacksmith in gleaming leather, as it were. Oh, I know! Maybe a—"

Thomas's lips captured Beth's mouth. The delicious rasp of his stubble lit her senses on fire, but it was his wide hands lifting her bottom and depositing her on the living room table that amped up her sensations.

That and the firm squeeze of his hands on her ass. The thrill of his grip traveled through every damn layer she was wearing and shot straight to her core.

"Let me assure you, my lady. I have a very questionable code of honor when it comes to you." The low growl in his throat caused her nipples to pebble instantly. She nearly scoffed at how sure of a thing she was around him. Because this man, her blacksmith, did all sorts of right things to her always-all-types-of-wrong body. "But if it's a bit of role play you enjoy, I may be able to satisfy you."

Thomas retreated from the living room and walked out of the doorway into another room. A moment later, he returned with a bayonet in one hand and a bottle of . . .

Oh my God. Is that champagne?

And what could those two things possibly have in common?

"Earlier this year, a French merchant was delivering four hundred bottles of champagne to an adjutant general of the Virginia militia. Unfortunately for the merchant, his ship took on damage during the voyage, and he had to dock in Boston for repairs." Thomas leaned the bayonet against the lip of the table but made sure it wasn't in accidental poking range to Beth. "He enlisted my services to help repair some of the rigging and such. The work was not that intensive and only took a few days, but even so, I quickly learned the man couldn't pay me in coin. So, we made a trade. I'm told this is quite special and expensive. But not nearly as precious as you are to me."

Thomas held up the bottle for Beth's inspection. But just as she went to grab it, he lowered the bottle and picked up the bayonet.

The movement happened so fast. A shrill slice rang out through the small room, followed by a loud pop. Frothy bubbles erupted out of the sabered bottle and cascaded over Thomas's hand. He quickly scooched back to avoid getting the overspill on his boots, but the mess was inevitable.

And was damn near the sexiest thing Beth had ever seen.

Thomas stalked closer to her, the champagne dripping carelessly onto her lap, and nestled in between the folds of her dress. A metal clang rang out as he let the bayonet fall to the floor. Then he grabbed the side of her neck and leaned the lip of the bottle toward her mouth.

"My lady . . ." He nodded. Fiery, intense heat burned in his hazel eyes.

Beth sat forward and opened her mouth. The moment the cool wine danced across her tongue, she sighed and wrapped her lips—carefully, to avoid getting cut—around the edge of the bottle.

The liquid was unlike what she would immediately associate with champagne. The wine was slightly pink based on the spilled drops on her apron, not a pale amber as she was used to. But the fizz was there, fast and strong, as the bubbles tumbled down the back of her throat with each greedy gulp she took.

Despite its differences, it was still comforting. Almost normal. A taste of home. Yet all mingled together with Thomas. And, boy, did that feel right.

Because somewhere along the line, her blacksmith had become more like home than any single-family suburban craftsman ever would.

Thomas's gaze never left her lips, which were still clamped tightly around the bottle. Watching him watching her was a heady rush. Her thighs cradled him more tightly to her. When she locked her ankles around the backs of his legs, he caught onto the hint and took the bottle back.

His mouth replaced the drink at her lips. Tongues tangled as Thomas eagerly lapped at the sweet stickiness dribbling down Beth's chin. Hands fumbled and skin scorched as they came together. Every nip, every tug pulled Beth closer to him, to his time. Each shiver of excitement that rose up at the beckoning of his tongue on her neck was a call she couldn't deny. Wouldn't deny. It was as if her soul had melded with his and was forged into a newer, stronger iron than could ever possibly exist on its own.

"I'll not take you rough again. I intend to take my time with you." Thomas's growl was intense, yet tempered. Like a lion holding back its killing strike so it could toy with its prey some more.

"Well, you'll get no objections from me, sir knight. Oh!"

Nearby lantern flames nearly blew out as Thomas grabbed and

quickly carried her to the bedroom. Her landing on the mattress was gentle, yet urgent. His hands wasted no time undoing the handkerchief draped over her shoulders and tucked into her gown and stays.

"No, wait!" She quickly remembered why she used the cover-up in the first place. But before her hands could stop Thomas's prying fingers, he captured them firmly against her breasts and held them there.

"I know what you're hiding from. Stop it." His abrasiveness took her off guard. Until he gentled his tone and only spoke once he had her full attention. "I will see all of you, Beth. I don't care what color the illness has turned your skin or what you perceive is right or wrong about the body writhing beneath me. Because there isn't a single thing about you that hasn't fired my blood since that first moment when you nearly lopped off my stones with a whack of your knee."

A short snort erupted out of Beth.

"Oh, you think my pain is funny?"

"Never," she said through a stifled giggle.

Thomas narrowed his eyes.

Then her skirts went up over her waist, covering her head and arms. Beth squealed as Thomas's rough hands snaked up the inside of her thighs. Tempting, torturing, drifting higher—or was it lower? Like hell if she cared to get it straight. Because he had essentially blindfolded her with her skirts. And played the same, devilish trick on her she had played on him before.

And, boy, did she not hate it.

Deft fingertips teased the folds of her opening, and Beth's hips jerked in response. Feathered kisses and hot breath swirled below and combined into a dizzying height of awareness. All at once, Thomas was everywhere. She never had a chance to feel self-conscious or nervous. Only aroused. Elated. Enraptured. And when the tip of his tongue breached her, with his hands on her thighs squeezing lightly, her body became a swirling eddy of sensation. Logical thoughts and reservations were flown wild as Thomas nursed her swollen clitoris. Each flick and lick caused her lower body to jerk in his hold. But he was relentless. The best kind of torture master.

Every time she floated higher, nearing her crest, he'd back off. Retreating to soft kisses and ticklish caresses. Only when she sighed in frustration did he resume his ministrations in earnest.

"Enough . . . with . . . the . . . teasing. I need you. Please." Beth was panting into her upturned apron and was pretty sure she looked about as sexy as a crazed animal caught in a bedsheet. The man was killing her!

"Yes, my lady." Thomas's low chuckle skated over every raw nerve ending he had exposed and only aroused her further.

"Yeah, well, your lady is about to wallop you with the nearest blunt object if you don't get up here."

At last, Thomas flipped down Beth's skirts and rose up over her, undoing her gown's fastenings. "Damn, I love your fire."

Beth sat up and they each worked to remove the other's clothes. Layer after layer after yet-another-damn layer fell to the floor, until Beth scooched back on the bed toward the headboard and looked at her bare skin. Her shoulders and chest were nearly completely green. The tops of her breasts were covered in the hue. The sight was scary and unnerving. Her already fast pulse began to quicken, though not for the reasons she'd like.

"Look at me." Thomas's voice was a muffled sound next to the panicked clamoring of warning bells in her mind. "Beth! You will look at me."

She glanced up at Thomas. Every beautiful tanned inch of him was on display. His chest, which hadn't looked half bad covered in sweat and rainwater in his forge, looked ten times as sinful. From his shoulders to abs and everything in between radiated power and strength. Even his cock, which stood proud and erect while he sat on his haunches, didn't shy away from scrutiny.

But it was his face that commanded her attention the most. She couldn't look away, which was exactly the right remedy when her body was betraying her.

Thomas's expression softened as he gently grasped her ankle, anchoring what he could of her to the moment. "Tomorrow morning, we shall find a way to use that dust on the ax and send you home. Your condition is but temporary. I swear on the souls of my wife and

181

son you will be restored to full health. And heaven help any obstacle that bars my way." Thomas nearly shook with the proclamation. His lips clipped shut and his hands fisted the quilt at his sides.

In that moment, Thomas had proven himself way more than an ally. He was the warrior in Beth's corner she didn't know she needed until this trip. But was it really a trip if she didn't want to go back? Her heart squeezed at the prospect. She had no idea what his plan was or how he thought to implement it, but her plan had slowly manifested over the past few days and had turned into more of a vision, a dream, a desire. Every sideways glance he threw her way when he probably thought she wasn't looking. Every whispered kiss under the moonlight. Every encouraging gesture he gave her to see Theodora or Annelise, and every word he hung on as she spoke of her profession. It all slammed together in a dumbstruck realization of Big Bang proportions.

Holy crap. I think I love this man.

The soul-crushing confession went off like a bomb in her chest. Beth's arms couldn't reach out to him fast enough. Only when he was fully in her arms did he relax against her. She smiled as he melted into her and the tension leaked out of his muscles. Their mouths collided in a frantic kiss. She stroked the broad planes of his back while he massaged her hip, her rib cage, her breasts. There wasn't a spot on her he didn't manage to trace and dote on in some way. The familiar pull between her legs ticked up with each slide of his tongue, each scrape of his fingernail across her nipple.

Her breath hitched as the firm head of his cock circled her opening. Almost hovering, a request for permission to enter. Beth smiled into Thomas's mouth as she grabbed him and centered him against her. He stilled briefly at the connection and, she suspected, her boldness.

"Now. Please," she panted.

"Yes, my lady."

Thomas thrust deeply into her. The motion wasn't fast or intrusive, yet was still done with purpose and attention. The invasion was the most welcome thing Beth's body had ever experienced. Her slick core cradled him as he slowly retreated and reentered her. Each time, she rose higher. But the connection turned deeper, more internal. When his intensity increased, so did the fire inside her. It was all intertwined and completely inseparable. Unbeknownst to her, she had wrapped herself entirely in Thomas and cradled him to her soul like a vital part of her makeup. She couldn't let him go if she wanted to.

Thomas's hips quickened their pace, and Beth's back arched with her release. His growl of satisfaction vibrated into the crook of her neck as they came together, their breaths and heartbeats mingling into one writhing, sated explosion.

Beth floated back down from her climax. Thomas's heavy breathing was a soothing weight to her jittery aftershocks. Then he curled his arms around her body and rolled to the side. She was cradled in his embrace from head to toe and would have drifted off to oblivion if he hadn't kissed her nose and demanded her attention with his whispered words.

"You have my love, Beth." He pushed a lock of hair out of her face and tenderly cupped her cheek. "For all of time, I am yours."

The words floated up to her mind, wrapped around her heart, and sank in her gut like a stone.

CHAPTER 26

Light puffs of air tickled across Thomas's bicep as he watched Beth sleep. Not only was she folded in on herself, but she had also blissfully wrapped around him in the night. Like a newly born forest animal clinging to a tree limb before it learned how to balance on its own. Her cheek was cushioned softly on his arm while her ankles wrapped around his lower legs. The length of her arm was draped loosely over his stomach. The entangled mess of limbs and skin was hot and slightly sweaty from where they had been pressed together for so long. His back ached from the strain of the position and his arm had long ago fallen asleep. Only one window was open, too, so the early summer air was a tad stifling.

He was in utter heaven.

And reminded him of all he would do to keep the woman in his arms alive.

Earlier, as the predawn sun began its slow rise up the hillside, he lay awake and pondered his options. Beth's soft snores and sleep-filled murmurs spurred him on and gave him the fortitude needed to formulate his next steps of how to send her back to her time.

Time.

Theirs had run out before he'd realized he wanted more, desperately needed more with Beth. The few short days they had been together weren't enough. They'd never be enough. His mind turned over with all the things he had yet to experience with her or do for her. The dagger, for one. It sat unfinished in his forge. The blade had been honed, true, but he hadn't yet completed the detail work. Nor had he told her how vital she had become to him. How he loved her fire and purpose and intelligence and . . .

Her. How he loved *her*.

Beth's hips began to squirm as her ankles unhooked from around his legs. Cool air kissed the spots on his skin that were now free of her touch. He hated the loss, despite the relief.

"Good morning." Beth's eyes were heavily lidded as she curled in impossibly closer against his chest.

He caged her in and kissed her temple. "You keep moving around like that, and it will be a very good morning indeed."

With every inch of her body flush against him, there was no use hiding his eagerness. Even his cock was drawn to her like a ship to a lighthouse as it pressed against her soft belly.

"Mmm . . ." She peppered light kisses along the pads of his chest. "Not a bad way to wake up. I wish I could start every morning like this."

The unspoken hung in the air between them. Once Beth had realized the implication of her words, she stilled in his arms. Thomas squeezed her closer to him, for the time had come to address what neither wanted to.

He cleared his throat. Unease choked him and nearly prevented him from saying what he needed to say. After he took a few more swallows, the quivering in his throat subsided and the confidence to speak returned.

"I've been thinking about how to send you home. Have you considered what might happen if you touch the green dust on the ax? Or perhaps breathe it in like you had done before you originally arrived?"

"I don't . . . I don't want to talk about it." Her words were soft and penetrating.

"I know, I do not either." He sat back a bit so he could look at her properly. Beth's eyes were more awake. The bright blue of them was stark and brilliant. The indignation in her gaze, however, pierced his gut with a silent dare.

Would he really send her away?

Hell, he couldn't do this.

"What do you wish?" The words fluttered across his lips before he could take them back. Because he didn't want her to leave. Not in the least. But if she stayed, the agony of the unknown was more than he was equipped to manage.

"I guess I . . ."

"I love you, Beth. Just know that whatever you decide, wherever your decision takes you, you have that." He brushed some hair away from her face and kissed her. It wasn't a passion-filled kiss or the urgent meeting of lips and tongues. Just a simple seal of a promise that she'd have his heart regardless.

"Ah!" Beth pulled back from the kiss and doubled over. Her head slammed into his shoulder as her knees scraped up his thighs.

"What's wrong? What is it?" Thomas frantically pulled back the bedsheet to examine her. He saw no outward sign of injury. No bleeding or rash. Well, aside from the green covering her skin. Panic gripped him at the need to fight a physical enemy, but he saw nothing.

"My stomach . . ." Beth said through short pants. Her eyes were clenched tight as she fought the onslaught of pain. She quickly threw the sheets off her and ran to the open side window near the bed. Her fingers clutched the lip of the windowsill as she stuck her head out and heaved, vomiting profusely over the edge. Thomas was there in an instant. Tremors skittered up her body as he pulled her hair away from her face and braced his arm across her stomach.

"Lean on me. Here . . ."

Another wave overtook her as her frame trembled in his arms. If not for his strength, she'd have collapsed to the floor, dead weight as she was. Fear gripped him like a vice.

"I'm fine . . . I think it stopped."

"Like hell you're fine." Thomas lifted her away from the window and settled her onto the bed.

Her complexion had turned ashen, and a sheen of sweat coated her forehead. Panic fueled his movements as he threw on his breeches and fetched her water. Seconds later he was dabbing her hot skin with a cool cloth and forcing her to drink. It was all he could do to be useful. He pressed on until her soft hand guided the cup away from her mouth.

"I think . . ." Beth's weak voice fumbled over the words they both didn't want to acknowledge.

"It's time," Thomas finished her statement. "Let us get you home, my lady." His slight nod was all the reassurance he could offer.

A bolder lie had never existed.

Beth's insides had been scraped raw. Hell, it was all she could do to stay upright as she sat on the edge of the bed. Barely upright, actually. The cool polished wood of one of the four posters did its best to gently support her forehead. But gentle was quickly turning into a dull prodding on her temple that wasn't doing wonders for her headache.

At least her stays weren't pinching into her sides. Thomas had helped her get dressed. At his insistence, he'd kept all the bindings loose. In case she needed to make a run for the window again. How romantic. Because puking while cinched up tight like a salami in sausage netting didn't make for a fun time.

Who are you kidding? Is any of this fun?

She shut her eyes as she clung more tightly to the bedpost.

The creaking of leather before her wasn't enough motivation for her to open her eyes, even though it signaled Thomas was hovering at her feet. She didn't need the auditory warning, though. The subtle smell of smoke and cedar always preceded him. Those scents had become her smelling salts, always managing to restore and revitalize her.

Not so much this morning. Every muscle in her body was lax and useless. She had never empathized more with Taser victims.

"One final sip. Come on."

Beth managed to crack an eye. A blurry image of Thomas squatting before her filled her field of vision. His expression was solemn, yet stoic. The pinched lines at the corners of his eyes and mouth gave away his concern. But he was trying to hold it all back for her. Trying to be strong for whatever the hell was happening to them.

"If you think I can lift that cup, you're dreaming."

"I think you can move mountains if you wanted to. Or at the very least, command me to move them for you."

"You know, most men don't like being bossed around."

"You can order me around all you'd like."

A smile pulled at her lips. The effort was immense, but the teasing helped lighten the mood. Kept her mind off the steaming pile of terrible inevitables she had stumbled into.

"Would you slay a dragon for me?"

Thomas hesitated a moment. "Hmm. That would depend."

"On?"

"The prize." His warm hand gripped hers.

"Ah. Well, I suppose it would be customary to provide you with a favor of my appreciation."

"Mm-hmm."

"How about . . ." Beth paused to pant for a moment. Even maintaining the breath needed for the conversation was challenging. But there was one final thing she needed to say to him. "How about . . . my love?"

The witty banter floated away as Thomas swallowed hard and cupped her cheek before the words had time to land. The solid strength in his grip was the most comforting thing she could recall. More so than the champagne, being a midwife, or even the jersey cotton sheets on her bed back home. Him. He was her ultimate comfort, and the relief at being able to finally tell him lightened her soul.

"Beth—" Thomas whipped his head around to look toward the doorway. The movement was so sudden. And when he didn't say anything, a chill shot up Beth's spine. He rose and left her in the bedroom.

Huh? Her heartbeat ticked like a metronome in her chest.

His heavy boots rushed into the bedroom a moment later. Then he knelt and lifted her into his arms.

"What's going on?" Panic kickstarted the waning adrenaline in her body.

"Don't make a sound and stay hidden."

"What? Thomas, what's going on?"

"Shhh." He carried her through the back door of the property. Without hesitation, he walked over to the nearby empty watering trough and squatted down with her in his arms. "Stay here and don't move. Keep your head low and don't make a sound. I'll come find you."

He laid her as gently as he could between the trough and the side of the house. A quick kiss was all the answer she got before he stood and ran back inside, shutting the door behind him.

A loud bang shook the house, followed by deep yells and dull crashes. Beth used her last ounce of strength to grip the edge of the windowsill above her head. Her arms were jelly and her legs were about as useless as a pudgy newborn's.

"C'mon, dammit. Work with me here."

She used the lip of the trough to shore up her body. The window was low enough, and the trough high enough, that if she knelt on its rim, she had enough support to peek through the window.

What she saw nearly had her heaving all over again.

A gang of nine men, all in mix-and-match soldiers' regalia, flooded Thomas's small living room. The place had been trashed. Pots and knickknacks lay broken and bent along the floor. The table in the center of the room had been upturned with its legs snapped off. The rocking chair, her favorite piece of furniture in Thomas's house, was splintered as one of the men took a cast-iron pot hanging from the mantel and bludgeoned the thing.

About half the men walked about the room, destroying everything in sight. The other half, however, had their hands on Thomas. And their weapons at his throat.

"Nice place you've got here."

Thomas was held in check by two soldiers who each had an arm. One was at his back, with an arm locked around his throat. A final one held the tip of a bayonet to his neck. A great cry erupted from Thomas. He yanked his left arm down and swept his leg out. The man on his left toppled, freeing Thomas on one side. Thomas gripped the arm around his neck and leaned over. The soldier behind him flew over Thomas's head and crashed into a chair. The man who spoke ducked out of the way as Thomas spun around. Snarls and curses left his mouth. Arms tensed and flexed with each punch. He fought like a berserker Viking, pummeling and pounding any man who came near enough. His massive size and strength were all he needed to break free of his attackers and send them flying, like fluff off dandelions.

Until a gunshot went off.

Beth's heart kicked at the noise. Outside of television, she had never witnessed a real gunshot before.

Thomas had been stunned as well. But before he could identify which of the men had fired the shot, a blade was at his chest and slashed across his pecs. With a cry, Thomas toppled over as all the men in the room descended upon him.

"Don't think for one moment that I won't kill you." The threat came from the other man. The one who had spoken earlier. The only one who wasn't actually fighting.

"What the fuck do you want, Hunterdon?" Thomas's words were clipped from how the men held his body and face to the floor. Even from her vantage point, Beth could see the muscles in his back heaving and tensing. Then Beth focused on the man who had issued the threat.

The man who held a musket, refreshed and reloaded, to Thomas's head. "Liberty," Hunterdon barked out. "And loyalty. Neither of which you've contributed to."

"I've told you. I'm not involved in your war. You pay for my services. If you don't like it, piss off and find another blacksmith. I care not for your cause." Thomas spat blood at the man's boots and was rewarded with a kick to the chin. Beth bit into her hand to keep from calling out. She would *not* make things worse for him by being discovered. Though, God, she had to help him somehow.

"I'm through talking. You always have excuses, Brannigan. Never solutions. So, this morning, you can explain to the good people of Boston all about your preferences and logic . . . as we make a public display of your treason. Take him and throw him in the cart."

The men grabbed Thomas by anything they could—sleeves, hair, throat—and lifted him upright. It was no small feat due to his size. Beth's stomach rolled again as fresh blood bloomed across his chest and dribbled down his stomach. As they dragged him out of the house, he kicked and thrashed. A soldier caught Thomas's boot in the back of his knee and briefly buckled. Another soldier elbowed Thomas in the ribs. He coughed and sputtered as he slackened in the men's hold.

In the wake of the destruction, Beth scanned the room. Everything was destroyed. Everything. Her arms and legs quivered as she struggled to remain upright, assessing the damage to Thomas's home. The mirror on the wall had been shattered, the quilt on the back of the rocking chair torn to shreds. Hot coals and ash from the hearth were spread all over the floor, singeing the rug and floorboards.

And then she saw it. Her ax.

It was lying underneath a large chest of drawers that had been thrown over, and its head had separated from the handle.

The divot. The small protective pocket of whatever remaining dust there was had been cracked open. Even from her far distance, the implications of what she saw were clear as day.

She had just lost her way home.

But she hardly had time to process the ramifications. Shouts outside spurred her to move. She let her body fall away from the window. Turned out, she had a real knack for falling. But once she was on the ground, movement wasn't so simple. Her legs wouldn't support her, no matter how hard she tried.

"Dammit!"

For lack of a better way to get around, she managed to get her elbows under her and army crawled around the back of the house. She had to get to Thomas. At least follow where they were taking him. Get help. Something!

But her muscles were exhausted. Beyond exhausted. The air around her weighed her down. She moved like she was swimming in peanut butter. Each lift of her arm was akin to a step up Mount Everest.

She finally rounded the corner of the house and did her best to keep low and out of sight. Thomas was on his feet, but men held him on all sides, with no fewer than three muskets pointed at his head.

Then he turned to face her. As if he sensed she wouldn't listen to him by staying put. His face was battered. Blood trickled down the back of his ear and painted a trail down his neck. But his chin was firm. Solid.

He locked eyes on her and quickly, so fast she nearly missed it, shook his head the slightest bit. *Stay put.*

It was his last act of protection. His final way of keeping her safe. And as he was loaded into the back of a horse cart, an inferno of pain bloomed in her gut. She went lax against the ground as her breathing became more strenuous. Beth shut her eyes as fate pummeled her life into a million shattered pieces.

Because she'd never had a choice in any of this all along.

CHAPTER 27

The city's custom house loomed large as the cart carrying Thomas slowed to a stop in the square. Pain flared across his chest where the knife had bitten into him. The ride had done his injuries no favors, but he was hardly focused on them. His muscles burned from the fight. Adrenaline crackled under his skin. He wasn't a violent man, but he knew his way around many a weapon.

Including the collection of various long and pointy objects currently aimed his way.

Thomas was a caged dog, but an intelligent one. The weapons trained on him went a long way to tip the scale away from his favor. So he willed himself to stay silent and still. But, blast, it was hard. His hands itched to take action, despite his injuries.

Half of Hunterdon's men were crammed into the back of the cart with him, while the rest had gone ahead on horseback. The man across from him—Will, he'd heard the others say, and the same one who he sent a message to a few nights ago—had unnerved him the most. Not because Thomas found him a threat. Far from it. But because Will's stare was ever present and hadn't moved from Thomas's direction ever since he had been dropped there.

"While I am flattered at the attention, you're hardly my type."

The jibe landed where Thomas intended. Will's lips pressed

together and his grip around the bayonet tightened. *I can at least throw verbal punches.* The satisfaction at Will's annoyance was small, yet satisfying.

"The redheaded cow. You fucking her, then?" He sneered.

The toe of Thomas's boot connected with Will's chin before the bastard had finished his sentence. The crunch was only mildly satisfying. He wanted his hands around the bastard's neck. To have his fingers press into soft flesh. To see whether he could wrap his large hands all the way around the greasy column tightly enough so his fingers could touch. In an instant, the other three men were on Thomas, holding him down. His mind had gone feral. Breath filled his lungs and his nostrils flared at the urge to strangle the man. Thomas's fingers curled at the thought.

The harsh tip of hot metal connected under his chin. The soldier's pressure on the knife sent the intended message as Thomas willed his body to calm.

The task was nearly impossible.

"What? Can't catch what you throw?" Will grinned as he wiped spittle from his face.

"Enough. Get him out. We're here."

Thomas's body was moved this way and that as he and the other men exited the cart. His mind hadn't yet been able to process his circumstances because he was too focused on Beth.

When Thomas was with Beth in his bedroom, he'd heard horses outside. He hadn't had horses on the property in years, and he never received visitors at his home. Always his forge.

Never had he been more grateful for his instincts.

Though self-preservation should have been at the forefront of his mind, his thoughts remained on Beth. No one knew she was there, and she was in no state to get help. Her body had nearly been dead weight in his arms as he carried her outside. Worry gnawed at his insides. How quickly would she deteriorate? Could he get back to her in time? No, he would. He had to. Because her ax—

"A nice, sizable crowd for a noontime demonstration. Glad to see the notices garnered attention."

Hunterdon's words broke through the moroseness of Thomas's

thoughts. All around them, people had started to gather. Men and women of all statuses and classes. Murmurs whispered through the swelling crowd. Many had papers in their hands.

What the devil is this?

"You are my honored guest, Brannigan." Hunterdon grabbed a piece of paper from a stack and held it up to Thomas's face. The men at his side held him firm as he took in the words.

The trueborn Sons of Liberty request the desired presence of the people to meet in front of the Custom House, at XII o'clock this day, to hear the public assignation of the blacksmith Thomas Brannigan as a loyalist to the British crown.

"This is a fucking lie, Hunterdon! I've made no such claim, and you bloody well know it!"

Hunterdon jumped in front of Thomas's face. "Actions go much further than words." He lowered his voice. "You supply their army with weapons, yet deny your kin the same courtesy."

"You are as deaf as you are blind. It is *business*. A fee for service. Or do your followers not yet know that you haven't the coin to pay them? Hmm?"

Hunterdon stood there, momentarily silenced, as his fists balled at his sides. The verbal slap had landed as Thomas intended.

"We *will* be heard, and our voice will carry into legislation," Hunterdon spat. "There is no louder voice than that of the people."

"Do you really think this action will be tolerated? With the state-house a block away, and the guards stationed outside the—"

But when Thomas looked to the custom house, his brows knitted in confusion. As long as he'd lived here, there had always been at least two British sentry guards in front of the custom house. Oftentimes more if diplomatic officials were in residence. The bluestone steps leading up to the entrance were barren, however. And at a time of day when traffic and business would be at their heaviest.

"Oh, yes. I should have mentioned that. You see, there has been a most unfortunate fire down at the docks. A British shipment of pine tar, I believe, right, Oliver?" Hunterdon turned to look at the man holding Thomas's arms behind his back.

"Right."

"Pity," he tsked. "I do believe the fire warden and all available enforcements were sent down to offer aid."

A low rumbling came from behind Thomas. Three of Hunterdon's men were rolling large wooden barrels into the center of the square. Two more men carrying burlap sacks joined the others. The tops of the sacks were open, and as the men walked by, a handful of feathers floated out and fell to the ground.

Thomas's gut sank like a stone.

"Lucky for us, we were able to procure a few barrels before everything went up in smoke."

"You started the fire," Thomas whispered as his mouth went dry.

"The route's all mapped out. We're ready," one of Hunterdon's men called down to him from horseback.

Thomas yanked against the arms that bound him. Two more men joined in the effort to restrain him and pulled a rope taut around his chest. The rough fibers scraped against his wound, reigniting sparks of pain that had previously ebbed.

More people joined the crowds standing around them. A woodsy scent wafted over as the lids of the pine tar barrels were pried open.

But the worst pain was flaring deep in his chest, behind the knife wound. Behind his ribs. Behind the fractured walls of his heart. Because, as the pieces of Hunterdon's torturous plan slowly fit together, despair dragged him down to hell's depths.

He wouldn't be able to return to Beth. Pain had not been Hunterdon's motivation, but a lengthy public ruination. One that would topple his business and his reputation.

Though that was all secondary to the true horror gripping his heart and why he had hoped to get back to Beth as quickly as possible.

When he was dragged out of his home and Hunterdon's men laid waste to the room, Thomas had spotted Beth's ax on the floor. With its head severed from its handle after a heavy oak chest of drawers had fallen on it.

The protective pocket at the junction point had been snapped, exposed. The dust on the weapon was likely gone and, with it, all hope of sending Beth back to her time. Of restoring her health. Her life.

"Welcome, everyone, to a demonstration of liberty!" Hunterdon's arms were outstretched as he addressed the crowd, as though he were a performer in the round. "We shall begin in a moment."

Hunterdon jogged over to another man near the barrels and spoke just loud enough so Thomas couldn't escape the words.

"One last thing, Gerald." Hunterdon pointed to the barrel of pine tar. "Heat it up."

White vapors were left in Emily's wake as she paced a circle around Beth. The lack of footprints in the dirt was infuriating. Emily longed to stomp, scream, and kick over everything in sight at what she had caused.

Poor Beth lay on the ground. Her cheek rested on the pad of her outstretched forearm as her eyes fluttered closed. Emily's skirts fanned out around her as she swooped down and placed her ear against Beth's back. Relief, however small it was, washed over Emily. But it was tenuous, like the hope of a threadbare blanket guarding against a blizzard.

Beth's heart still beat, but barely. Her lungs still inflated, but shallowly. And the green coloring previously hidden under her garments crept higher up her neck, until it just scarcely kissed the bottom of her chin.

"No, no, no . . ."

Thomas couldn't suffer the loss of this woman.

For the relationship between the two had blossomed into more than Emily had originally bargained for. Her intent had been to find a like-minded companion for Thomas. One who was a craftsman, a mentor. A friend. For that was what she thought he needed. Someone to steer his ship back into calmer waters.

She had been horribly wrong in the most enlightening of ways.

Miss Beth had done far more for him than any grizzled old blacksmith from the future ever could. Her softness, her nurturing heart. Those were the missing pieces of the healing process Emily couldn't predict. Her foolishness and naivete were ever present. Of course Miss Beth would be a splendid healer. She brought new babes into the world. It came as no surprise she was able to birth a new light inside of Thomas as well.

But the evidence of Emily's horribly laid plan rested in the muck. Its target was unconscious and unaware of what was about to happen.

Emily rested her hands on top of Beth's outstretched palm. She couldn't grip the woman's hand. Couldn't feel her slowing heart rate as its tempo softened to a scant patter. Couldn't rub warmth into Beth's palms as the blood lessened its circulation to her extremities. All she could do was sit there as dry tears threatened to form but would never fall—

Emily gasped as a speckle of dust rose up from Beth's chest. It was infinitesimal. Barely noticeable. Until others joined it. As each new fleck formed, the particles floated away from Beth and toward Emily's spirit form.

Her essence.

A swirling cloud of dust enveloped Beth's body, until her form no longer lay on the ground. And only after every last bit of essence was returned to Emily did the spirit fall back on her bottom and wail into the day's harsh sunlight.

CHAPTER 28

Hunterdon's words had become a buzzing in Thomas's ear. The bastard must have loved the sound of his own voice enough to come on himself from just hearing it. Thomas scoffed as the man strutted around the square with his showmanship on full display more so than his cause. Lies dripped from his mouth like acid. Phrases like *traitor* and *disloyal* and *thief among us* grated over Thomas's skin. Every blaspheme spouted from Hunterdon was another hammered nail in Thomas's professional coffin.

"He outfitted the British while our own went unarmed . . ."

Clang.

"He grew fat off foreign profits . . ."

Clang.

"No integrity for Boston's people or its hardworking tradesmen . . ."

Clang.

Unfortunately, the crowd around him ate up every word like a fresh meat pie. The occasional yes-that's-right turned into a more raucous he-can't-be-trusted as Hunterdon's speech went on.

Thomas's focus remained inward. Nothing could be done about the crowd or his reputation. Hunterdon had seen to that. So his mind centered on what he could control. His arms and legs, thankfully, had been freed. Though his captors replaced their hands around him with three musket barrels pointed at his head. A bit excessive, but he could hardly fault them for the added insurance in their security. He was grateful, too, as standing freely allowed his nausea to ebb and feeling to return fully to his arms and legs. Likewise, despite the gash across his chest, his strength was as solid as he could hope for.

Too bad he had no hope left for anything else. For his future. For Beth.

"Let's get to it, shall we? Shirt off, gents."

The collar of Thomas's shirt was pulled tight against his neck. His sleeves and back were ripped away in one clean fashion. He winced as his arms were yanked and his shoulder rolled inward. The toes of his boots tripped over his stripped-away shirt as he was pushed, gun to his back, next to the barrel of pine tar.

A swift kick to the back of the knees and he buckled. The cobblestones bit into Thomas's palms as he fell forward on all fours. Clumps of his hair, slick with sweat, fell into his face, obscuring his vision. His stomach twisted in revolt at the aroma as the smoking hot pine tar was moved closer to him.

He had heard mention of tarring and feathering being a favorite form of torture of the Sons of Liberty. The tactic had been used to disparage and humiliate the opposition, to ruin a reputation more so than permanently maim or injure. Hence the parade route for the victim once they'd been defiled.

Never had he heard of them boiling the tar. Until now.

Thomas's biceps curled in resistance. His nails scraped along the stones as the world spun to pieces around him. Ever since Emily died a hairsbreadth after their poor son, he'd floated through his days. He ate only when his stomach growled at him to do so. He slept only when exhaustion dragged him under. Routine had been his savior. Metal his cold bedfellow. For iron couldn't hurt him. There was no love to lose or anguish to heal from when hammering at his anvil. Only a billet of rawness that needed to be pressed into the whims of the highest bidder.

Somewhere along the way, he had lost his desire to be his own advocate. His wants had faded into the background of monotony, while a hardened survival instinct had sprouted up like an invasive weed, choking out every possibility of intrigue or inspiration.

Until Beth stumbled into his path.

Thomas hung his head. His hair draped over his features even more so, like a shroud cast over the deceased. Any thoughts of her, any glimmers of happiness that might have broken through his countenance, were his to protect, even in his vulnerable, exposed state. Off to his side, a soldier laid out wide brushes, while another used a long rod to stir the barrel of tar. Wisps of smoke wafted up, causing his nose to twitch in light of the impending punishment.

A shaky breath rattled out of him as he shut his eyes, sweat nearly blinding him. An image of Beth, with her vibrant red hair and solemn blue eyes, painted the backs of his lids. Despite her circumstances in her time, she was damn proud of her skills, even when those who should love her for them claimed indifference. Her tenacity in her trade, along with her encouragement and understanding, was infectious. Only in her wake had his urge to toy with his metal craft been reignited.

Maybe Hunterdon was right, to a degree. Thomas had just been following the money, and he'd been content to do so as time went on.

Until he wasn't. Until Beth had come along and forced him to say his son's name out loud for the first time in years. Until she'd laid her warm, soft hands on his cold, hardened body and kissed away all the despair that had chained him to his anvil and his misguided duties.

Wood screeched against stone as the barrel was brought closer to him.

"On your face or on your feet, it makes no matter to me." Hunterdon's catcall was rabble-rousing and incendiary to the masses. Cries and roars shot up from around him. Some demanded he rise to take his punishment. Others called for his head to remain low in shame.

Thomas glanced up through the tufts of hair covering his face. Bodies in front of bodies clogged his vision. Nameless faces of a jury stared back at him as they looked on to Hunterdon to deliver their verdict and his sentencing. None of these people knew him. Knew his grief or motivations or losses.

Only Beth knew him and had cared for him regardless. And damn that he'd never gotten the chance to tell her it was the same for him.

No, more than the same. He loved her. From every smile on her face to every light in her heart, he loved her and always would.

The faces in front of him blurred. His throat clenched and strained as he tried to swallow down his anguish.

Through his torment, his sight managed to latch on to a swoosh across his field of vision. The movement was slow, yet steady and kept repeating, like a pendulum clock swaying in front of him. As Thomas squinted to try and focus, the five fingers of a hand sharpened.

A wave. Someone was waving at him. One of the people in the crowd, a woman with a bundle clutched to her chest, was moving her hand back and forth, as if she was trying to get his attention. The movement was subdued, as she stood toward the front of the crowd, but she was far back enough that her gestures wouldn't immediately be noticed by others.

Except for Thomas.

Confusion and curiosity pushed to the surface. The warm wetness that trickled down his neck, the flaring pain across his chest and his shoulder, sank to the back of his mind as he forced all his senses to focus on what he was seeing before him.

The woman with long dark hair held an infant wrapped to her bosom, and she was most certainly waving at him. Her lips thinned a second before harsh hands gripped his shoulders, holding him steady. Still, her infernal free hand continued to wave a subtle greeting in front of her chest. What was he to say?

Thank you so much for coming out to my public ruination. Perhaps later we can meet to swap scone recipes and soap formulations.

Panic hammered along his skin, and irritation gnawed at him. A confusing mix, to be sure, and one he had no time to parse out. He needed a plan, dammit! Yet as he squinted closer at the woman, her fingers waved faster. More urgently. No, she was not waving a greeting. She was trying to get his attention. Then her fingers shifted from an open palm to a single finger pointing off to Thomas's left.

What?

Thomas dropped his lead low and subtly pivoted his neck to the left. Past the edge of the crowd. Past the carts and carriages amassed in the street. Until he saw a single horse, bridled but without a saddle, poking its head out from around the cobbler's corner shop. The reins of the animal extended behind the building. He couldn't see who held them.

Until a mop of shaggy light brown hair and an aproned torso peeked out from behind the wall. The man looked at Thomas and offered up the reins in his fist.

Francis.

Thomas's head whipped back around to look for the woman in the crowd. When his eyes fell on her, a larger connection fused together.

Theodora.

Her nod was slight and meant only for him. It was a nod of encouragement. As if she had faith in him to do what? Could he possibly . . . ?

Theodora rocked the babe in her arms and shifted his weight against her other shoulder. Her nodding was persistent and unflappable despite the scene. They believed him. Believed his innocence and motives. And, of course, believed in Beth. For they would not have known each other at all unless Beth hadn't forged ahead and insisted on helping her deliver their infant son—

"Aah!"

Sharp pain coursed down his back. Scratchy bristles dripped hot pine tar along his skin. The initial contact prickled and flared as he twisted his back away from the onslaught. The pain was intense, jarring, incendiary.

And just enough for Thomas's resolve to snap into place.

His hands clenched into fists as he dug his knuckles into the stone. A great cry rose up from his chest, silencing the onlookers. Thomas heaved himself off the ground. His arms flung wild. The men at his shoulders stumbled back. The man to his right tripped over the barrel in surprise, floundering back on his arse. Gasps and cries fluttered through the crowd. Hunterdon barked orders.

But they were all gnats to Thomas. Annoying buzzes that faded to the background as he straightened and ran toward the horse. His legs were sluggish at first but quickly gained momentum. The people gathered at that side quickly shuffled away, giving him a wide berth. Like any member of a crowd, they were content to condemn in voice but not aid in action. So they parted for him and saved him the trouble of plowing them into the ground.

His feet slowed only slightly when he reached the chestnut mare. One smooth leap and Thomas was sitting astride the horse. No words were exchanged as Francis quickly threw him the reins. Thomas merely nodded. It was all he could offer in his way of thanks in the moment.

"Hah!" He clicked his heels against the horse and sped off away from the melee.

Adrenaline pumped furiously in his chest. He had to get to Beth and see her well. For he didn't think his soul could survive another loss.

CHAPTER 29

S luggish didn't even begin to describe Beth's body movements or the brain scramble that sloshed around in her frontal lobe. Her eyelids were like the iron gates of a castle clamped down to protect against an invasion. She tried to raise them, but the effort was immense. She'd rather just stay sleeping, sprawled out on her side, lost in the best dream of her life. Where a hulking blacksmith had peeled away all her layers of insecurity and self-doubt until he revealed the shining gem of potential and determination underneath.

And love. A whole lot of love. The giving, receiving, wrapping around her tight kind of love, until she was smothered in the knowledge and warmth that her soul was protected and cared for by another. Who loved her just as she was and for everything she would be. A soft sigh ghosted out of Beth's lips as the image of her blacksmith came to mind—

Her left shoulder floated backward from its lack of support. The rest of her body joined in on the descent. She rolled over and, with a thud, landed on her back. Ain't nothing holding back those eyelids now as they shuttered open. Her lower back pinched in pain as the boning of her stays bit into her skin from the sharp twist her body just managed. A chunk of her hip had been nipped when she'd landed on the hard floor.

Wait . . . stays.

Beth dropped her chin and glanced down at her body—and was immediately greeted with the flesh of her breasts. Not in a bra, but pushed up in a boned, yet loosely cinched, corset-type device, which her now-online brain told her she'd been wearing daily for the last two weeks.

And those puppies were a matching set of pale and pasty. Not a hint of green in sight. Beth dropped her head back on the floor. She had never been so happy to get an eyeful of her always-too-large breasts.

"Holy crap. I'm back." She panted in disbelief as she stared at a rickety ceiling fan making its lazy rotations overhead. Dust particles fluttered down from the fan blades and danced in the afternoon sun's illumination.

Dust. Shit.

The slight tickle was the only warning she had before an angry sneeze spewed out of her. And another one. After the third face full of snot, Beth finally got wise to the situation and rolled over. Scratchy laminate floors greeted her palms. So, not the linoleum of her house, then. And she didn't have ceiling fans at home because she hated the heat and had insisted on a house with central air conditioning.

Beth shot up and looked around. Shades of brown, brass, and silver filled her vision as she scanned the room. Wooden tables were covered with knickknacks and books. Beige price stickers dotted everything, while a glass jewelry case to her left reflected rainbows on the wall.

A loud honk made her jump. Was that . . . ?

Beth flew to the window and pushed the dark green drapes aside. Cars, trucks, and buses clogged the street in front of her. Horns blared and middle fingers were thrown as a red sedan with out-of-state license plates tried to make the light but got stuck in the middle of the intersection and successfully blocked out all other traffic.

It was like a long-lost love note from her city. *Welcome back, Beth. And remember, don't block the box.*

"I'm back!" Beth threw her fists in the air before clamping her hands over her mouth.

The antique shop was empty but she expected the shopkeeper to come and investigate the noise any second. Her eyes stayed trained on the beaded curtain in the back entryway that led downstairs. Staticky radio voices in thick Boston accents pricked her ears from down below, yet there was no other movement. No footfalls on old wooden stairs. No screeching of chair legs across the floor as if someone were to stand and see to the noise.

Nothing. Some security system this guy had.

Beth briefly entertained the idea of calling out and putting in more of an effort to make her presence known. But a pewter mug on the table next to her caught her attention.

The thing was polished to a high shine. Or as high of a shine as you could get on something that was umpteen years old. She lifted it up, held it in front of her, and examined her reflection.

She hadn't had an opportunity to look at herself, really *look* at herself, in days. Her eyes, despite the physical hell she'd just been through, were brighter. When she smiled, the apples of her cheeks squeezed into comfortable cushions, as if they had spent much time in their new positions and enjoyed returning to the setup. Hints of laugh lines crinkled at the corners of her eyes. The pad of her finger easily smoothed them away, but her skin protested the new arrangement. Happiness looked good on her.

The thought jarred her for a moment.

She had been happy. For the first time in a long time, Beth had been floating on cloud nine, where all the pieces had fallen into place. Her body knew it. She knew it. And dammit, her heart knew it, too.

Beth dropped her gaze over the rest of her features, down to her neck, shoulders, and upper chest. No green anywhere.

Her throat tightened as she forced a smile on her face. Thomas had stayed true to his word to protect her. Through sheer stubbornness and some unknown force of nature, the man had managed to make sure she got sent back to her time. Back home. In full health. Just as he promised he would. He'd given her exactly what she'd wanted. To return home.

Then why the hell did every bone in her body scream out in protest at the decision?

This is wrong. I shouldn't be here.

Did she want to make it back home? Originally, sure. But that was before her body had memorized every hard plane and stubbled angle of Thomas's physique. Before she'd settled into a routine with a man who would bring her a cup of tea and a sweet biscuit as she worked by his side every day. Who anticipated her needs without a word needing to be spoken. Who encouraged her to see to the care of expectant mothers and sent her off with a sparkle of pride in his eye. Who cared for her, despite climbing and descending a Mount Everest of grief after losing his wife and son.

The pewter mug dropped from her hand and thudded as it skipped across the floor. Tears pricked her eyes as she looked out at Boston's midday traffic.

Thomas!

Her last vision of him came flooding back in an instant. Of men with bayonets pointed at his throat. Of being held down and pummeled by fist after fist, the blood saturating his shirt. Of being dragged this way and that as Hunterdon and his goons forced him into a carriage, all while they held a musket to his head.

And then the last memory she'd ever have of Thomas bloomed in the front of her mind.

Her blacksmith, battered and bloodied, looking back at where she lay, partially hidden behind the house. His eyes connected with hers, though briefly. Then he discreetly shook his head.

His last unspoken words to her. *Stay there.*

It was the final interaction she'd ever have with him, and it was solely about him keeping her safe.

Beth's lip quivered as the loss settled in. The actions had been there, even when the words hadn't been.

He loved her. In every way a man should love a woman. But, God, was he safe? Was he alive? She had to hope, had to believe he survived the assault. But how would she ever know? She didn't have her ax anymore. There was no way for her to go back to him, to see the extent of his injuries or worse . . .

And stupid, foolish Beth. As the enormity of her loss and the uncertainty of his circumstances sank in, her pain from so many unanswered questions only magnified with each new memory of just how much he had shown his love for her all along.

Tucking strands of hair out of her face as she focused on learning how to write with a quill.

Patiently teaching her how to draw out a billet at the anvil, even though she'd wasted many chunks of iron with her mistakes.

Softly kneading the tension out of her arms each day as her muscles struggled to adapt to new skills.

She loved Thomas. He had become her person. Her other half. But she never got the opportunity to tell him until it was too late.

Or ask him how one was supposed to soldier on when life offered up the most precious thing and fate shit all over it.

Thomas's boots landed in the soft grass before the horse had a chance to come to a full stop.

"Beth!"

He ran around the back of his house and nearly tripped over himself when the trough came into view. His knees hit the ground in front of it. Beth's absence punched him in the chest. Had Hunterdon's men seen her? No. Thankfully, she'd understood his silent message and stayed hidden where she was. There were no other marks in the dirt aside from her own. Thomas rose and rushed into the house through the back door. It took him five seconds to scan every possible space.

Beth wasn't there.

He slowed his frantic pace as he entered the living room. Shattered glass and broken furniture covered the floor. The destruction was uninspired and unorganized. Anything that could be knocked over was. Anything that could have been snapped or smashed lay in pieces at his feet. He glanced at the rocking chair in the corner, or what was left of it. The frame had been kicked and splintered beyond recognition. The small trunk behind it lay on its side. The quilts and blankets within were ripped to shreds, with yarn snaking over broken planks of wood like ivy on a grave.

Then Thomas walked over to the front door and knelt to inspect the toppled chest of drawers. There was nothing under it, other than its contents.

The ax was gone.

Thomas fell back on his arse and dropped his head in his hands. *Had she done it? Had she made it back to her time safely?*

As he sat there, he ran through every possible scenario of how Beth could escape. He left no detail out. He considered her health, her appearance, her stamina. He considered her speed, the distance they were to other people, her knowledge (or lack thereof) of riding on horseback or where she was in relation to the city. The time of day, Hunterdon's men, the food and drink Beth had access to. Thomas threw all of it into the kettle in his mind and swirled the contents around . . . and came out with nothing.

There was no solution, no possibility made available by the laws of nature, that would result in her not being here or in close proximity to the property.

Unless she had successfully traveled back to her time.

Thomas swiped his hand down his face and exhaled. She was safe. He'd done it. He'd fulfilled his promise to her in the way he never could to Emily. But damn, the loss hurt. More than hurt. Glass pricked the backs of his legs and his back twisted painfully against the cooled sticky tar, but those were as superficial as a bee sting. For inside his chest, a cancer bloomed. The infection was slow to start, creeping outward and upward around his heart.

Shaky legs saw Thomas upright. Hunterdon had more of a winning hand than he'd realized. The bastard hadn't just taken away Thomas's hard-earned reputation and successful business. He hadn't just forced him to pack up his belongings and leave Boston in search of a new town or city welcoming a journeyman blacksmith.

No. Hunterdon's damage was more debilitating. He had robbed Thomas of his final moments with his soul mate.

Death would have been a kinder punishment.

As Thomas moved to his bedroom in search of a satchel to begin packing his wares, a slight shiver ghosted across his skin. He turned his head to the side, keeping an ear open for any noises. All was silent, so he slowly walked over to his trunk.

His nerves stood on end as he unloaded items. Probably due to his grief. That had been a common reaction for him in the days following his family's death. Yet as he fisted the fabrics, he tried to shake off the prickle of unease at his back.

The kind he got when he knew he was being watched.

CHAPTER 30

The harsh clang of metal on metal jarred Emily out of her morose thoughts. Thomas had thrown a handful of iron files into his trunk. He hadn't bothered to organize them or bundle them into clusters of different sizes, as he'd always done. Instead, they were all clamored together in a pile on top of various hammers, odd bits of metal scraps, and a few half-finished blunted blades.

She had never seen him so careless with his tools.

For the days that followed, Emily hovered around Thomas like a second shadow . . . ever since Beth had returned to her time and Thomas had returned, battered and berserk, to his home. At first, his behavior and mood were like a recurring nightmare one had long outgrown but was horrified to experience again. Every bright spark she had seen blossom in Thomas since Beth came along had been extinguished like a hot blade thrown into a quench basin. The light in his hazel eyes immediately had gone dark.

Emily had witnessed it before, when she first came to know her spirit form. But those days had been maddeningly confusing, both for her and Thomas. Now, however? The signs were like a musician's song being performed for the same townspeople. Predictable and without hope that the next song would be better.

Initially, Thomas closed down in all ways. He boarded up his forge and brought to his home every last unfinished and completed weapon he kept there. One of the hardest blows was the lack of surprise on his patrons' faces as he delivered what he could of their orders. Most items were partially executed. Some orders he was able to fulfill as a fragmented inventory. For all, however, he was given no final payment. Emily's stomach fluttered in protest as she watched him on each visit he made. His eyes remained downcast, while his customers silently parted ways with him, regardless of how long they'd employed his services or how large of an order they'd placed with him.

Emily nearly vibrated with fury when Thomas delivered the last of his stock to its owner. Oh, how she prayed she could be a vengeful spirit. One with the ability to haunt and terrorize Hunterdon in his sleep. Surely, frightening children's stories must have had some basis in fact. She had even paid the man a visit. Yet try as she might, no matter how hard she screamed and howled, she could not tip over even a single tankard of ale. Her hand movements were just that: movements of her ethereal form. She could kick, punch, and grasp at every part of Hunterdon's body and he wouldn't feel a thing.

Despair for an eternal spirit was an immortal punishment.

Thomas's hulking form passed in front of Emily. She looked up and watched him walk out the front door to load another satchel onto the horse cart.

And that was how she and Thomas spent their last days together. She would stay close to him and serve as a useless sponge for his grief while he would move through the motions of packing up his life and leaving once again.

Guilt weighed heavily on her heart. Yes, her time on the mortal plane was long over, but as a direct result of her meddling in it, she had cost Thomas his second chance at happiness. She glanced up at the bare wooden walls around her. What hadn't been destroyed by Hunterdon's men was packed away in the cart outside. This room, this house, was once again a set of walls. Walls that had once offered Thomas a fresh start from insufferable grief.

This time around, she was the chief cause of his pain. The fault lay with her.

Emily bit her lip and squeezed her eyes shut. Her front teeth clamped down harder on her bottom lip, while her fingernails dug into the back of her opposing hand. She hesitated, waiting for the sting of pain to register. For the slightest punishment of her own doing to reverberate up through her body.

Nothing. She couldn't even kick her own behind or cause herself some pain to atone for her own foolishness.

She exhaled a deep breath her lungs had no use for but bellowed out anyway. The action reminded her of blowing out a candle or coaxing life into banked coals. Like the bellows at Thomas's forge.

The forge.

That had been the start of this whole mess, hadn't it? Emily had chosen to leave her essence in the forge for someone to find in the future. She had originally hoped it'd be a blacksmith or future metalworker. Someone to mentor Thomas in his profession. But then Miss Beth had stumbled upon it . . .

Emily whipped outside the front door and scattered in the wind. She hadn't even looked back to check on Thomas or his progress. The house was mostly empty anyway. He would surely set out on the road today.

But what if she could recreate her original experiment? Travel to the future and leave her essence in the forge as she did before? Would Miss Beth find it again? Would circumstances happen the same? She could hardly wrap her head around the possibilities, but she was willing to try. She was willing to do whatever she could to right the terrible wrong she had brought on the man who deserved none of it.

The thrum of the vibrations around Emily was electrifying as she reformed along a walkway in front of the antique shop. Giant carriages whooshed past her like stampeding wild horses. Dark gray smoke sputtered from the rear of the roving beasts. All around her, people clogged passageways and harsh noises jockeyed for positions to be heard above all others. Emily shut her eyes, shook her head slightly to tune it all out, and ghosted through the shop's front door.

The shop was empty of people, filled to the brim with various items. Some she vaguely recognized and others, though they had the wear and appearance of old age, looked vastly more modern. One particular item in the corner caught her eye. Emily moved toward the small table where the ornately carved metal apparatus, along with its matching coils, sat. A small white piece of paper housed in a hard casing lay propped against its framework.

Vintage Ornate French Victorian Style Rotary Telephone.

She hadn't the faintest inkling of what a telephone was, nor what most of those words described. But that wasn't what drew her to the item. Emily floated her fingers over the ornately carved patterns against the gold metal. The telephone sat raised on four feet, with each one carved to look like a flower petal. All around the boxy shape were ribs of branches and vines, curling this way and that. Clusters of grapes and recessed sunbursts filled in the sunken spaces and wrapped around the whole item. The handle was the most ornately carved area. In the center, where she suspected one's palm would lay, were grids of crisscrosses and raised leaves blanketed over them as if the leaves had freshly fallen from trees.

The craftsmanship was all so lifelike. Every praiseworthy phrase she could think to describe it, with her simple vocabulary, fell short to attest to its beauty. The intricacies tugged at her heart, and images of Thomas painstakingly crafting the baby rattle for Elliot flooded her memories and revitalized her mission.

She needed to get Beth back to Thomas.

Emily whipped around to the table near the front entrance, the one with the nails and musket balls she recognized from her time. The items called to her like a homing beacon. She put her palm out, which had already developed a light coating of green dust from her travels there, and reached for the closest thing, a tin soldier mold.

"What in the bloody hell do you think you're doing?"

Emily gasped and turned around. Her hands flew to her chest. Melanie, the closest thing Emily had to a friend since entering her new existence, glared back at her. Dark lashes slanted across stern brows as Melanie crossed her arms over her chest.

A storm cloud would have had a cheerier countenance.

"I made a mistake, Mel. A bad one. A catastrophic one."

Melanie sighed and pinched the bridge of her nose. "I told you it was a bad idea to go about meddling. What have you done now?"

"I thought I could help Thomas." Emily's throat tightened as she forced the words out. "I thought . . . if I could just help him find that spark again, he could get past his sadness . . . get past the deaths. You remember our original plan?"

Melanie nodded solemnly.

"It worked . . . until it didn't. The woman who was sent to him—"

"A woman?" Melanie shrieked. "You sent a woman to your husband? I thought you wanted to send another blacksmith or tradesman."

"I did! But it didn't turn out that way. And I couldn't be gladder for it."

"You'll need to be explaining yourself." Melanie shook her head.

"She's exactly what Thomas needs. This woman has made terrific strides toward making him whole again, and I couldn't want more for him." Emily dug her fingers into her scalp and closed her eyes. "But she's gone now. Back to her time. She took my essence into her body and it brought her home. But it'll kill him, Melanie." She dropped her hands and pleaded with Melanie. "The loss will kill him."

"So, what, then? You fix to just repeat what you did before? And hope she'll stumble along into this shop and touch what you intend her to?"

"I don't know! Maybe?" Emily threw her arms up and paced up and down the small aisle. Her vapors sharply changed direction as they followed, like a small child tugged reluctantly along with its mother. After she'd made the lap a dozen times, she turned back to Melanie. Her shoulders hung low in defeat.

"Don't be batting your doe eyes at me, Em. I can't fix your mess. What's done is done. But . . ." Melanie rocked her head back and forth as she mulled over an idea. "There may be a way to increase your chances. *May*, I say. High hopes have no place with afterlifers. I need you to know that." She gripped Emily's shoulders and shook her slightly. "There's the devil's chance in heaven that your woman will return to this exact spot. But there is a place she's much more likely to connect with."

"Where is it? Tell me."

"Close your eyes first."

"Don't blather at me about trying to remain calm again—"

"If your mind ran half as fast as your mouth, I dare say you may not be in this mess you've made." Melanie rolled her eyes. "Are you prepared to listen to me or prattle on in a panic?"

Emily slumped under Melanie's very valid, though very infuriating point. It was all she could do not to stomp her foot and cry out about life not being fair. Though that was exactly the truth of things, wasn't it? It wasn't fair that her son had died before he had a chance to live. It wasn't fair she'd been taken shortly after, and her sainted husband had been left to mourn and bury his young family.

It wasn't fair that Beth had stumbled into Emily's line of fire, or that Thomas had come alive again with a woman who, through Emily's misjudgment of risk, could never stay by his side.

"Close. Your. Eyes."

Emily's lids slammed shut at Melanie's insistence.

"Your spirit is likely to still remember a bit of the lass, even if only faintly. Focus on her. What do you see?"

"How am I supposed to—"

"Well, you're not going to be seeing much if you're too busy running that mouth of yours. Now, focus. Picture her in your mind. Start there and see where it leads you."

Emily exhaled and shook out her arms. *Focus, Emily. Focus.*

She calmed herself as much as she could and thought of the woman who had found her essence. Slowly, a blurred image began to form in her mind. Bright red hair framed a solemn face kissed with freckles and determination. In her vision, Beth's skin was free of green taint and radiated vibrant health. Emily's eyebrows softened at the image. Then, slowly, the haze around Beth's tendrils sharpened, revealing a wall of glass framed inside a brick house. The glass had panes, as if it could move from one side to another. The image expanded wider still, and Emily could see the fabric chair Beth reclined upon atop the stone patio. She appeared comfortable and relaxed, though sullen.

Minute vibrations rumbled just below the surface of Emily's frame. They were incredibly faint, yet insistent. They tugged at her, and her instinct was to follow. Emily's eyes flew open.

"What did you see?" Melanie urged.

"Her house. Beth is at her house." She panted in amazement. "It is not in the city, but in a town just outside of it."

"How do you know that?"

"I . . . I don't know, but I can feel it. I know how to get there."

Melanie stood up straight and put her hands on her hips. "Well, then. Let's get you in closer range to that woman. It's the best chance you've got to improve the situation you've cocked up."

Emily swallowed down her nerves and scattered into the air.

CHAPTER 31

The crisp chardonnay glided down the back of Beth's throat as she looked out at her backyard. The glass's condensation rubbed off on her hand when she settled her drink on the stone patio beneath her. Beth quickly wiped it dry on her khaki shorts.

She hated when her palms got wet. For the last several days, she couldn't get her palms to stop sweating. Ever since she woke up in that antique shop and was hammered with the knowledge that she'd never see Thomas again.

The sweating had become a psychosomatic reaction. Almost as if her body, her own skin, was protesting the new environment. Though it wasn't new. Far from it. She had chosen it all. Beth had purchased this home with the intent to share it with Kyle. To live there as a couple. Sure, it wasn't massive, but it was home. And it had everything she needed.

Except she couldn't stand the place. The cream-colored paint on the walls, which she had originally picked as a neutral yet calming shade, reeked of institutional hallways and dated office buildings. The giant gray microfiber sectional in the living room, which she'd never loved but had given into so Kyle could watch the Patriots with his buddies, was a mammoth eyesore and made the craftsman's modest living room feel like a narrow cave about to collapse in on itself.

None of it fit anymore. The house, the furniture, the neighborhood. All of it choked her like a boa constrictor. The feeling was acute and worsening. Yesterday, when she returned from grocery shopping, she rolled her car into the garage like she always had. But as the garage door slowly descended behind her, blocking her into the confined space, her hands clenched around the steering wheel. The hammering in her heart thrummed louder against her chest wall as her palms struggled to find purchase against the solid leather in her hands before she quickly wiped the sweat off on her thighs. And that had happened about a billion times since she arrived back home.

Beth peered out at the muddy hole in the middle of her backyard where she and Amanda had ruined Kyle's clothes. Her lip curled up at the memory. Damn, that had hit the spot. But as she let the cool wave of revenge roll over her and drift back out to sea, she was surprised that the payback hadn't had more lasting powers. Her emotions were muddied, just like the puddle.

Mud had seemed like an accurate analogy for her life. Since her time with Thomas, everything had become as clear as mud. Life in her own time, it turned out, had moved right along in parallel to the days she had been in the past. Because of her humiliating experience with Kyle, she hadn't yet told her employer about his cheating or the fact that she no longer needed the previously approved two weeks off she had scheduled for her honeymoon. Boy, had that time off worked out in her favor. She hadn't returned to her job yet and had graciously asked her colleagues to cover for a few more days. But the drive that had fueled her before was different as well.

Boston, at least the Boston she'd called her home for most of her life, didn't resonate as home anymore. And though she loved her fellow midwives, she absolutely did not love the hospital hierarchy and the professional disapproval that often came with it.

But with Thomas, she had been valued—by both him and the women who sought her help, and for more reasons than the boxes she could check during a prenatal visit. She had been seen and admired and . . . loved.

And, wow, was that such a monumental gift, even if it did come in long-gone wrapping paper and trimmings that only existed in her memories.

Boston was toxic. It was time for a change.

I just wish Thomas was here to help me do it.

Beth grabbed her wine glass and sipped as she pulled out her phone. A few taps and swipes took her to local realtors. Their large smiles, blindingly white teeth, and perfectly quaffed hair gave Beth the assurance that any of them would be happy to take a cut of her money in exchange for her house's listing. She clicked on one at random, filled out her basic information on their contact form, and hit submit.

She took another sip and savored the flavor as she sloshed it over her tongue. The glass had dried off significantly, and the wine had warmed up so it more closely matched the humidity outside. Her tongue painted the flavor across her lips as she recalled the champagne she and Thomas had shared.

Her eyes quivered, doing their best to hold back tears, as the memories flooded back. Sticky mouths, tangled tongues, and brushed kisses along scorched skin poked through the fissures of her mind. As if Thomas, in all his awesome strength, was determined to bust through Beth's protective casing of their time together and hammer home his force in her life.

The split was crippling. Her body lived in the present, but everything that colored the marrow of Beth Carmichael nee fake-McCrary nee nearly-Donovan-for-a-hot-second-because-she-almost-changed-her-name was left in the past.

With Thomas.

Who had picked up his life after a devastating tragedy and moved hundreds of miles away, without the benefit of trains or cars, to a port city where he could thrive in his trade.

Beth scratched at the lawn chair's vinyl armrest as a thought occurred to her. "Could I do that?" she whispered.

Gears, so rusted and encased in old-as-time habits, slowly began to turn over as a new path took shape in her mind.

When she was with Theodora and Francis, the need for a good midwife had been made painfully clear. And given the tumultuous time and the habits of the people, it wasn't surprising that the residence arrangement for the former midwife went by the wayside and the working class was left with no one.

The Boston of her time was so clogged with fancy hospitals and bright and shiny medical centers that they overwhelmed the choices for well-woman care. And as long as those sites also offered multifaceted healthcare centers, with everything from top-notch cancer treatment to state-of-the-art fertility management, the top-dollar funding hardly ever went to midwifery practices.

If Beth stayed in Boston, she'd always be just a midwife.

But there were plenty of suburban or even rural towns along the Mid-Atlantic where a woman's best option was a women's wellness clinic or birthing center. Where a full-fledged hospital was a targeted, intended destination instead of the medical equivalent of a coffee shop that popped up on every corner.

"I could do that." The affirmation was louder in both her ears and her heart. It rose in tempo as the gears slowly knit together, forming a cohesive mechanism that would fuel her next steps.

Beth sprang from her chair and ran inside to fire up her laptop.

Emily reformed in front of the large panel of glass at the back of Beth's house. Melanie joined her a moment later.

"This is it. I did it." Emily's eyes roamed across the brick facade before she turned around to face the yard.

"Does she have pigs?" Melanie squinted at the large muddy puddle in the center of the lawn.

Emily shook her head. "I don't know."

"Well, that's a pretty sizable pile of muck for someone who doesn't tend to pigs. Odd." Melanie rested her fists on her hips.

"I'm not here for mud, Mel."

"Oh, don't I know it. I'd say you've already stepped in more than enough of it."

Emily rolled her eyes and turned to enter the house. She met no resistance as she coasted through the glass.

But if she had been whole again, she'd have reduced it to shards with a tap of her finger. Emily's spirit was alive with energy and panicked urgency. She glanced around the house, but her eyes weren't registering images. All thoughts were consumed with sending Beth back to Thomas. Her hand pumped with the need to scatter and disperse her essence on anything and everything.

It seemed as good a plan as any.

Emily tamped down her unease at not recognizing most of what was around her. Determination and pure stubbornness powered through her fear of the unknown. In one bold move, she swiped her palm across the nearest counter. The stool in front of her was next. Every flat surface and possible item that Beth would touch was fair game as Emily spun through the kitchen.

"Stop! What are you doing?"

"What should have happened all along." Emily hardly recognized her own voice. She had become a whirlwind of activity as she fluttered about Beth's home.

"Stop, Emily," Melanie yelled, but Emily was too engrossed in her task to heed the warning.

Just as Emily reached for an apple that sat proudly in the center of the fruit bowl on top of the small table, Melanie reformed in front of her. The reappearance was so fast, it nearly caused Emily to topple backward.

"You are not infinite." Melanie's words grated like gravel under carriage wheels. "What I see before me is all I will ever see of you."

Emily reared back at the words.

"Now you stop to listen." Melanie shook her head. "Perhaps if you spent a fair bit more time among your own kind instead of chained to your living husband like an anchor to a cast-off ship, you'd have more sense than you do. So hear this now, and listen well. You are not infinite. Your essence is all that's left of you. It is not something that can be spread so thin that you'd dilute your own spirit. This single being," she said, her fingers curled into claws and pointing at herself, "is all we've got left."

Emily glanced down at her hand. Her essence was mostly gone. Only a mere smudge remained on the tip of her thumb. Melanie's words hardly seemed like much of a threat. But she had been right about one thing. Emily had hardly embraced her spirit form or mingled much with others like her. How could she? When Thomas had been left behind to suffer like he did.

"You think you're the only one to leave a loved one behind?" Melanie scoffed. "Am I not standing before you? Is grief so singular that only you and your husband have a claim to it? Well, I'm glad your foolishness isn't catching. I, for one, am content to know that me and my wee one are not just bones and blood at the bottom of the sea. I have no qualms with this existence." She held her hands out to her sides before slowly lowering them. "But I can tell you do. You grieve every bit as much as him, don't you? And the pain hasn't waned . . . because you won't let it. That's what this is really about, isn't it?"

Emily fisted her hands as she stared at her friend. The only other spirit she'd ever bothered to talk to or connect with. Because Melanie was right. Emily had refused to accept her fate. She had never been good at change, especially not when she had no say in the matter. So, it had been far easier to remain as close to the same as she could.

Regardless of how much it made her heart bleed.

But she could change all that. If Thomas was happy, Emily could be, too.

Deep thumping drew her gaze to a stairwell at the far side of the kitchen. Beth barreled downstairs, with a rectangular flat object cradled under her arm. She sidled up to the table in the center of the kitchen— and infuriatingly managed to avoid touching any of the things Emily had dusted—and laid the item flat on the surface. Beth opened the object like a box, separating the top portion from the bottom and setting it upright. Instantly, bright light flared out of it. Beth grabbed a stool from the corner—another item Emily hadn't yet touched—and tapped her fingers out along the bottom portion. Minute clicking sounds filled the kitchen as Beth stared intently at the object in front of her.

Emily homed in on Beth's fingers as they flew in a seemingly random pattern across the clicking panel.

A panel filled with indentations and divots perfect for catching her essence . . . and which Beth was repeatedly connecting with.

Emily's gaze shot to the spirit at her side. Melanie thinned her lips and gave a terse shake of her head. It was all the warning Emily got. But her decision had already been made.

Emily wheeled around to Beth, intent on swiping the last remnant of her available essence along the clicking panel beneath Beth's fingertips. Melanie lunged in front of her, the spirit's vapors clouding Emily's clear view—

A loud crash startled the women.

The slim rectangular object Beth had been touching lay open on the floor. Shattered spiderwebs were cracked along its glassy surface, while tiny fragments of metal were strewn about on the kitchen tile. Next to it, Beth lay on her side, knees tucked up under her and arms nestled close to her chest like a newborn babe. Emily sucked in a breath as tremors racked the woman's frame.

"What have you done?" Melanie shrieked in horror.

Emily went over her actions in her mind, replaying the careless temper tantrum that had consumed her since she entered Beth's house. Her goal since arriving had been widespread and less targeted. She hadn't paid mind to the nuances of where Beth might be, only that Emily was intent on making the connection happen in any way possible.

But they hadn't connected. Of that she was certain.

"No." Emily slowly shook her head. "It is not my doing. She hadn't yet touched my essence. I've taken no part in this."

"Oh, like bloody hell you've taken no part in this. Look at the poor woman!"

Beth's limbs were tense and crunched, as if she were being squeezed to fit into a traveling trunk. Her teeth were clamped tight and no sound came, though her body was held rigid as if it were protecting itself against a tidal wave crashing down.

Had this been what the poor woman endured the first time?

Dammit all! She was so stupid and naïve. Those being the kinder phrases Emily was inclined to call herself. Because her bullheaded stubbornness had whittled away at any remaining sense of what she truly wanted.

She was tired. Grief was exhausting, and even more so when one carried around such a load not only for herself, but for her husband. And without an end in sight for any of it.

Tears trickled out of the corners of Beth's eyes as her body fought against whatever force was bearing down on her.

Emily turned to Melanie. "I don't know what to do. I don't want this anymore. I want it to stop."

Melanie opened her mouth to speak, but she never got the chance.

A deep, bellowing voice filled the small house, startling the women. The sound was louder than any other sound of the living she'd experienced. It reverberated through the walls of the house and vibrated up her spine. Emily looked around for the source, but saw nothing until . . .

There, floating on the wall behind Beth's writhing body, was a patch of light no bigger than a person's shadow, flickering in place, like a dancing sunspot on top of the sea. And then she heard the voice again.

"Emily. Enough."

CHAPTER 32

The light on the wall was mesmerizing as Emily squinted more closely at the spectacle. It was bright and beautiful, with every varied color in the rainbow warring for position. Emily glanced around for the source, for surely something with a reflective surface was throwing the light. But even as she swung her head around the entire open floor of the house, her instinct was twisting knots in her stomach.

Something was wrong.

And then the voice bellowed again. "Leave us."

Melanie gasped at Emily's side. Her vapors thinned to mere tendrils as the spirit was transported away. Emily flew back until her bum hit the edge of the kitchen counter. Her fingers dug into the granite and a new sensation, one that hadn't paralyzed her so fully in quite some time, gripped her heart.

Fear.

"Calm. Calm . . ."

The sunspot before her glowed brighter. As it did, Emily's hands relaxed their hold on the counter. Her arms slackened in their iron defenses. The paralyzing fear had quickly started to melt away, like winter's ice cracking and thawing under spring's new blossoming sun.

She hadn't the faintest notion of what was happening or what that voice was, but her body, her spirit, had settled in its agitation.

As Emily relaxed further, the sunspot dimmed its brightness to as it was before.

"It is time for you to be called home."

The baritone voice seeped into Emily's mind and came to rest inside her. The muscles in Emily's face pulled a wide smile at the intrusion. Any notion of fear had left her. She remained with only light and peace. But even through the transformation, she refused to shake her inquisitive nature.

"What are you?" The words came out shakier than she would have liked. All her senses were a jumble of confusion.

"I am a spirit sentry." The news was shared as if it was a great certainty of life and not something Emily has just been told for the first time.

She turned to where Melanie had stood. Her first instinct had always been to ask her friend when Emily needed information related to the spirit world. But the empty space at her side was all the reminder she needed that she was alone. With a force that could transport spirits to and fro at will.

She tried to muster up that fear again. To call upon those deeply ingrained survival instincts so key to a person's existence.

But they didn't come. By some manner, the sentry had suppressed those feelings, those skills.

Melanie would have known what to do. She would have been able to tell Emily exactly what was floating across the wall and why Emily couldn't help but seem to trust the floating sunspot.

The reality of her situation plowed into her like a ship sailing without a crew to man it. How much of her spirit life had she shirked for all her desire to stay close to Thomas? For the five years since her illness, she'd refused to accept her death. And, in return, had tasked herself with quelling Thomas's grief. But in doing so, she had never accepted her new existence as well.

The result had left her stuck in the middle between a life she could no longer have and an existence she wanted nothing to do with.

And Beth was the one who had to pay the price for Emily's stubbornness.

"I . . . I must confess, I do not know what you are." Her words were shaky but resigned.

"That is surprising, as you are not new to this life."

"Yes, I . . . have much to learn still." Her eyes remained downcast on the floor. While her fear had certainly dissipated, white-hot shame had bloomed in its place.

"I am one of many who watch over the spirit world."

"I didn't know we needed watching." Gosh, did she sound like a petulant child.

The sentry didn't immediately respond as it floated across to the adjacent wall, the one closest to where Beth lay. Emily glanced down at the woman on the floor. Her tremors had ceased and her body had slackened. The tips of her fingernails no longer bit into her palms and the tense lines of pain along her brow had smoothed out. She appeared peaceful. At rest.

"The lives of this woman and those you left behind are no longer concerns of yours. You are being called home."

"You said that before. What does that mean? Home to where?"

"To rest."

Rest.

The idea sounded so splendid and inviting. Like taking a break from one's chores for a quick lie down in a flowered meadow. To kick off one's shoes for a moment and focus on each blade of grass as it tickled the skin. To be without conscience or care. No guilt, no pain.

No grief.

"But what about Beth?" Even as exhaustion weighed heavily on Emily, her mind couldn't stray far from the family she'd left behind and her selfish actions that had caused more harm than good. "I can't just leave her there. I . . . I don't know why she fell ill suddenly. Yes, I intended to send her back again, but she hadn't touched my essence. Not yet, at least. I'm certain of it. I was arguing with Melanie and then she—"

"The woman will be fine." The resolution in the baritone voice was absolute and brooked no questions. Yet she needed to know more. Perhaps she had begun to resign herself to whatever the sentry had in store for her, but she hadn't come all this way only to abandon Beth and Thomas.

Her stubbornness, like her grief and impulsivity, could flow in many directions as well.

"The living cannot witness sentries. When we are near, their bodies collapse and we take over their minds. Fear not. The woman is deeply dreaming and will not have any recollection of this encounter."

The expression on Beth's face had changed from one of tension and pain to calm and happiness. The last time Emily had witnessed that peace in Beth was when the woman had been with Thomas. Curiosity poked at Emily as she wondered what Beth was dreaming about. Certainly, the poor woman deserved happiness just as much as Thomas did.

The realization refueled Emily's plan. Despite the sentry, she still had demands to make. "I will go with you, but you must save Beth first."

"We do not get involved in affairs of the living."

Emily ran up to the wall and stood a few feet away from the sunspot. It was odd to argue with a patch of light, but nothing about the circumstances were everyday occurrences in her world.

"Beth is in this position because of me, and I cannot move forward unless I know those I'm leaving behind are seen to."

"That is the problem I am here to solve."

Emily reared back at the unexpected proclamation. Before her, the sunspot swirled and expanded. She expected it to take the shape of a man or at least appear as a body capable of eliciting commands in such a low voice. Something she could sternly address and stand up to. But no such manifestation ever occurred. The lights before her remained disorienting.

"You are at risk of diminishing your spirit."

Emily shook her head in confusion.

"You have not yet learned the ways of your existence, yet you proceed without caution or care."

"What is diminishing, precisely?" Her voice had softened as the seriousness of the situation was pressed upon her. She dared not miss a word the sentry said.

"Your essence. The very makeup of your form. It is what allows you to appear as you once were and binds your soul to this world. Once you have passed on from the living, your essence becomes solid. A tangible reminder of the intangible. But it is not endless."

"But Melanie told me about spirits traveling through time repeatedly. They always leave their essence behind when they do. Are you telling me they just poof out of existence? What else is this afterlife for, then? Why not just have us be dead and done with it?"

The questions flowed quickly and poured out of her like water rushing out of a newly broken dam. She was acting immature, but she no longer cared. Between her death and grief, there was only so much room one had left for riddles and mind games.

"You have not learned the ways of your existence."

"Yes, yes, you've already said that—"

"If you continue along your current path, the spirits of you and your son will soon cease to exist."

Emily's arms fell at her sides. The mention of her son slammed her attention back to the presence before her.

"Your essence is diminishing, as is that of your son. Spirits have been given the gift of time travel in the afterlife. But it is a gift, and not one to be abused. Interference with the living is discouraged."

Emily nodded. "Yes, Melanie mentioned that last bit."

"It is discouraged because every time the living takes in a spirit's essence, whether by accident or insistence, it is a danger to the spirit's existence. Their spirit is lessened because of it. But you, Emily . . . you have been intentional in your travels and your interactions with the living. You risk scattering your essence so profusely that you would diminish yourself and your son into nothing. I am here to tell you that your actions, if continued, will cause you to be extinguished from this plane. And if you are gone, you will take with you the soul of your son."

The words sank heavily into Emily's gut as she walked away from the sentry and glided over to the back door. The whole of the situation finally formed in her mind, and the truth of it lay bitter on her tongue.

For she could not continue as she had been. That had been made clear.

She had not managed to assess her circumstances fully until that moment. She had been so young when she passed. A new wife and barely a mother. And then it all ended. The depression she had fallen into as a spirit had been immense and only fueled more so by Thomas going down a path that would lead to his own depression as well.

The situation had become all-consuming and impossible to manage. And desperate, especially given her newfound existence and resources.

But she was not alive any longer, and neither was her son. The thought of Elliot's precious soul not living on with her in the afterlife was crushing and something she had carelessly never considered.

There was so much she'd never considered. So much she hadn't bothered to learn.

"It is time to rest, Emily." The baritone words filled the first floor of the house and nestled their way into every pore of her skin.

Comfort, acceptance, and peace flooded through her, mending the holes in her soul with light and warmth. Emily took a deep breath and shut her eyes. When she opened them, the spirit of her son lay nestled in the crook of her arm. His eyes were open and bright and stared straight at her.

And gave her the courage to let go.

She slowly turned and walked back to face the sunspot on the wall. "I am tired."

The admission was mountainous and had been held captive inside her fragile frame for too long. For a moment, she was inclined to call it back, as the lightness inside her was so unnerving without her burden. But one did not grow without change, despite the initial unease. And as more seconds ticked by after she set her weight free, that unease settled inside her. The wrinkles of her grief were ironed flat like a bride's wedding gown.

It was glorious.

"I wish to rest, to be done with it." Relief filled the void where Emily's burden had been.

Her response, however, was met with silence. So she pressed on her final request before the opportunity escaped her.

"But before I go, I must plead again for one thing. Please, if it is within your power at all, help Beth. Thomas needs her. They need each other, and I can't bear the knowledge that they will be left behind in the world apart from each other after having been thrown together because of my toying. Please. I cannot stomach the thought of myself as the cause of their pain."

The sunspot on the wall grew brighter and its swirling sea of colors pulsed with vibrancy. The warmth of the light radiated out from the wall and cascaded over Emily's spirit. It was a waterfall of comfort and calm, like submerging into a hot spring that leached out all the poison and tension from one's body.

Emily's eyes closed at the onslaught, and she smiled for the first time in a long time. Dry tears formed at the corners of her eyes. She opened them to blink away the wetness that would never fall and was consumed with the bright white light encompassing the house. Then she gasped as the sentry entered her mind, intimately speaking to her its final decision. The connection was marvelous and freeing. The smile across Emily's face stretched as wide as it ever had.

Wisps of her spirit floated up off her arms, higher and higher until they collided with the sunspot on the wall and were enfolded into the celestial embrace. More of Emily's spirit rose up, her vapors being siphoned off to be welcomed into the other being. But she wasn't worried or alarmed. Far from it. The change was soothing and much needed. The weight of her whole existence departed and in its place were the ease and lightness of being cared for.

The sunspot flared even brighter as the last of Emily's spirit was called home. But right before the spirit sentry dimmed its presence and left the house, it floated over to Beth, who still lay on the floor. The light draped over her sleeping form like a warm tide ushering stranded creatures home. Once every inch of Beth was illuminated, the sentry's presence pulsed until fluctuations flowed in time with the woman's heartbeat.

After a few minutes, the light receded and dimmed. Nothing was left behind.

CHAPTER 33

Thomas groaned as he kicked out his leg and adjusted his bottom against the hard seat of his wagon. Though the new position was a welcome change for his cramped legs and locked knees, the tingles running up and down his lower extremities were not. At least his blood was thankful for the new route to travel freely. He wished he could say the same for his mare and wagon. Though he supposed he ought to be grateful. If it weren't for the animal to care for, he highly doubted he'd even stop to notice his own discomfort.

The pathetic truth of the matter was that he had no choice. His whole damn body betrayed him constantly. In the time since he left Boston, he'd been on the road. It was no surprise he headed south. Without any real compass or destination—or care, for that matter—his mind forced his body to go in the only other direction it knew. He hadn't the sense or the interest to argue.

Every divot and crest along each dirt road he traveled rocked his tired frame. When the wheels of the cart would rise and fall over a slight hill, his shoulders and torso would sway like a rowboat lost from its mooring. Only when the wheels leveled out on the ground again did his body right itself. As if the mechanics of motion had more of an interest in his posture than he did.

Not far off.

The long barren stretches between towns had been the worst. The roads were less traveled and, therefore, not as smoothed and trampled down. Swaying over the barrage of bumps and hills would inevitably lull his mind into a sleep he fought tooth and nail to prevent. Where his nightmares always flooded up like darkness eclipsing the sun.

The image of his Beth, ashen as chalk and weak as a newborn, lying in the patchy grass behind his house. Vibrant red tendrils lay flat and limp over her outstretched arm. An arm that had reached for him, begged for him to aid her. Her lips, so flushed and soft in his memory, fell cracked and open in a perennially silent cry for his help.

The most haunting was her eyes. For in his nightmares, they never beamed the brilliant sapphire blue he knew them to be. A blue that would chase the storm clouds in his mind away and melt the hardest ice shards around his heart.

No. In those fitful respites of forced sleep, his love's eyes were the same as the pale green taint that consumed her body. An ever-present reminder of his knack for welcoming tragedy.

And his pathetically weak will gave it such power over him.

Thomas's knuckles scraped against the new hairs under his chin. He had never been one for beards, mostly because the itching was damn insufferable in the early days of growth. As his fingernail scraped along the underside of his throat, he nearly laughed at the irony of how little he had come to care. Basic grooming had devolved in its importance. Pride and preference had previously dictated the details of his image for his profession. Since he handled every aspect of his business, from weapons creation to customer introductions, his appearance mattered. Boston's elite hadn't wanted to do business with a ragamuffin blacksmith who was as greasy and filthy as the oil in his quench basin.

The opinions of Boston's wealthy merchants had since become as useful to him as an overflowing piss pot.

Impatient chuffing interrupted the horse's steady clomping.

"Yes, yes, all right. We'll stop." Thomas sighed in annoyance, though at what? The horse for needing to rest and eat? At least the beast had the good sense to make its needs known. Thomas's own sense of self-preservation had vanished when he lost Beth.

Thomas unlatched the horse from the wagon leads and walked it over to a flat, grassy area. Far enough away from the road that it wouldn't get spooked by any travelers, but near enough that Thomas could easily recall the creature to his side. Thomas leaned against a wide oak tree and watched as the mare walked to the nearby creek and eagerly lapped at the water. His arms crossed his chest as the stillness of the meadow did its best to impart some serenity into his riled frame.

It was useless.

He missed his forge. Missed the strain in his muscles as he fought with a clump of iron. Missed the heat scorching his brow and singing his fingers as he carefully poured molten pewter into molds. His limbs, his heart—hell, even his teeth—would come alive and brace for the auditory impact of his hammer as its repercussions filled his body. And with each swing, he'd turn his upper body a bit. Ever so slightly. Just so he could catch a glimpse of the flames' glow flickering across Beth's alabaster skin . . .

"Dammit! God-*fucking*-dammit!" Thomas collapsed to the ground. The hard earth met his legs with a jolt, but the pain was not nearly enough. He rose up on his knees, balled his hands into fists, and unleashed his fury against the oak tree. Punch after punch met the aged, craggy tree trunk. His chest got tighter as his muscles burned with the exertion. But he welcomed all of it. Every jab was aimed at an enemy he had been powerless to protect against.

His thighs burned as they held him steady while his arms hammered against the trunk in a rage. The old tree stood still and stoic, even as bits of bark flew off in all directions. As if it mocked his tirade and chided him for what it was: a tantrum of a man who hadn't yet learned how to deal with defeat.

Flecks of blood caught his chin and dolloped the white of his cravat around his neck. Pain blossomed along his knuckles as the exposed wood bit into his ragged flesh. Thomas swallowed back the torment and was relentless in his attack.

He waited for Beth's smooth hand to calmly rest on his shoulder. For her sweet and encouraging whisper in his ear that he had done enough, spent enough, endured enough. That he could rest and she was well, thriving and surviving in her own time without him.

She never came.

Warm wetness dripped onto his lashes before falling hard onto the bridge of his nose. He couldn't tell whether it was sweat, blood, tears, or a mixture of everything. But only when his vision strained for clarity and his fists began to deaden with numbness did he collapse on his arse, an exhausted puddle of unspent emotions and blazing uncertainties.

Thomas sprawled out in the grass as his breathing struggled to return to normal. His ear lay flat against his outstretched arm, dulling the ambient murmurs of the meadow and creek. Even those were too loud. He brought up the palm of his other hand, wet and sticky from the brawl—if he could even call it that—and held it flush against his other ear. At once, the sounds around him fell away. All that remained was the *womp womp* of his heart as it still beat, despite his preference.

I can't do this anymore.

As the thought entered his mind, he blinked away the sweat and cloudiness and managed to focus on a copse of wildflowers farther down the field, nestled along a row of trees. The bright purples and faded oranges stood out like grave markers, even though they were protected in the shade. Their stems, though far away, were visible enough as they reluctantly floated and swayed in the hot summer breeze. They, too, appeared to take umbrage with their lack of say in their own circumstances.

Thomas squeezed his eyes shut to drain them of any lingering would-be tears, then blinked them open. Sunspots, bright and random, illuminated the patch of wildflowers briefly before dancing to the bushes behind them. Strange how the light moved from one area to the other, as if it couldn't make up its mind on where it should settle. The rainbow hues fluttered and pulsed in each beam of light as they moved all throughout the bushes. Thomas lowered his hand from his ear as he lay there, mesmerized by the brilliance before him.

A sharp whinny from the mare had Thomas looking back at the creek. The animal had stepped back from the water's edge and neighed its brief agitation before resuming its drink. More than likely, a river otter had startled the horse, and she was not appreciative of the intrusion.

Best get used to disappointment, my friend.

Once Thomas was content that all was well with his mare, he returned his attention to the sunlit wildflowers and nearly had the breath sucked out of him.

The sunspots were gone. The shady dwelling of the wildflowers had been restored. But behind the flowers, poking out from the row of overgrown bushes, was a hand. A pale, open-palmed hand.

Thomas scrambled to his feet and withdrew the knife from his boot. He waited for the bushes to rustle, for the rest of the arm to move or for any number of unexpected headaches to jump out and attack.

"To hell with it." He was tired of waiting, and his muscles agreed.

On light feet, he jogged over toward the outstretched hand. He kept his blade out, uncertain whether his presence would be welcomed or eschewed. Slowly, he rounded the far bush that hid the rest of the body. His eyes tracked the open palm and followed it down the exposed forearm. Down the delicate elbow and rounded shoulder.

Red hair stopped him in his tracks.

His knife fell to the ground. Less than a heartbeat later, Thomas was on his knees beside Beth.

She lay still among the patches of shaded wildflowers. But her complexion was healthy and whole. No green tinge or ashen pallor overtaking her beauty. And speaking of beauty . . .

Thomas sprang to his feet and peered around the road, the creek, the road again. Then he was down at her side, closer than before. Almost hovering, nearly smothering her exposed body.

She was barefoot and her legs were entirely exposed up to her mid-thigh. She wore no gown, shift, or any other undergarments he could see. Just shortened beige breeches that were fastened about her waist and covered far too little of her legs. Her bodice was no different. A tight scrap of fabric stretched across her breasts and stomach, leaving every curve and bend to no one's imagination. Two thin straps that wrapped over her shoulders on either side seemed to hold the gray garment in place, but that was all. Her neck, shoulders, and arms were otherwise entirely bare.

The shock of it all overwhelmed him. He needed to touch her, convince himself that she was real. That this wasn't the damn nightmare playing tricks on his mind again. When he extended his hands out to her face, which was peaceful and resplendent in sleep, bloodied knuckles and torn skin stared back at him.

Thomas cursed as he ran to the creek. Like hell he'd touch her looking like a mongrel.

He dunked his hands in the cool water and wiped away any possible speck of his loss of control. The open skin stung at the contact, but the pain quickly abated and washed into the water with the rest of the blood and grime. Once he was content with the job, he shook out his hands and wiped them along his thighs.

"Thomas? Is that you?" Beth's voice, his favorite sound he never expected to hear again, halted his movements.

Slowly, with cautious leaden steps, he turned to face her. He dared not move quickly lest it all was a figment of his fever dreams. He couldn't stomach the notion that he'd turn around hurriedly, only to frighten away a skittish memory that was never there in the first place.

But she was no memory.

Before him stood Beth. Her hair fell in soft waves around her shoulders, and her palms covered her nose and mouth. Blue eyes rimmed with cautious tears stared back at him. Eyes he'd gladly give his life to see one last time. But could he be certain she was real?

"Beth . . ." Words died in his throat. She was there. She had to be. Separated by the mere length of his wagon instead of the length of centuries.

"I . . ." His voice betrayed him.

She dropped her hands from her face and smiled the biggest, brightest, happiest smile his shriveled hopeless heart could never have dreamed to witness again. She was here, and she was his. She had come back to him. But how? He couldn't comprehend any of it, but he hardly cared.

Damn, did he love that woman. And he wouldn't risk another moment going by without telling her.

"Beth . . ." Thomas swallowed past the newly formed lump in his throat. "I . . ." She was real, but his skeptical brain refused to quell its suspicion. None of it made any sense. How was she back here? The logical questions brutally wrestled with his hopeful heart.

Words and emotions clashed inside him, robbing Thomas of any coherent thoughts. Until he said the only thing his jostled mind could offer up.

"Beth . . . I . . . fought a tree."

CHAPTER 34

Beth's mind was slow to catch onto the situation. Her brain was like an engine that refused to turn over and power the rest of her body. But though the critical thinking portion of the show hadn't yet raised its curtain, her sensory network was all about the eye-high kicks and jazz hands. Long blades of soft grass tickled her bare feet as she lay in a field she didn't remember being in. Hot sun kissed her shoulders and heated the freckles on the bridge of her nose. But the most obvious, and welcome, change was the lack of pain.

When Beth had been at her laptop in her kitchen, her stomach had gone into a sudden rebellion of anything and everything. Iron grips and excruciating vices twisted every organ in her body as she fell to the linoleum floor. Her limbs had seized, and it was all she could do to fight against whatever painful paralysis ensnared her. And then . . .

It all stopped. Soft rustling at her side stirred her senses. As she opened her eyes, her vision was flooded with a bright blue sky and poofy cotton candy clouds. Sun, grass, and the hint of wild lavender took the place of her vanilla-scented candle and bleach floor cleaner.

Then her fried brain leaned on experience and jammed those jagged puzzle pieces into place.

Holy crap. It happened again.

Weak legs miraculously pushed her to a standing, upright position.

Verdant, lush greenery filled her vision instead of her tiled kitchen backsplash and stainless steel appliances. Beth's heart hammered faster, not out of fear or worry, but out of hope. And wasn't that a kick in the pants? Because who in their right mind, when faced with an inexplicable circumstance that had direct implications on their survival, immediately had happy tummy flutters?

This gal, apparently.

Grunting and grumbling mixed with the sounds of trickling water behind her. When curiosity had her turning toward the noise, giddy excitement and wonder had her glued to the spot.

Broad planes of a muscled back her hands itched to touch rose up and down. Even with only visible shirt sleeves and a cut leather vest draping the form, recognition was instant and soul deep.

Thomas was on his knees in front of the water, frantically washing away something that clearly irked him. His movements were quick and slightly sloppy given the splashing. His curses, however, were soft and endearing, if that was even possible.

Her blacksmith, the man she needed and loved more than her lungs needed air, was in front of her. In the flesh. In another time.

And he was flustered as all get out.

"Thomas? Is that you?"

Wobbly legs carried her forward. Her hands covered her mouth and nose as she waited for a response. Then the nerves kicked into high gear and she stopped walking. *What if I'm wrong?*

The man at the water froze. Slowly, like a lithe hunter around skittish prey, he rose and turned.

Silence had never been so loud. An eruption of emotions bubbled up and clogged every pore of her body. Elation at seeing him again. Relief that the door had reopened. Uncertainty at where in time she was (though the horse and wagon were big frickin' clues). Fear that she couldn't return . . .

No, not fear. Excitement. Because everything she needed was standing in front of her and all around her.

The man before her, however, stood still in his own apparent uncertainty. His confused brow, his hesitant stance, the slack-jawed expression. She had never seen Thomas so thrown, as if he'd just witnessed the creek's water turn bright purple and his horse sprout wings. And he had a beard—at least, the beginnings of one.

The whole image was delicious. She dropped her hands and smiled, tears pricking her eyes as he stammered out her name. To her surprise, Thomas struggled. The few words he managed to speak came out a disjointed jumble. He was literally tongue-tied.

And then he spoke. "Beth . . . I . . . fought a tree."

Cue the brakes.

Beth quirked her head to the side and padded toward him. "Did you?"

Thomas ran his hands down his exhausted face before extending them, knuckles up, in front of her. He looked down at them. "No, I meant—"

Beth's hands gently gripped his. Though she craved to run her thumbs along his battered skin, she carefully skirted around his wounds. "You truly are a brave knight."

Then her instincts took the wheel. She stood on her toes and kissed him, silencing any more nerves. The connection was electric and just so *right*. Like aloe on burned skin. One needed the other to be whole.

Strong arms clasped around her waist. The uncertainty that had previously painted Thomas's stilted words got lost real dang quick. His grip tightened and Beth melted into his solid form. Lifetimes passed before they broke away, begrudgingly coming up for air.

"Is this real, then?" Thomas whispered.

Beth shrugged her shoulder. "You feel pretty darn real to me."

"How— No, it matters not. I'll not question it."

Beth wrapped her arms around him and laid her ear against his chest. The steady patter of his heartbeat was like her favorite wind chime that had adorned her grandmother's porch when she was a child. A sound that she instantly associated with love and safety.

"That sounds like a great plan."

They stood there in silence until the moment rushed in full force and slammed its significance straight into Beth's head. While fear hadn't exactly reared its fangs quite yet, questions began to sprout up like weeds through neatly trimmed grass.

Was she exactly where she was before? Had it still only been a few days? What had happened to Hunterdon? And Mrs. Potter, were they still looking for her? Had Thomas—

"I love you, Beth."

Thomas's words were gruff, yet smooth as they washed over her rapid-fire mental inquisition. She relaxed her grip and looked up at him. The face staring back at her was all sorts of solemn, brook-no-arguments, and serious as a heart attack.

And a man in love.

"I won't question the why of it or take another second for granted. You're here, breathing in my arms and warming my heart. When I left you, I had nothing but hope that you would listen, that you would stay hidden. Your ax had been broken, the dust gone. In my panic, all I had was blind hope that you'd somehow survive. I never thought in all my days that I'd have you in my arms again. When I returned to the house, I couldn't find a single trace of you. Not a hair or footprint. Nothing. Just memories."

Thomas cleared his throat as he cupped her face in his palms. "Stay with me. For however long we have. I need you by my side. Always. As a partner and wife who is more than my equal in every way."

The proclamation chased away any doubts or concerns left lingering in Beth's mind. All the uncertainty had been replaced with mountains of heck-yes and oceans of she-can't-possibly-love-this-man-more.

Her cheeks hurt at how hard she smiled. Before her mouth had an opportunity to fumble her words, she kissed him again, hard. She would never get tired of this. His scent, his taste, his confidence in her, his love. All of it. Thomas had become her own form of adrenaline and motivation. To fulfill his ideals of the woman he knew her to be, regardless of the time period. His love was a gift she would happily spend a lifetime thanking him for.

But just before he turned his head to deepen the kiss, she pulled away. "I have one condition."

He growled his annoyance as he leaned forward, trying to chase her lips. "It's yours. Declare it quickly."

"Oh, but I like this. You're so squirmy and impatient. Ow!" The squeeze of his large hand against her backside was all the information she needed as to how short his fuse had gotten. "What happened to all your knightly chivalry?" she squeaked.

"The devil can take it. Speak now or forfeit your chance."

"Well, any good knight should give his lady a favor, right?"

"Mmm," Thomas mumbled as he kissed up the column of her neck. "I seem to recall this discussion."

"You owe me a knife."

His warm lips stopped just behind her ear. Then he pulled back. "You want a knife?"

"Since I don't have my ax anymore, and I know how insistent you are that I always have protection—"

Warm hands left her body as Thomas jogged back to his wagon. She had to swallow down a laugh at how fast he rifled through the sacks and trunks. Protection had always been a prickly point for Thomas, and it was also the thing that had brought them together in the first place. She no more knew her way around a knife than an ax or any other edged weapon, but the purpose and fire her request sparked in Thomas was rewarding on both ends.

Even if a good knee to the groin against baddies was still her go-to method of protecting herself.

Thomas appeared at her side a moment later and held out an object wrapped in a piece of cloth.

"I didn't mean immediately," she teased him as she peeled back the layers of fabric. "Oh my God! Is this—"

"Yes. It's the blade we made together. In truth, I had intended to adorn it more fully. I wished to mimic the pattern of your ax's handle and engrave it onto the hilt. Time did not allow for it, however." The disappointment in his voice was apparent. "Still, it's a good blade. It should fit your hand comfortably, and I've honed the edge so be mindful when—"

Beth threw her palm over his mouth as she held the knife in her hand. Everything about it was perfect, from the size to the handle shape to the man who'd made it.

Or who'd made it with her. As a partner.

Beth looked up. Thomas's hazel eyes stayed trained on her, assessing, waiting. Slowly, she lowered her hand from his mouth and replaced it with a soft, lingering kiss. A kiss full of commitment and promise and love.

"I love it. And I love you. And . . ."

"And?"

"And I'm *really* loving your beard. That's got to stay."

Thomas chuckled. "As you'd like, my lady."

It had been decided. Across the world, spirit sentries amassed against every imaginable backdrop to call the restless spirits home. For good. Countless orbs of light pulsed and grew brighter as flecks of green and wisps of white rose up from their surroundings like iron filings to a magnet. Spirits from all throughout time were being called home to rest once and for all.

No human on the mortal plane would see the sentries. It was as it had always been. The gatekeepers of the spirit world had stood as protectors both to those who had passed on and to those left behind. The separation was imperative and eternal. For that was the way of life and death. It could be no other way.

Until it had all changed. Spirits had learned of their essence, the very thing that allowed them to exist in spirit form beyond their time on the mortal plane. And also, the very thing that allowed spirits to visit their loved ones freely, though unnoticed and without intervention for the living.

Yet with time traveling came the occasional involvement in the human world. Spirits had discovered a side effect of leaving their essence behind for the living to embrace. After a few mortals traveled through the planes of time, the damage had been set in motion. For each time a spirit initiated the travel, their essence withered with each trip and violated the sacred duty of the sentries.

So action had to be taken.

Waves of green dust floated through the air, forming a solid collection of particles that melted into balls of light. Every speck of a spirit's essence was collected en masse from the mortal plane. None would remain, and neither would any wandering spirits.

The final eddies of white vapors swirled around the sentries, accompanying the green clouds of dust, and melted into the light with no resistance. Almost as if every unattached soul sighed in relief at finally being called home.

To rest.

The immense sunspots in the sky flared with their last bursts of energy before shimmering out of existence, leaving to guard the spirit world once more.

EPILOGUE

Two years later

The subtle creak of the door was all the warning Thomas got before a visitor entered his forge. But unlike when he had his shop in Boston, he hardly minded the interruption. Especially when his Beth was the one who loved to pay him a visit around noon every so often and bring him a meal.

He closed his ledger and laid it back on the desk. His wife—and it gave him a thrill every time he referred to her in the manner—beamed a smile only for him as she walked over and settled her satchel of food on the table.

"It was a girl! The third one in the last month or so. I'm telling you, there must be something in the water here that leans heavily toward girl power. Not that I'm complaining. I just won't envy these parents when their kids hit the teenage years, that's for sure. Speaking as a former teenage girl, of course."

Beth swiped her arm across her forehead and did her best to pin her loose hair back into her bonnet. The movements were so normal, so routine, yet he'd never tire of them.

"Alex, you can take your leave now." The words came out harsher than Thomas intended. But he always craved alone time with his wife and quickly learned that, as a partner to the town's busiest midwife, he was often third or fourth in line for her attention at any moment.

And he wouldn't trade a thing for it.

A young man stood over a shelf toward the back of the forge. The coals in the fire were banked, and no new projects were scheduled to have their forging commence that day. No, it was a day for dreaded inventory and supply restocking.

"Are you certain, sir? I've not yet finished putting all of the new delivery's supplies away."

"I'm certain. Go see Mrs. Angler. Here . . ." Thomas took some coin from a purse in his desk and handed it to the lad. "I'm sure she'll have some biscuits for you."

"Yes, sir! Thank you. And good afternoon, Mrs. Brannigan!"

"Bye, Alex." Beth smiled to herself as Thomas's apprentice eagerly left the shop, content with the surprise early dismissal.

"Come here," Thomas growled.

Before Beth could respond, he sat in the chair at his desk, gripped her waist, and draped her across his lap. He ate up her surprised squeal with a hungry kiss. The weight of her in his hands, the taste of her on his tongue—it was all a miracle he had no right to, but he would never stop being grateful.

When Beth returned to him, his purpose and direction had changed course. He'd had no desire to return to Maryland. Only a desire to keep Beth by his side for as long as possible. But he had no idea where to go or, more urgently, how he could reestablish his profession and provide for her after Hunterdon had smeared his good name. And he had her own skills to look after as well, for she would never abide sitting idle while her hands itched to care for women in need.

His immediate concern, however, had been to see her fed, properly clothed, and sheltered. So shortly after she returned to him, he'd turned back on the road he'd traveled and settled them both at an inn he recalled passing. The town had been unremarkable in its makeup. Just another moderately sized traveler's town, with a few merchants and enough tradesmen to peddle wares but not so many as the bloat and barrage of a city like Boston demanded.

Once he had been content that Beth was tucked in their room and safely resting for the night, Thomas ventured downstairs to speak with the barkeep.

The town they had chosen to stay in was called Collinsford, and the beer man had confirmed Thomas's original suspicions.

"Oh, we get plenty of people passing through, like yourself, most of whom are on their way to New York. But we get by just fine for our size." The barkeep rattled on as he dried out pewter mugs with a dingy rag. "Agriculture is our main industry. Several of the families own quite a bit of farmland and see to the needs of not only the townsfolk, but of the larger settlements as well. Plenty of cattle, live-stock, and the like. And we keep busy with the sheep's wool, that's for certain. Plenty of woolen fabrics, linens, and such. As I said, we get along more than well enough for our size and do our best to keep our noses out of things that don't concern us. If we lacked for anything, however, I'd say it was in our skilled trades. Not as many stick around for that."

Thomas pressed the man on that last bit, as his curiosity was piqued.

"We lack a bit of the bright and shiny, I suppose. When the young ones come of age, they wish to explore the cities and learn skills there. Fewer stay behind with their families, and I can't say I blame them outright. But it leaves us lacking. We haven't a cooper, for example, and our blacksmith has been getting on in years."

Thomas tried on the thought of staying in this town with Beth. Far enough away from the dramas of the cities, but it had population enough, with the need for skilled laborers. And families, too. But an agricultural town would hardly have the need for the weapons Thomas had been used to producing en masse. No, his ironworks would be different for farmers than soldiers. More horseshoes, hoes, cowbells, and even more items suiting the daily needs of the town, like pots and pans, candleholders and fireplace racks. But items where a bit of artistry and creativity could be useful, if not appreciated.

The variety of a more mundane daily life excited him, absurdly enough.

He never imagined how agreeable Beth would be to the arrangement. But he should have known better than to sell her mind short.

She was delighted, mostly at the prospect of her usefulness to the townsfolk. But as the days and weeks passed, and Beth remained at his side, in his time, Thomas allowed his happiness to fully sink in. There had always been a worry in the back of his mind that some force would take her from him again, that he would be powerless to keep her. But as time progressed and wooden planks rose to form their new house and his new forge, their day-to-day lives solidified into a welcome and heavenly routine.

The people of the town took to his Beth like a cat to cream. There were two midwives the town turned to for aid, but they were getting on in years and were more than elated to have a young person help the cause. Especially one who was already as proficient as Beth.

She took to the task in great stride and had quickly become a revered figure in the community.

And even though Thomas was able to successfully establish himself as a blacksmith in the town—and well enough to take on an apprentice of his own a year later—his accomplishments were paltry compared to Beth's achievements. More often than not, people recognized him through his association with Beth. He had never had a more fitting or proud relationship.

That was, until he took the title of husband. Shortly after he acquired Alex as his apprentice, he and Beth were married in a small ceremony by the town's minister. Just the two of them and the silver rings he'd made in secret. It had been one of the happiest days of his life.

"You know, girls aren't this bad omen I make them out to be," Beth murmured across his lips.

"Mmm, so you have demonstrated." His arms tightened around her waist and settled naturally against her full hips as he kissed up her neck.

"Boys can be quite the handful as well," she said, exposing more of her neck.

"I shall endeavor to prove that statement correct." He dusted his fingers across the edge of the handkerchief draped over her shoulders, trying his best to feel more of her.

"What I'm saying is . . . oh . . ." Beth dropped her head back when Thomas kissed the spot behind her ear he knew she loved.

"Oh?"

"Yes . . . I mean . . . what I'm saying is boys and girls can both have their challenges. But also their own wonders."

"I'd very much like to sample more of your wonders."

"Thomas." The breathy panting from a moment ago had vanished. The tone of his name implied something earnest and urgent.

He immediately pulled back. "What's wrong?"

"Nothing's wrong. In fact, everything is a thousand percent right." Beth smiled wide at him and toyed with the shells of his ears. "I'm pregnant."

The slight whisper and crackle of the banked fire was the only sound in the forge. Well, aside from the hammering behind Thomas's ribs as his mind turned over the news she'd just shared. Perhaps he'd heard the words wrong.

Or perhaps he hadn't.

"You're . . . We're . . ."

"Yup." She removed his hands from her waist and repositioned them across her stomach. He didn't know what he should think or feel. Joy and gratitude ballooned so large in his heart he couldn't even form words. All he could do was move his hands across her midsection, where a miraculous new life lived, and do his best to cradle it, protect it from harm.

"You're going to be a father. No, you're going to be the best father this child could ever be lucky enough to know. And he or she *will* know you, Thomas, because you and the baby have me. And I'm not going to let a darn thing tear apart our family."

Thomas's throat tensed. In one sweeping, solid gesture, this woman cut the head off the only monster left from Thomas's past. Her vow that this child would live to see his family was ironclad. Beth stated it without an ounce of hesitation or uncertainty because she had been sent to him with the knowledge and expertise of a time that largely prevented widespread death in infancy.

"You are the greatest gift of my days, Beth Brannigan." Thomas's whispered words were barely audible as he gently traced the curve of her lips, the apples of her cheeks, every part of her he'd never tire of loving. "A father!" he bellowed.

"Oof!" Beth yelped as Thomas rose from his chair and twirled her around the forge. Only after he'd held and kissed her thoroughly did he let her feet touch the floor. Her cheeks were flushed and her hair was mussed. She was utterly perfect.

"Wait. Don't move. I have something for you as well."

"Well, I doubt it can top my announcement, but you're welcome to try." She laughed.

Thomas ran to his desk, removed a satchel, and immediately returned to her side. "Open it."

Beth quirked an eyebrow as she lifted the item out. But as soon as her hand grasped the handle, her face fell. She looked more closely, and her mouth dropped.

In her hand was the ax that Beth had carried when she first slammed into him two years ago. The same one that had dangled in her pocket every time she would visit his forge in Boston. The same weapon that had housed the magic that brought her into his life.

"My ax . . . but . . . how?"

"I had been sketching its likeness from memory for months. The etchings were the most difficult to remember, but I had studied it enough that I think the representation is fairly accurate. Do you—"

Beth threw herself at her husband and nearly knocked the wind out of him. Yet he stood strong, as he always would whenever she was in his arms. And as he would when holding his future child. *Their* future child.

"I love you," she said through tears. "I love you so much. I can't believe you made this . . . that you remembered. I mean, you remembered *everything*."

"And you've given me everything," he soothed into her ear.

He held her a moment longer, relishing the feel of her soul in his arms, until she backed away and looked at him.

"To be clear, just because this is a baby ax does *not* make it an appropriate baby gift. Understand?"

Thomas threw his head back in laughter as he cupped her head close to his heart. "Of course, my lady."

Thank you so much for reading *Forged by the Past!* If you loved seeing Thomas and Beth's relationship grow, let your friends know. Help other readers fall in love with this couple by leaving a review.

Can we keep in touch? Do you want to read what happens when one woman finds her soulmate in the spirit world, but in order to claim him, she must give up everything she's every known and worked for? Claim *Honored by the Past,* a prequel novella, when you sign up to my newsletter to find out whether a sinfully gorgeous spirit can convince a jaded woman to leave her past behind for love. Enjoy!

Are you a fan of paranormal romance? Find out what happens when a fallen angel, who spends his nights vanquishing demons, stumbles upon a mortal woman who get stuck in the crossfire. Can he protect her from the fatal target on her back while the soul bond between them grows stronger with each touch? Start reading *Angel's Target,* the first book in the Elemental Angels series.

Scan the QR code to dive into *Honored by the Past* and *Angel's Target* today!

ACKNOWLEDGMENTS

This book will always have a special place in my heart because of where I was in my life when I wrote it. *Forged by the Past* was the first book I published as a full-time author, and my list of people to thank is too vast to list in a few short sentences...but I'm going to try.

I'm a member of several online writing groups for self-published authors. The inspiration and encouragement I have received from complete strangers in these groups has done more for my career than I can say. Thank you to the members of The Writing Gals, Elana Johnson's Indie Inspiration, and Lee Savino's Millionaire Author Mastermind.

A special thanks to Sarah Stewart for keeping me accountable, even when I didn't want to be, and to Jessi Gage for being a wonderful critique partner.

And, as always, many thanks to my husband, Ben. He took a leap of faith with me, and trusted, against all odds, that a net would appear...and it did.

ABOUT THE AUTHOR

Aimee Robinson is a lover of romance novels in all forms. Her absolute favorites, though, are the ones that offer a little bit of something *extra*: time travel, guardian angels, good old-fashioned meddlesome grandmothers with a supernatural secret to hide, you name it.

She believes romance novels should transport you from the humdrum to the swoonworthy, preferably while being curled up on the couch with chocolate and tea (or wine...or both!). Aimee's overactive imagination lends itself to fun tales with emotional adventures, sexy snark, and happily ever afters.

When not writing or reading, Aimee enjoys spending time with her husband and keeping up with her two young sons.

Printed in the USA
CPSIA information can be obtained
at www.ICGtesting.com
LVHW091647171223
766724LV00040B/468